THE LEGACY SERIES

SERIES TITLES

Like Human
Janet Goldberg

The Hopefuls
Elizabeth Oness

Never Stop Exiting
Michael Hopkins

Broken Heart Syndrome
Anne Colwell

The Mexican Messiah: A Novella & Stories
Jay Kauffmann

Close to a Flame
Colleen Alles

American Animism
Jamey Gallagher

Keeping What's Best Left Kept Secret
David Ricchiute

Soaked
Toby LeBlanc

The Path of Totality
Marie Zhuikov

Shocker in Gloomtown
Dan Libman

The Continental Divide
Bob Johnson

The Three Devils and Other Stories
William Luvaas

The Correct Response
Manfred Gabriel

Welcome Back to the World: A Novella & Stories
Rob Davidson

Greyhound Cowboy and Other Stories
Ken Post

Hoist House: A Novella & Stories
Jenny Robertson

Finding the Bones: Stories & A Novella
Nikki Kallio

Self-Defense
Corey Mertes

Where Are Your People From?
James B. De Monte

Sometimes Creek
Steve Fox

The Plagues
Joe Baumann

The Clayfields
Elise Gregory

Kind of Blue
Christopher Chambers

Evangelina Everyday
Dawn Burns

Township
Jamie Lyn Smith

Responsible Adults
Patricia Ann McNair

Great Escapes from Detroit
Joseph O'Malley

Nothing to Lose
Kim Suhr

The Appointed Hour
Susanne Davis

Yes, No, I Don't Know

Kathryn Gahl's remarkable talent is on full display in *Yes, No, I Don't Know*, a 24-story collection that varies impressively in content, structure, and tone. A story might capture the emotions of a single sexual encounter, while others encapsulate an entire life. A story might be harrowing, hilarious, or heartbreaking—or contain all three qualities. And throughout, Kathryn Gahl's prose is filled with striking imagery, original metaphors, and precise detail. *Yes, No, I Don't Know* is a wonderful collection.

—LARRY WATSON
author of *Montana, 1948* and *Let Him Go*

Kathryn Gahl is a multi-talented writer, a savant comfortable in nearly any genre. These stories cement her place as a Wisconsin literary luminary and an important voice in Midwestern letters. I'll read anything Gahl writes, and more often than not, I am delighted, surprised, and in awe.

—NICKOLAS BUTLER
author of *Shotgun Lovesongs* and *A Forty Year Kiss*

In *Yes, No, I Don't Know*, Kathryn Gahl dramatizes the vulnerabilities of intimacy in two dozen stories distinguished by their emotional intensity, beautiful poetic prose, and lovely waves of significant detail. The ambivalence of the book's moving title story is woven throughout these remarkable narratives, which follow characters on the move, seekers and dreamers obedient only to their physical and spiritual yearning. Like the hitchhiking couple who get into a dangerous stranger's car, Kathryn Gahl is fearless; she'll go where she pleases, and these stories take us along for the ride.

—RON RINDO
author of *Life, and Death, and Giants*

Gahl's *Yes, No, I Don't Know* is what you'd get if Joyce Carol Oates and Raymond Carver had a baby and then sent it off to be raised by Joan Didion. Complex, morally grey, and always compelling, these stories perplex and interrogate the human condition with tenderness and stark truth. Gahl's mastery with poetic language and syntax is in full display and from page one, the reader can feel they are being led by a true storymaster. I didn't want this collection to end and found myself slowing down as the pages dwindled to prolong the experience.

—WENDY WIMMER
author of *Entry Level*

Behind the gossipy classrooms and smoldering barns of small Midwestern towns, Kathryn Gahl is listening with a poet's ear and a dancer's flourish. Down on their luck but determined to connect, her characters dwell in "the morning side of midnight," where waltzes twirl into awkward tangles and fathers race to save their children—and where everyone should know better but no one chooses to act better, until, sometimes, they do. From first sorrows to fresh losses, this collection hums with the music of enmeshment, in all of its bright and bittersweet notes.

—REBECCA MEACHAM
author of *Feather Rousing*

With sharp-edged precision—and a deep understanding of the culture of the upper Midwest—Kathryn Gahl illuminates how the hopes and dreams of her eclectic characters collide with the realities of their lives. Bold and compulsively readable, this is an astounding, astonishing collection.

—THERESA KAMINSKI
author of *Queen of the West: The Life and Times of Dale Evans*

This is the stuff of rural myth come to life. The characters in these stories have secrets…some they keep even from themselves. With mentions of nylons rolled to ankles and girdles, Elmer's glue and strip poker in the back of a school bus, Gahl immerses us in the times and places of her stories. She shows us the heavy load we carry after seeing something we'd rather not. She reminds us that the people we think have it all often have a whole lot less than that—and keep on going anyway.

—KIM SUHR
author of *Close Call*

Kathryn Gahl's stories are found everywhere—along the weedy edges of gravel roads, farms steaming in the heat, towns iced over in January, kitchens. Normal and strange, with a sense of detail that is unfailing, she shows us in our world in all our flawed glory. And Gahl's prose is gorgeous, a treasure—rhythmic, musical, and precise—telling American tales that flash like summer lightning. Her aim is true.

—BARRY WIGHTMAN
author of *Pepperland*

In Kathryn Gahl's first fiction collection, the much-published poet creates memorable images throughout. An old man, post-stroke in a nursing home, contemplates the best and worst of his life and waits for death as two adult children hold his exit in their hands. A feverish, bullied school girl, whose grandfather is her best friend, dreams of fitting in, in a dizzying tale of adolescence, meningitis, and distracted parents. This is an eclectic assembly of vignettes and short stories, sure to surprise, provoke, and enlighten.

—JEFF ELZINGA
author of *The Distance Between Stars*

The first lines of each story in Kathryn Gahl's collection feel like encountering a door opened just a crack. There's glowing light beyond that door with music and hushed conversation—entire worlds inside a single dresser drawer that belonged to one main character's deceased wife. These are imperfect, gritty, often vulnerable human characters, and you can't help but come in when they beckon and join them for a strong cup of coffee and a slice of pecan pie on a chipped plate. Gahl has an unbelievably keen eye for all the artifacts and moments that make a life, a life.

—EMILIE LINDEMANN
author of *Ghost(ed) Woman & the Electric Purple Pants*

Kathryn Gahl's sharp, poetic prose dances along the page with light-footed grace. With an expert hand, Gahl crafts stories that sparkle with emotional clarity, capturing the ache and wonder of existence. This collection is full of wit, tenderness, and grandeur. Truly a remarkable work of art that I found myself savoring long after the last word.

—RICHIE ZABOROWSKE
Neenah Public Library

YES, NO, I DON'T KNOW

stories

Kathryn Gahl

CORNERSTONE PRESS
UNIVERSITY OF WISCONSIN-STEVENS POINT

Cornerstone Press, Stevens Point, Wisconsin 54481
Copyright © 2026 Kathryn Gahl
www.uwsp.edu/cornerstone

Printed in the United States of America.

Library of Congress Control Number: 2026930352
ISBN: 978-1-968148-25-6

Cover image © Jamie Heiden 2025

This is a work of fiction. Names, characters, businesses, places, events, and incidents are either the products of the author's imagination or used in a fictitious manner. Any resemblance to actual persons, living or dead, or actual events is purely coincidental.

Cornerstone Press titles are produced in courses and internships offered by the Department of English at the University of Wisconsin–Stevens Point.

DIRECTOR & PUBLISHER
Dr. Ross K. Tangedal

EXECUTIVE EDITORS
Jeff Snowbarger, Freesia McKee

EDITORIAL DIRECTOR
Brett Hill

SENIOR EDITORS
Paige Biever, Ellie Atkinson

PRESS STAFF
Lilly Kulbeck, Brianna Loving, Abby Paulsen, Samantha Bjork, Sophie McPherson, Andrew Bryant, McKenna Bartel, Gwen Goetter, Kim Janesch

to Bobbo, who found me

STORIES

Miles

Foggy water. Watery fog. It enveloped the Alaskan ferry until the boat's Chief Engineer, Miles Gopon, saw more than fog. He saw sheets of lace. Pink lace. Panties. They landed like soft light on the pilothouse floor, the last piece she removed before lifting one foot, then the other, and walking toward him.

He shook his head. He was woozy and he knew it. Who was she? It was four in the morning. Was he sleeping on the job? He shook his head again, and then pressed his leathery fingers against a huge marine map. He squinted and scowled, shoulders hunched, knees locked. His six-foot frame, once hefty with flesh was leaner, wanting—a man at fifty. He pressed his temples in a circular motion and peered into the fog. A line on his forehead twitched, a spasm he quickly controlled. Then, with self-assurance, he spoke. "Thirty degrees north."

"Aye, aye, Chief," a man in a crisp white uniform replied. The man, by title but not by experience, was the boat's Captain. The Captain turned to the wheelsman and barked, "Thirty degrees north!"

Miles lowered his head. He gazed over his half-moon bifocals at the sweaty wheelsman, a young buck probably the same age as the improbable panty girl: twenty-five. Miles wondered what illusion (his first wife called it *mimsy delusion*)

1

drifted through the kid's head during a watch at the wheel. In the ten years Miles had been navigating the Inside Passage, calling the shots and making decisions, he never asked the guy playing Captain or the brawny wheelsman what they thought about when executing two degrees north, turning eight degrees southeast, or holding steady as she goes. What mattered to Miles was not their fantasies but the engines below, the grunting of coal-fired furnaces, and the fog that could run them aground. And oh the passengers—in those days, working-class types come to make a killing: build the pipeline, carve out roads and sewers, and staff the taverns, fishing boats, and Bartlett-Memorial Hospital, the only sick house in Juneau.

It had been a week since he had noticed a real twenty-five year old arriving for summer assignment. She was power-walking the deck in blue jeans, shiny blue clogs, and a red wool blazer, hand-sewn, she boasted. He had stood outside the Crew Only door, puffing his pipe. It was after supper, his belly swollen from bean soup and extra slices of soda bread. "Evening, Ma'am," he said, nodding and touching the edge of his black beret in a modified salute.

On her first lap, she ignored him. On the second, she accelerated her pace, breath quickening and chin jutted forward, her arms swinging. On the third lap, she stopped, pivoted to face him, and planted her feet. "I am not a *mam*," she said slowly, looking past his shoulder at the rosewater light. And then, fixing her eyes on his shoulder, she added, "*Mam*, by the way, is colloquial for Mamma." With her eyes on the beret, she concluded, "And I'm no *mam*."

"I see that," he said. "I stand corrected." He removed the beret in a swooping manner to let her know he found her fresh and potentially generous. She returned the gesture with a practiced look that was flirtatious but hardly provocative, the best for a pigeon-toed girl from Nebraska. Then two burly women walked by, holding hands. A teenage boy with a guitar came right behind them, scratching out a Dylan tune. "We carry a ship of fools," Miles said. "And I'm one of them."

She studied him with the rehearsed face of a nurse, making clinical notations of a sun-blotched forehead, broken blood vessels around the nose, a receding hairline. He wore oil-stained coveralls zipped only to the waist. The high-water britches were tugged upward by his distended belly. Her mental notations made him nervous. Deliberately, he set the beret on his head at what seemed the quintessential sexy angle.

"Nice hat," she said, but it was awkward.

"It's a beret."

"You're *French* then," she said, her tone changing, an expectation that here finally was a ticket to adventure.

"Not that I know of."

"Then . . ."

"Then why? Because it makes me look unlikely. And I like being unlikely."

"Oooh."

"I expect you do, too," he said. "Or you wouldn't be here."

She frowned. "Am I that transparent?"

He frowned back. "With all due respect, might I stroll with you?"

"Sure."

They lapped the deck several times, working the light banter of the lonely. She: *Are those gulls or seagulls? How'd the ship get its name? How do you cope with the midnight sun?* He: *That's an impressive red blazer you've got there. I once knew a guy who was a cornhusker, always in a fight. I'm glad the ship didn't get wrangled up in Wrangell.*

Eventually, he paused at the Crew Only door. "Want to see how my world lives?"

"Uhh, sure."

He unlatched a door and they stepped in. After their eyes adjusted to the grainy light, he unlatched a second door and motioned her in. She scanned the rumpled bunk, stained coffee cups, and soapstone pipes face down on a stack of *Popular Mechanics* magazines. "It has a lived-in look," he joked.

"So do you."

His face fell. He had no comeback.

"I like it," she said.

Whether she meant she liked his face or his cabin did not matter. It was a cue and it was the only cue he needed. It took three hours to make it to her waist, and his seasoned, middle-age approach was worth every minute, every drawn-out luxurious minute for she seemed willing, confused, young, and unbearably soft. And somewhere in there was trust, too, something new for him and full of trepidation.

As for her: she was drawn to the crepe layers beneath his eyes, how he tapped his pipe, how he had walked on the balls of his feet with urgency, too much in a hurry to use the whole foot. He smelled of new life, exploding aromas of tobacco, oranges, and motor oil. He even claimed to be a father, yet no family photos bathed the close walls, only posters of Alaska: sky, mountains, rivers, and birds. He had a past but had left it where it belonged, he said, *in the past.* She liked that, she thought.

"So," she noted in their second hour together when they still sat at the two-by-three foot table hinged to the cabin wall, shots of Scotch untouched. "Let me get this straight, three wives and two children, one stillborn."

He spun the curly hairs of his mustache. "Perhaps," he said, "it was two wives and three children." He had intended to sound cheery, amusing, but hearing the truth out loud suddenly felled him the way a good driving rain flattened the wild rushes along the water. He broke his gaze on her and stared at the cabin door. He rubbed his palms together, the skin over his hands moving, lolling with regret. Then he heard her lovely chest fill with air and, still fixated on the door, waited for the typical female retort of *Uughhh.* When it didn't come, he looked at her. She had pinched her lips together and above them, her eyes had gone gray, flat washers with holes in the middle. "Look," he said, arms upswept like a priest at Easter. "Sometimes I can't remember my own story, what with the Scotch and all." Her face tightened. For a moment she shook all over. "It's the twelve on, twelve off," he said rapidly. "I work to drink to sleep to work."

At that, her pupils dilated, brackish whirlpools trying to spin all of him. She stifled a sigh. She felt lightheaded. He seemed to be all that had been drilled out of her—naughty, risky, somehow banned. He might be what so many young girls needed: a Project, someone to work on and improve, although right then and there, she could not enunciate that. Right then and there, he was a whirling mass of something, drawing her right toward the forbidden center. She tried to speak but what she came up with sounded naïve and dumb. So she simply sat there.

He welcomed her reserve by pulling on his mustache. He ironed the salt-and-pepper hairs, working from center to edge in a rhythmic fashion. Then he said he was *crazy* about her. She took in the information with a glassy little girl look and he continued pulling at the mustache, his signature tic when he was uneasy.

The tic accelerated the vortex she had fallen into. She giggled, a release of some sort finally coming. Then she asked if his name was really Miles. It mattered, deeply. After this summer, she wanted to change Ann Gray to something more. More what? Suzanne could be a start. She had read *Change a name, change a life* and she hadn't come this far to adopt a man's name, to settle for that kind of change. Was Suzanne Gray too timid? What about a name like Suzanne Blackstone? Or Suzanne Tresor Blackstone? A totally new identity.

"Miles it is," he said. "I swear."

"*Miles to go before I sleep.*"

He grinned. "God, I hope not." He reached across the table and lifted her hand, kissing fingernails, suckling the silky curve of each knuckle, the fresh tan on back of the hand, the inside of the wrist with its taut skin and bounding pulse. Then he paused as was his custom and asked, "What's *your* name?"

She felt an obsession coming on. His lips were drenching her fingers in heat. "Suzanne," she said, flushing. "Suzanne Blackstone."

"Wonderful." He kiss-kissed each finger again until she crumbled into tiny pieces. Then picked up each piece and sashayed around the table. He patted his lap. She sat down, straddling his coverall thighs. "What was your first wife like?" she asked, searching for a benchmark, for a chance to acquire knowledge that she had no idea how to apply.

"Huh?"

"Generally speaking, what was she like?"

Miles stroked the mustache. "Generally speaking," he said, "she was generally speaking." His eyes twinkled. "Any more questions?"

Outside, waves splashed the ship's sides and, had they looked, gulls rode eddies of air behind the boat, diving for churned-up fish. Inside, she studied him, shaking her head from side to side, though for his part he had no interest in more questions. He unbuttoned her blouse. The five buttons popped through each buttonhole easily. Next, he unhooked her bra. She went limp. He ran weathered palms up her spine, across the shoulders, and around the front.

She let out a startled cry. He placed his index finger over his lips, and she got the message, quieting. Then his sweet tobacco mouth opened and she pushed her ample breasts to him with pride. He cradled them and she made small singing sounds, a hum of notes rising uncontrollably from her pelvis and along her thighs, her lines voluptuous and charged.

At that, he stopped.

He put his ear to the welling space between her breasts. The sound of heartbeats filled her rib cage, the ruffle and drum of the Divine. He returned to action, beside himself with licking, an unrelenting fervor while she held on for his feathery tongue strokes.

"Let's go to your place," he whispered.

She nodded. He offered to dress her. She let him, interrupting his methods, kissing his forehead and earlobes, gliding her buttocks back and forth with a lazy island smile. She was not particularly striking, a girl with glasses and a cowlick. She was round-shouldered and he *had* noticed she moved like a pigeon. He fastened the last button and then held her red blazer. She threaded in one arm, then the other, before he hugged her from behind and realized he was hard, at last, blessedly hard.

He unlocked the door and stepped out onto the deck. When the coast was clear, he motioned for her, standing three feet away, as if they were strangers. A sliver of a moon held up the sky. Stars and gulls filled spaces between puffy clouds.

She walked ahead of him, trembling, excited by possibility and not wanting this to end. In her mind, the only possibility was to extend the possibility until she was certain he would not take advantage. And so she changed her mind, not allowing him to enter her cabin, neither that night nor the next, though she did dine with him in the office's dining quarters, a big move on his part to acknowledge her public presence in his private, lonesome gut.

"Tell me where it hurts," she said as the waiter set down plates of buttery whitefish.

"Where doesn't it?"

Under the table, she wiggled her foot between his legs. Lines around his lips spread into a homespun smile. The tip of her tongue lobbed back and forth along her upper lip until he said they should eat while the food was warm. And they did. And he talked more and her foot again found its place, the numbers of wives and children soon irrelevant. For what mattered was how his life of blazing infidelity was unraveling, and how her life as a helper took him in, their time at table merry and downright playful.

By the time the boat docked in Juneau, he knew hope for the first time in years: address, phone number, work schedule at the hospital. In two weeks the boat would be back, he'd be back, he'd cautiously climb all over her at the tacky apartment she was to share with a secretary from Montana. The Lower 48 could go to hell as far as he was concerned. Those get-rich-quickers had come to rape Alaska and make him find another place to hide out. But maybe, he speculated, it wasn't a place he needed. Maybe it was this person, an earthy young woman who could hold the emptiness inside him, someone who understood but did not pity what a Downs baby had done to dreams the second time around. Aw, hell, he oughta leave her alone. She had twice his energy. She was undefiled and spotless, round and full, vibrant. She had a beautiful structure, at least as much as he had seen. He wanted her. As the engines fired up and the dockhands let go the chains around the pilings, sending him out to sea for another two weeks, he wanted her so badly he went to starboard and threw up.

And she, in the weeks that followed, wanted him too. After orientation on days, she came home to pine-paneled walls in a prefab thrown together that spring. She stood at the window and watched the bulldozer backfill a swamp across the street for a trailer court where, by summer's end, salmonella and its attendant diarrhea would seize the latest arrivals. The hospital would be full, she working double shifts, glad to fend off hours when the Alaskan midnight glowed and, alone behind room-darkening shades, she would think of his oil-stained nail beds, jelly belly laugh, that wistfulness when he talked of rocky necks, mountain goats, and salmon that swam upstream to spawn and die.

Each time after he left the dock, she tasted him for hours. He was Scotch, full-bodied and sweet with a warm afterglow. She herself was three-two beer, heady, and reminiscent of sawdust and strains of polka music. And now they had met. Whether flirting at the greasy spoon in town or watching bald eagles soar, her vision swelled. And his? It could only be said that his exploded ever since they stood on the deck (the very spot where they first met) and looked at the line where sea met sky. He called it a mystical place, similar to the end of a rainbow or the prisms inside the geode he sent via post to *My Suzanne*.

By mid-summer, their ideas of sharing a runaway life jelled.

Until a Tuesday evening when she arrived early at the place where he stayed when ashore, a room at the Juneau Hotel. It wasn't only his room. It was a room the ferry line rented; a rotating cast of officers was assigned it when ashore. He had expected her close to midnight, after her evening shift from which she *never* got out on time. But by eight p.m. she had garnered a "low census," meaning enough patients had been discharged that a full staff wasn't needed. She jumped at the chance to leave work early. It meant less money, more of him.

She fairly skipped down the sidewalks between the hospital and hotel. Slabs of cement tilted this way and that. Tufts of switch grass poked between the cracks, defiant against the changing landscape. He had said the room was on the first floor, that she was to simply walk past the front desk clerk, an Indian who had fallen out of a tree, had bumps on his head, and was living off his Native American Pipeline Payout.

From the street, she saw the only room with light, a pearly blue beam. Then she did something she had never done before: she spied. Stepping off the functional but treacherous sidewalk, she climbed the small stony incline to the lit room. The shade was down, but not completely. The window was ajar. She heard a man's voice, clearly not Miles's, say, *I'm going to give you something I need to give you.* She had an overwhelming itch to say *Boo.* Instead, she inched closer. *I will eat until you say I can't take it any more,* another man said. She held her breath. She peered in and, beneath the shade, saw Miles sitting on the edge of the bed. The TV was on and he was hunched forward, naked. His left hand supported him on the bed. In flickering light, his right hand was at work. He labored rhythmically, neck veins bulging and mouth ajar while a siliconized woman moaned on the television. She studied the screen. Two men wet with sweat labored over the woman, one entering her mouth, the other a perineal orifice. It was unclear which orifice.

She scrambled down the embankment in a panic. She had an urge to run. But she was Suzanne now, not Ann. She entered the hotel and stopped at the front desk. The Indian, as described, seemed slow but she engaged him in conversation, buying time till she thought Miles would be finished. Then, she made her way down the hall and knocked on his door.

"Who's there?"

"Who do you think *who's there?*"

Behind his door, the TV went mute. A chair scraped the wooden floor. The double-hung window wobbled in its sash, a crunk-clunk sound as it closed. Then, the door opened. "It can't be true," Miles said. He wore faded jeans, nothing else. "*What* are you doing here?"

"I thought I was invited." She crossed her arms against her churning stomach.

"Well, sure. Come on in."

She did not move. She hugged herself tighter. A tear began to form in her left eye, but she cut it off by squinting, then gritting her teeth.

"Wow," he said. "Bad night at work? Hey, you got out early. How's that for a change?" A man came down the hall; the two of them stood there, transfixed and speechless while the man shuffled past. The man arrived at his door, fumbled his key in the lock, and swore. He tried again, succeeded, and then slammed the door as he disappeared. They remained under the transom, frozen, eyeing each other.

She spoke first. "That was disgusting."

"What?"

She glared at him, arms still folded tightly. She drummed the fingers of her right hand along her left forearm.

"Sorry," he said. "I should have closed the shade all the way, but it's stuffy in this pit."

"That," she repeated, "was disgusting."

"I didn't want to rush you." He fetched a shirt. "Look, come on in, we can talk about this. You of all people should understand biology."

"That was beyond biology," she said. "*That* was debasement."

"Shit," he said. He felt caught. He felt like the very essence of all he scorned. He shot her a look. "You were inaccessible," he said. "I didn't want to rush you. We've got a thing, you and me. You know it. I know it."

"You know nothing." She kicked him in the shin, her face registering surprise at her own spontaneity.

"Good," he said. "That's good."

By the end of summer he thought of how he had waited until the next time the boat docked, then marched right up to the nurses' station in new trousers and a button-down shirt clean out of the crinkly package, his few wiry hairs slicked to one side, beret in one hand, the other jiggling something in his pocket.

"Suzanne Blackstone," he said with a wink to the ward clerk. "It's a surprise." The freckled clerk looked up from her sandwich, puzzled.

"Nebraska," he said, adding a head nod to the wink.

"We've got an Ann Gray from Nebraska," the clerk replied, pushing a wad of food into her cheek. "That little cornhusker's gone to Seattle on a transport, going to take a little R&R while there, something about the midnight sun, how she can't sleep."

"Suzanne Blackstone from Nebraska," he said.

"Sorry, bud," the clerk said as the phone rang and she answered it.

He paled and walked back to the hotel. He borrowed the desk clerk's shiny new Dodge Charger and drove out to the Mendenhall Glacier. There he got out of the car. He tasted the view. He heard the ice from the hundred-foot high wall crackle and crash into the collecting pool. Didn't she know what a big deal it was that he had taken her down to the engine room and up to the pilothouse? Only authorized personnel were allowed there. Didn't she know this was all *her* fault? That way she set her face, fresh from the prairie, with a display of curiosity, followed by sincere interest, and then the sincere, kind nursiness. *Of course* he had confessed, unloaded the story about his greedy kids, how he couldn't take it anymore, and those two testy Glendale wives in the rat race. *Even if you're winning the race*, he had told her, *you're still a rat.*

She had laughed and gotten him to confess even more—how bad he felt when he watched porn, worse after. But a man needed a release, and if his real woman (that's *you,* Suzanne) was inaccessible, then he did what he did. She had pouted and said she didn't like knowing about a problem she couldn't do anything about. *Problem,* he had replied. *Problem? The only problem was my willingness to wait, for you.*

He continued to stand at the mile-wide wall of ice, ironing his mustache. He looked to the sky spackling into pink and purple and gold. He felt the old stiffness at the back of his knees. A hunk of ice crashed. He feared that in another decade the tree-spotted valley he had just driven through would be clotted by condos, gas stations, and strip malls. Little by little, glaciers would melt and salmon would die before reaching their spawning beds. How would he survive? With another greenhorn Captain? A double-Scotch doubled? He spit.

The magnificent ice before him fissured and fell. It was getting late but he had nothing better to do. So he stood there, trying hard not to think and in the void he recalled how the bar maid had let him use the phone and he had yelled above the Stones on the jukebox, shouted over the pinball machines, and railed beyond the boatload of thrill-seekers pouring into the bar and crowding him while he professed to her how they'd hike the mountain to a salmon bake, take the train to Skagway, and fly into Kodiak—*now there's a place we can hide out,* he predicted.

At some point the phone line must have fizzled into dead air; he wasn't sure when. Still, he was believing that she had heard him when another chunk of glacier crashed, a giant drop destined for meltdown. He picked at his teeth with a pocketknife. Night was coming slowly and he was ridiculously cold, for August. His ankles hurt. His lips were blue. He tugged at his beret and zipped up his windbreaker. A sheet of clouds moved in and moved out while he kept watch, waiting. And then at midnight, a bunch of round and full and vibrant stars emerged, and he watched them flirt in the vast blackness.

Pecan Pie

June 1970. Good a time as any to hitchhike from Chicago to Florida. Like Frank says, school's out, jobs are scarce and Mia has this uncle in Tampa with a restaurant. If we can smile on our feet, we'll stay and wait tables for the summer.

Illinois is one long-ass state, riding in Dodge Chargers and Chevelles, plus a seed farmer in a pickup who drops them at a bus station where they sleep overnight. Come morning, they wander to the Texaco and meet a semi driver who drives them straight through Kentucky and Tennessee, pretty places, pretty poor. And before this story rolls on, Frank says it's important to know Mia's size and shape. Jet black hair down to flat little buttocks, white skin without a blemish. Barbie doll bones, like Frank says with breathless adoration. In other words, Asian, on the road with a white guy in sandals and a backpack, hair the color of sand, and freckles starting to emerge from the sun and, Frank grins, from the love state I was in with Mia. Which was all youth cool. Until Mississippi. Folks there are disturbed by an unending Vietnam War, but worse, impending forced integration mandated by a federal court. And so, there they are in a state of turmoil, Mississippi sun beating down on dirt roads speckled with dogtrot houses—wood-frame, tin-roof dwellings with open-air hallways running down the middle. A train hooting in the distance, Coca-Cola and donuts in their bellies from breakfast. And Mia in front of Frank, both their thumbs in the air to catch a ride.

An old beat-up black Cadillac roars past, twenty miles over the speed limit, so fast they can't see the driver. Next, a Chevy short-bed crawls past, the driver giving them the finger. That's when the Caddie backs up and its passenger door swings open. A deep voice says, Looks like y'all need a ride.

Yes sir, Frank says. They scoot into the front seat. The seat's wide, with Mia in the middle sidled up to Frank. The Caddie purrs and Frank glances at the white man. He's built like a billboard with broad shoulders. Fat had deposited itself everywhere and run out of room so that now it piled up like drifts, crowding the backsides of his bare arms.

Pistons spit as they reach the crest of a hill and the man says, Blowin' up a storm over yonder, you'd a been drenched. Tell me, miss, what brings y'all to these parts?

I'm in school, Mia says.

They ain't got schools from where y'all come from, I reckon.

That's when Frank notices the shotgun in the back seat and says, you can let us out at the next intersection. No response. They drive on in drenching heat until the man stops at a wood frame house. I'm slap worn out, the man says, adding, how's about a lemonade?

We'll be on our way, Mia says, slicing her elbow into Frank's ribs before the man grabs the gun, opens their door, and gestures toward a slanting screen door. They get out.

Daisy! The man yells. We got company! For the following hours, food and fury crisscross a gray Formica kitchen table edged in chrome. Corn bread, the oil embargo, and sagging used car sales. Chitlins and the government. Lemonade and lazy hippies. When the pecan pie arrives, the man lights a Camel and says, I got me a son. 'Bout your age. How old are you?

Nineteen, Frank says.

The man turns his bald head at Mia. Gotta tell 'ya, first time I seen one of you close up.

Scooter! Daisy shouts.

Hush your mouth, woman. His breath shortens. He chews the inside of his cheek. Then, he looks Frank dead-in-the-eye and says, We went over there to kill them people. And. We. Got. Killed. His hills of flesh quiver. A red flush creeps up his jowls. And then it begins, a slow squall, a stall, before he weeps. It's a long, bawling, gut-wrenching scene.

That night, Frank and Mia sleep in the son's bedroom. Straw tick mattress, fresh sheets, soldier photo on the bedstand, a young boy in olive green, hat with a stiff brim, mouth set in determination.

In the morning, after another piece of pecan pie, Scooter man-hugs Frank, a long hug he can't let go. Daisy dabs her eyes. And then Frank and Mia hit the road, two thumbs up, confident they will hitch another ride.

Sure

After he left the family, she took them to London to live with an aunt, drove to Gary where the steel mills were booming, put them on the orphan train and bit her lip. He hit the road to Albuquerque on his Harley, saw his daughter one time across the ball field, took a liking to firearms and nude beaches. Once, she turned on the gas, opened her legs to a realtor promising help, drove deliberately into the lagoon. He chipped his tooth chewing ice, built a back-story about lumberjacking, and felt his hemorrhoids fire up.

Sometimes, she left them alone when the sitter bailed, worked the night shift while they slept, wasted time tracking a deadbeat dad. He allowed no room for indecision, rented a room from a widow, and made a baby with the babe from the bar.

Meanwhile, in Iowa, she took them to Grandma's house, clipped coupons, went off to college and graduated cum laude. He took a job selling used cars in Long Beach, began to see himself as exceptional, said he suffered from seasonal affective disorder.

She indulged in hot baths, scoured Goodwill for school clothes, and patched the roof. Every now and then, he adjusted his nuts, his address, his reason. She cracked her knuckles, told the kids to knock it off, and paid the collection agency five dollars a month. Sometimes, she got drunk on screwdrivers. He took up with the priest, stock car racing, and single malt Scotch. Sometimes, he cried in his sleep on Saturday. She lost weight, gained weight, raised African Greys. He basically disappeared, joined the Yacht Club, nearly choked on a chicken bone.

She pawned her wedding ring, nailed a second job at Wal-Mart, suppressed an ugly impulse. Twice, he went to jail, to Miami, to the library. Three times, she went to church, the cop shop, the food pantry. He worked the boats of the Inside Passage, hired out as a hired hand in Montana, lost his thumb at the shoe factory. She got breast cancer, a raise, a refinance. He engaged in conversation about life, literature, and love, underwent a vasectomy, thought he recognized his son going down the escalator.

After he left the family, they saw one another twenty years later and were hard put to remember the exact point in time where the wind shifted, when it put their boat in irons. "Here's something to ponder," she said, reading from her iPad. "*Most of your pain is self-chosen.*"

"Still looking to blame," he said.

"Looking at Gibran."

"LeBron," he retorted.

She was ready to smile, but held back. "LeBron," she said.

"Lebron *James*," he added.

She looked to the lowering sun. "Sure," she said.

Wife

Wife. It is not what every man wants. But at some
point in time, it is what most men get. That was what
Irvin Kramer, our bus driver with the permanent four o'clock
shadow and bitten fingernails, said. No one knew Irvin and
no one wanted to. We didn't know if he himself was married
and if he was, his wife probably wore pink girdles, nylons
rolled down around her ankles, and orthopedic shoes clung
with cowshit. The subject of wife came up because of Lacey
Miller. She was the freshman girl from a family of five boys,
all older. She had curls the color of honey and eyelashes the
color of straw. Every torqued up guy on our bus wanted to
get into Lacey's pants, including me, a puny freshman.

It was a typical, boring Monday when the after-school bus
stopped at Lacey's gravel driveway. She stood up, gathered
books in her arms, and walked four rows to the front of the
bus. She stared straight ahead. She knew not to look any of
us horndogs in the eye.

"Thanks, Mr. Kramer," she said, and floated down the
steps. Soon as the door closed, senior guys in the back seats
whooped and hollered.

At that, Irvin stood up and faced his adolescent charges.
"Wife," Irvin said. "You clowns in the peanut gallery back
there need a wife?"

"Hell no," Skeeter replied. A couple of guys stood, thumping Skeeter, pushing and shoving one another, a street party full of courage and nerve. Skeeter, for one small minute, probably felt heroic.

"Then let her alone," Irvin said, "because she'll grow into a wife. Now sit down and shut up." Skeeter sat down, fast, having lost position with the band of bullies. The bullies likewise drooped their heads and sat. I felt sorry for Skeeter. He was the kid with hay fever and psoriasis. He stuttered. That day, though, he didn't stutter. He belted out *hell no* with such gusto for a moment I thought his speech therapy was working. He couldn't wait to get off the bus at his stop, one before mine, and when he stomped to the front of the bus, he looked straight ahead, just like Lacey. Irvin opened the door and Skeeter paused. I thought he was going to deck Irvin, the way he stopped, confident, dead in his tracks. He locked his knees. His chest rose. Then he yelled, "Fucker!" and bolted out the door. The bus engine growled and pulled away. I watched Skeeter scuffle to his dilapidated house. It had a crumbling concrete birdbath on the lawn and a broken swing hanging cockeyed from an old elm. Skeeter picked up a handful of gravel and pitched it at vines clinging to the silo. Sparrows in the vines scattered like buckshot.

Irvin's theory of how to grow a wife was never mentioned again and from then on, Lacey sat in the front seat, just to the right of Irvin. I sat behind her, staring at her bouncy curls. When she got on each morning, she looked at the floor. I figured her older brothers had given her a few tips. Meanwhile, boys at the back of the bus found strip poker, dog-eared *Playboys* and *Penthouses*, hunting stories, rifle comparisons, or chewing tobacco to amuse themselves. As for me, I looked and listened. Sometimes I did my homework. Mostly though, I daydreamed. And often I thought about Irvin's wife advice. I didn't know what a wife was those years in high school, so how could I believe I would get one? It made as much sense that Lacey would be a wife as it did that my sort-of girlfriend, Pauley, would be a wife—mine or anyone else's. Pauley was a basketball star. She could set a pick, take flight, roll hard to the glass. She had a gravity-defying drive and crossover charm. Her three-on-one break and pullup jumper had nothing to do with ring-around-the-collar. Or that new thing for frying pans, Teflon. She would never Scotchguard a floral print sofa. She would never say that tie doesn't match, what *were* you thinking? Pauley was a wild card. She could call anyone's bluff.

She sat behind me on the hour-long ride from Frankfurt High School to our farmhouses. One time she poked me on the shoulder. I turned. She grinned and said, "Watch this." She got up and went to the back of the bus. Strip poker was in progress, unknown to Irvin. He had his eyes on the road, negotiating slick roads during a pounding rain. Pauley wedged between Duane (missing pants and a belt) and Kenny (already without shoes and socks). Guys' jackets were bunched against the emergency rear-exit door. Pauley took off her windbreaker. She added it to the pile. For a moment, it seemed the game would be called. Skeeter, who had won two rounds with a straight flush and four-of-a-kind, fidgeted. Strip poker was one thing. A stripped girl another. Skeeter looked to the humongous rear-view mirror above Irvin's head. One more trip to the principal's office and he'd be suspended. Irvin wasn't after Skeeter that day, though. With rain pelting the bus, Irvin dead-eyed the road, his shoulders hunched with responsibility.

"Anybody want out?" Skeeter said to the poker players. No one moved. "Okay," Skeeter said. "Deal." Jimmy dealt, which set the stage for various combinations of truth and dare. At the end of each hand, everyone but the winner removed a piece of clothing. In no time, I saw Duane's zit-marked shoulders, Jimmy's sunken chest and Pauley's sports bra. The game had never gotten quite that far before, but fierce weather had extended our ride. Jimmy was shuffling the cards for another deal when Irvin slammed on the brakes. We all lurched forward in our seats. A beech tree, felled by lightning, blocked Cardinal Road. Everyone scrambled to put on coats, caps and shoes. The entire bus piled out and beneath sheets of cold rain, we rolled the severed beech into the ditch.

My mother loved those bus stories. The poker one in particular would have tickled her. She was thirty-nine with a green thumb and a blown aneurysm behind her green eyes when Dad and I lost her earlier in the fall. She had said Pauley was a tomboy. "Believe it or not," she had said, "I was one too." I stared at my mother. Impossible. Then she showed me a photo of her with her bicycle. Age twelve. Zipped hair. Peddle-pusher pants. My mother, the tomboy. When she died, however, she was obviously a wife. If I could have told her about Lacey and Irvin, she would have said something to make me think. "Lacey's the kind of girl with *maid* in her future," my mother might have said, "not *wife*."

"Maid, wife. What's the difference, Mom?"

My mother's eyes would have twinkled. A maid gets paid for washing and cooking and cleaning, she would have said, but a wife does it for free. Mom was never pissed off that she cooked and cleaned. She and Dad were bookends. They took care of one another and me in the middle. Sometimes they kissed and hugged in front of me. It never felt weird. It felt balanced. It was Skeeter who lacked balance. If Mom were alive, she would have told me, go cheer him up. So after Dad's hot tamales and baked beans, I walked half a mile to his house to surprise him. Skeeter sometimes showed up at my house, unannounced after chores, to eat Butter Brickle ice cream and potato chips. Then he shuffled back to his dad sitting in front of the Zenith boob tube. His Dad clutched a Budweiser while his mom threw the shuttle on her weaving machine and every now and then said, *Ronny, you keep drinking and you'll meet your Savior sooner than you can say Jesus.* As I walked into Skeeter's yard, I saw his parents at their usual posts, stonewalled. The only lights in the house came from the Zenith and a naked yellow bulb above Mrs. Karsteadt's head. Usually Skeeter sat in the straight-back chair next to his Dad. But he wasn't there. I was about to head back home when I heard a noise from the barn. I figured it was a possum or fox scaring up the chickens. So I walked closer, only to hear commotion from the south end of the barn where the pig pens were. Damn, I wished I'd brought my BB gun. At least I could scare the critter off.

Rather than open the big barn door, I went in through the milk house. Three noiseless doors and I stood at one end of the murky, long alley. Some cows were still upright, their stanchions clinking as they chewed their cuds. Other cows had laid down and were asleep. With catlike steps, I stole my way to the south end of the barn. A few bats zipped overhead and I stood stock-still, held my breath. The sound I heard was a pig all right, but not the graveled pitch of one giving birth, or of a sow in heat fighting the boar. No, this sound was like one being rounded up for bacon, a 300-pounder climbing up a wooden gangway into the livestock truck. There was no truck in sight, though. And Skeeter's dad wasn't out here herding anything.

The sound continued, low, grunting. It became a moan, more like a sheep in distress. The fiery grunts spurted faster and faster, but in the dead air between them, I heard something else. It was a human, breathing, growling, groaning, and somehow fighting, too. My breath froze. I worried that Skeeter in his stupid way had taken his *Playboy* and Budweiser to the barn and been attacked by the boar. My heart raced. I had to do something. I punched my legs into overdrive and raced full-tilt down to the commotion. There I found Skeeter, pants down, pale skinny ass pumping a Hampshire hog. The baffled porker tried to wriggle free but Skeeter's fingers dug into the animal's skin and held on. Over and over the barrel of Skeeter's penis rammed the daylight out of that sow. In, out, in, out, the two of them screaming and squealing.

Finally, Skeeter caught sight of me and tumbled backwards, caught up in his own dropped pant legs. He righted himself, pulled up the pants, and cinched his belt. I felt blood drain from my entire body. Skeeter looked past me down the barn alley. "Old man thinks I'm at your place," he said.

"Sure, sure," I said. I felt cemented in place. Skeeter stared at me, face flushed, hands in his pockets. It was then we both realized the pig was still thrashing about, tied to the bottom board of the pen. Bailer twine crisscrossed its neck and front legs and it was fighting the restraint. I nodded toward the pig. Skeeter looked back at me with BB eyeballs. Then he reached into his pocket and pulled out a Swiss army knife, stolen, no doubt. His hands shook as he flipped open the correct blade. He snapped the bailer twine. The pig thrashed some more and finally swung itself upright on little horned feet. It rumbled to the corner of the pen, and stood there, heaving. My legs began to tingle. I pivoted away from Skeeter and the pen and the pig. All the way down the alley, Skeeter drilled the back of my head, I could feel it. I opened the milk house door and turned. I couldn't see him, but I knew he was in the shadows somewhere. I cupped my hands and yelled, "I won't say a word. Scout's honor." Then I careened through two more milk house doors and raced out of his yard. I walked home in the moonless night. There wasn't a car or truck on the road. Halfway home, I wondered if Skeeter had stayed in the barn to slit his wrists. But I wasn't going back. Somewhere I'd heard you don't die from wrist-slitting. You just got scars. And more teasing. And you're still horny.

That night I sat at my window all night, thinking, there must be something bigger out there than this. Boise, that was it. I thought of the Harley Dad promised me when I turned eighteen, and now I heard him say, you'll be in hog heaven.

I looked at the gunmetal sky, thinking of that Harley. I felt strange and confused. I could hear Irvin's short speech that day on the bus. It is not what every man wants, but at some point in time, it is what most men get. That's what he said because he didn't want to say the real deal, and that is this. It is not what every man gets, but at every point in time, it is what every man wants. To touch. And be touched. And that year, I would grow to understand how either one could tear you in two.

Sugarplum

F ear hung round the old lady's ankles like her nylons, rolled down in summer heat and left there, limp. By early evening, those violet-gray rolls looked as if the skin of Agnes, the old lady, had fallen upon itself. Now Agnes watched Mary Clare zip a dishrag back and forth on the kitchen table, Formica dulled from countless wipings and detergents. "Missed some, Sweetie," Agnes said, and motioned her daughter to pork-chop grease near a vase of lilacs. Mary Clare swished again and returned to the sink, seemingly perturbed.

Agnes sighed, pulled a hankie from her brassiere and dabbed her neck. She yearned for a cool evening to tug the nylons back up and hook them in garters, an apparatus descended, she once thought, from a chastity belt. Agnes knew women named Chastity, Prudence, and Deliverance. She herself hadn't been named with such luck. Some saint, Agnes, had descended upon her, an Irish predilection to foreshadow destiny with baptism, and a name. Throughout her life, Agnes had tried to become her namesake, the patron saint of virginity. People were ignorant, though, thinking virginity meant no sex, when it meant power, self-assurance, a woman complete to herself. Well, she had failed at that too, and now at Mary Clare's, her namesake was the farthest thing from her mind. She patted one side pocket of her

26

apron, then the other, in search of her address book. Not finding it, she said, "What day is it again?"

"Monday, Mom. Monday." Mary Clare dipped plates from sink to stacking rack and did not face her mother.

"I know it's Monday," Agnes said as she checked the apron's front chest pocket and found an address book with broken spine. Rubber bands stretched both lengthwise and crosswise around the ragged book. "What *day?*"

Mary Clare grabbed a towel and vigorously dried one plate at a time. "You mean *date.*"

"Tell me what I mean, and then tell me something else," Agnes said, cheeks red. She stretched one of the rubber bands to remove it. With a snap, it broke.

"It's not time to move on, Mom, if that's what you're worried about," Mary Clare said without breaking the rhythm of her work. She clacked one plate, then another into the cabinet before she said, "You go to Frank's *next* week."

Agnes carefully adjusted the remaining rubber band, pouched out the apron's chest pocket, and dropped in the little book. With the flat of her hand, she anchored one arm on the table, one on the chair. Biceps once round and ready to carry milk pails now revealed nothing but bone, with papery skin collapsed like an emptied udder. She edged her chair back with considerable effort.

Mary Clare draped the towel over her shoulder and faced Agnes. "Need help?"

"I'm fine," Agnes said, rope-like veins bulging in her neck. She worked at momentum, produced one, two, three *oomph's* and swung upright, slightly dizzy, just as Mary Clare raced to the jiggly table, caught the vase of lilacs, and fumed, "You sure?"

"That's it, Mary Clare," Agnes said and stomped her foot. The jellyroll nylons waggled into a momentary coolness around her swollen ankles. With one hand affixed on the wall, she took two steps, steadying herself on the thick-heeled, sensible shoes. She repositioned the hand, then two more careful steps. She made her way like this to the living room, imagining all the while that someone expected her and she had kept them waiting.

In fact, by the time she got there, Agnes had walked into a space even Mary Clare—Mary Clare with fifty-eight years of life—barely knew. It was the place where Edward Francis St. John was alive and well.

Edward Francis and Agnes Catherine, both eighteen, had lived in a small clapboard just outside Green Bay, Wisconsin. In fields around them were Jersey cows with velvet skin and brown liquid eyes. Grass was green like the Ireland their parents described, but the land here grew more than potatoes. And winter blew less cruel with feather quilts, wood stoves, and Guinness. It was 1905: people went to bed with the sun, got up with the sun. Nature dictated when to plant and harvest while Pope Pius X decreed rules to live by. *The hell with the Pope,* Agnes's favorite brother Ben said, mostly when drinking, but everyone knew he didn't mean it. He was a man "full of the devil," a great Irish compliment for a jokester. Ben had given Agnes her first shot of Jameson down at the creek and announced, "Whiskey rolls confession and communion into one easy sacrament." When later Ben announced the same to Edward, hard at work digging postholes, Edward nodded in silence, lifted a shovel full of black earth, pitched it, and wedged down the shovel again, quicker, embarrassed.

Edward Francis St. John. The name was sure, deep. She repeated it now and re-lived the first time he showed up with barn painters—suntanned, with ebony curls and a seventeen-year-old's laugh. She had studied his high, smooth forehead, round cheeks, and full lips. They took in each other, slowly, because they had been raised with caution. *Bodies-are-sinful* warnings moved over their landscape like clouds that shrunk a vast sky into more shadow than sun.

From little on, both Agnes and Edward had learned to offer sleep and every moment of the night to God, to place themselves in His most sacred side and beseech Him to keep them from sin. Families placed petitions in the Sacred Heart of Jesus, so when the Eternal Father saw their plea (for good children or good crops) covered with the mantle of Jesus's precious blood, He would not refuse it.

Accordingly, Agnes prayed while she scanned Edward and that hardy group of barn painters. *Bless my lips, Sweet Jesus, that I will say nothing to displease Thee.* Then she looked Edward straight in the eye and asked, "How long you been living around here?" Papa stood next to her and nodded, a man short on words.

"About a month," Edward said and looked at her but quickly focused on Papa, as if *he* had asked the question. Edward knew how to act, she figured, how to get along in the world. He seemed true and good.

"Been here my whole life," she said. "Papa and Mama were born in Ireland, but me and my brothers, we're all born in America."

"I'm American too," he said.

"Good," Papa said. "Let's get that barn painted."

After the painting job, the crew moved on. By late September, Edward was back for good, living two miles away on the old Smith farm. Agnes and Edward saw each other at roof-raising parties and barn dances; they danced the jig and Do-Si-Do and seemed, folks said, close as a brother and sister. At Grange Hall, they ate Irish teacakes and studied a huge chromolithograph of Custer's Last Fight—a symbol the nation had left one century and was moving on. Farmers from several sections got together at Grange Hall, mostly to gossip. Agnes remembered some gossip in particular, about the Smiths, who had left their apple orchard for Canada. Word drifted back. The Smiths were *wrong*. Their crops up there failed. It was the first time Agnes heard *wrong* outside of St. Michael's, and that night she opened her prayer book and repeated, "Help me to be faithful in doing what is *right*, no matter what the cost may be."

After what happened to Edward, the notion of *cost* grated her. It raised its scratchy, horrible voice at times she least expected it, like in Mary Clare's kitchen after dinner when she only wanted to know when her stay was up with Mary Clare and she'd move on to Jimmy's, or did Mary Clare say Frank's? She was an old woman without a home and every three months went to live with a different child.

Child. But not one with Edward Francis St. John. She heard his voice.

"Sure is a purdy dress, Agnes." He bowed slightly. Every muscle in his six-foot frame curled toward her.

"Thank you." Agnes didn't know what else to say.

"You make it yourself?" He stood a respectful distance away.

"Oh, I did. Yes, I did."

"Well," he said bashfully, "you must be one talented girl."

"Mama says that. Did Mama tell you to say that?"

He winked, his eyebrows lifted and she felt the soar of a teeter-totter when he said, "Thought it up myself."

And so it went. Field flower bouquets, evening walks along Dooley Road, apple picking in the Smiths' orchard, now owned by Edward's parents. Sometimes Agnes and Edward sat in the parlor with a stereopticon and went through a basket of stereographs of the St. Louis World's Fair. He peered at a stereo drawing of ice skaters, skimming across ice in summer at the Fair. *Unbelievable*, he said and handed her the stereopticon. She squinted into it.

"Maybe we could go to the next fair," he said and butterflies started in her belly. She remembered him now, imagined their apple-picking scene captured on a stereograph, wind and fleshy fruit and all, for her to view over and over. She had been hot from reach-pick-stoop, reach-pick-stoop, and had rolled down cotton hose to her ankles. She and Edward worked diligently, setting each apple carefully in bushel baskets because any bruise would rot the apple over winter. When they had filled half a dozen bushels, they propped themselves against an ancient Granny Smith and welcomed the chilly breezes and cool grass. They each ate an apple, then Edward stood and pitched the cores over the fence. He sat back down, a tad closer, and placed his hand on her porcelain-white leg. Her skin rippled.

"Now Edward," she said, but it was weak.

"I never felt a girl's leg," he said. "It, it's nice." His face whistled with innocence.

"What's it like?" she said and lowered her hand on top of his. She remembered that afternoon together, remembered it over and over and sixty years later, still wondered: did he interpret her hand as a signal to stop? Or to go?

"What's it like," she repeated.

"It's like, like…" He kneaded several times, then lightened the effort, as if only by contrast, by figuring out what it *wasn't* that he could say what it *was*. "It's like something someone ought to tell you. Smart people—priests and nuns—the ones close to God, the ones who know *everything*, why don't they tell us?"

"Keep talking." She closed her eyes and relaxed into the tree, into the rich, raw smell of fat apples and Indian summer. She wanted to taste his words, feel his palm, without distractions of empty bushel baskets and trees heavy with fruit.

His breathing changed. His palm loosened, did not move. "To touch another human being," he said, solemn as a cantor, "is to touch God."

"That's why men fight?"

"Not *that* kind of touch," he said. "Come to think, maybe we fight when we're angry with God." He sprang up, made two fists and punched the air. "When Uncle Simon's drunk, he's a rabid dog." He paused. "But my Pappy? He's a happy drunk."

Agnes felt like a bird that had flown into a window, confused and nervous. She had veered him to talk about fighting, though she envisioned him to be gentle, righteous. He was looking at the unpicked trees when she said, "So. To touch a woman . . ."

"Maybe touch isn't the right word," he said and plopped down, Indian-style, across from her.

"Feel. Is *feel* a better word?" she said, her feet incredibly hot.

"Maybe. Maybe we—you and me—could make up a word for it, after we're married."

If she hadn't been seated, she'd a fainted. His proposal, shy yet secure, surprised her and from that moment in the orchard, he led the way. He was steady, assured. He would know what to do and she would follow. She would submit, the same way she did to Papa, Mama, the teachings of the Church.

The following spring, Edward's Pappy helped them purchase forty acres and ten cows. They married in June, the altar of St. Michael's sweet and airy with lilacs of white, French blue, pale purple. Agnes had dipped her locks of hair in ammonia, wrapped them around a safety pin and heated them with an iron. It was her first permanent, permanent as love. She wore Mama's wedding dress, aged satin and lace the color of beeswax. She was but a girl with little need, Papa said, of *rouge* from the Sears catalog. Her breasts were high, her waist tiny. Edward wore his black-earth Sunday suit and a starched white shirt with plumb-straight pleats.

After the wedding Mass they turned and faced the congregation. Edward brought one hand to his waist, crooked an elbow. Her small hand slid into that waiting space as if she'd found a field where she could run free.

"I love you," he said and stiffened the other arm, her sentinel and protector. Her soldier for God.

"And I love you, too," she replied. Then they descended Father Maloney's altar where they had been reminded *Your body is God's temple,* and, *May the Almighty Father teach you to put into action your better impulses.* They were all smiles, gliding across the cold stone floor, then through arched, olive doors into the churchyard and a shower of rice. She caught Ben's eye, his look sweet but sad. It must have been too much to see his baby sister marry. And then the crowd swept them away to a dinner of steaks, potatoes swaddled in cream, Mama's green beans, biscuits, and preserves. And of course a dance, with whiskey, spilled ale, toasts, and fiddle music that swelled past midnight. When they finally left the dance hall, the horses whinnied and clomped the dirt, eager to take the bride and groom to their farmhouse where *God Bless Our Home* hung over the door.

Within the week, Edward laid the Holy Bible, bound in leather with gilded edges, on a lace-covered table in the parlor, ready for Father Maloney's home visit. In the pantry Agnes placed *The Farmer's Bible,* a Haynes-Cooper mail order catalog, their secular hope for salvation from want.

They never once ordered from Haynes-Cooper, not even stereographs. There wasn't money—not unless Agnes sold more eggs. They used the Victrola wedding gift and Victor Dance Record a few times, but it wasn't like barn dances. They anticipated a relentless cycle of tilling, planting, harvesting, plowing. They planned to make babies, soda bread, quilts, and hay—all with little care for biology and psychology. Kotex hadn't been invented and once a month white rags, some tinged with pink, hung on the line. Agnes still remembered her rags, stained, no matter how many times she scrubbed them, fluttering in the breezes that first year she married, month after month despite recitations for grace, patience, worthiness, each a repetitive plea to send them a child.

While they waited, they worked. Edward cleaned out the chicken coop, resoled barn shoes, oiled the horse harnesses, even put harness oil on Sunday shoes to make them last longer. Agnes bottle-fed sick calves, made butter from soured cream, and rendered fat into soap. They slept in a Mission-style bed, grateful for its size; they could sleep without touching. Touch disturbed sleep and without sleep they could not manage the farm.

They took on rural rhythms, balanced Sunday church with Friday outings: Agnes's sewing circle and Edward's night with the boys at Sheehan's. She could still see Sheehan's Tap: swinging shuttered doors and front windows cluttered with potted ferns, posters, and advertising displays. Inside, Edward said he liked to stand at the long mahogany bar, one shoe resting on the brass foot rail. He drank beer for a nickel and straight whiskey for a dime. Each man treated the group to a round of drinks and was expected to stay long enough to be treated, in turn, by others. Men with great voices, men with great laughs, including Ben, subdued themselves when they recounted that last time Edward joined them.

Once Agnes got the whole story, tumbled it over in her mind 'til it wore thin, she never talked about it, not to Ben, not to her children. Let Mary Clare think she was an old, confused woman when the trance came over her and she simply left the room. That was better than letting Mary Clare and Frank and *any* of the kids, or, my God, grandkids, know that her first husband, Edward Francis St. John, sensitive and kind Edward Francis St. John, had taken his own life. God strike her dead if she told anyone. Keeping the secret had worked, for here she was, seventy-eight years old. But the older she got, she realized long life only gave her more time to mourn the night Edward opened the door to the all-male world at Sheehan's Tap.

Every man there that night had spent the day haying. Each man rested his elbows on the shiny, cool bar the way a sailor might lean on the railing of a ship, gaze out at dark water, hear its rolling and wonder about the next port-o-call.

"Well. If it ain't Edward Francis." The words came from Ben when Edward came through the door. Ben confessed he'd said it, said it loud, started a little bar talk. Man talk, he told Agnes. Besides, they were brothers-in-law, that gave him rights, to poke fun.

"Hey, Ben." Edward pushed a stool aside and ordered a tall cool one.

"Edward," Ben said. "How's Agnes?"

"Dandy."

"Like you," Ben said and ordered two more beers. "It's up to the bull," he said, and pushed a foamy glass in front of Edward, who pressed his lips together. "The cow waits for the bull," Ben said. "Honest injun."

Ben told Agnes he didn't *mean anything* when he said *You're not a man.* Agnes considered this, that ribbing and kidding were ways to talk about unmentionables. No one knew Edward like she did, though, a man so attuned to God's Word he could have been a priest. Edward never would have guessed that people were like animals, that he had colors in him like the glistening pink thing that erupted out of the bull, made a cow fuss and fume. And Agnes had no idea. It took her second husband, an educated schoolteacher, to caress and stroke, press her until she gushed.

"Aw, Agnes," Ben said. "It was just bar talk. Men drink and loosen up, in fun, you understand? Naw, a woman wouldn't understand." Nonetheless, Ben continued with the story like a penitent in Father Maloney's confessional, admitting it was not the first time the men needled Edward.

"No baby on the way?" someone started.

"Not yet," Edward answered and downed another beer. It had been over a year since the wedding.

"Young bull like you?" someone said. Another called him a mule. "To break a mule, begin at his head," someone added. "Maybe he can only fart," said another, for mules were notorious for farting. The barkeep howled along with everyone.

More beer and shots of Jameson hardened the fun until, Ben said, the talk swung to whose cousin was coming to town and whose farm was next for haying and so on. Eventually the place settled into a *real nice* evening of drinking, and Ben, startled to hear the news next morning, said yes, Edward had left Sheehan's early, before closing.

Yet Agnes didn't hear him come home that night. She didn't feel the mattress move or smell his sugary breath. In the morning her hand strayed to his leg to push him out for milking, but he was already up, probably tending to a sick heifer. A good farmer, he would have tied up the horses, checked on the heifer before coming to bed. She arose, pinned back her long hair and went out into the August morning. Six a.m., birds sang from behind curtains of leaves high above, and in the field, cows bellered to be milked. Two horses, still on the carriage, wandered up and down the lane, thirsty and tired. She panicked, ran to the barn where the door was partially open. She thrust her wiry body against the crisscrossed door. She got it going and it slid slowly along the track. She stepped inside. A few bandy roosters squawked at her. She squinted her eyes in the barn's coming light.

"Edward! Edward!" she yelled, her nightgown dragging across loose straw on the floor. She felt his presence, yet he did not answer, and she feared he had fallen through a hay hole and suffocated. She raced down the alley, and there, with morning sun cracking through slats of barn board, she found him.

Edward Francis St. John hung from a rope on the middle barn beam. She shrieked and ran to him, except her legs would not move. She tripped on her nightgown and landed face down. Her nose was bleeding, her face a mulch of hay seeds, dirt and saliva. Star, the horse named for markings on her face, was pacing back and forth in her stall when Agnes entered. Now the high-strung mare broke out and thundered across the wide-plank floor. A milk can, evidently Edward's last foothold on this earth, laid on its side not that far from where he swayed. Star knocked the can and its tinny noise rolled through the barn. At the same time, Star's sudden blow to Edward sent him into a spin. The horse, at gallop by the time she reached where Agnes lay in the gutter, burst through the half-open door and knocked it off its track.

Agnes opened her mouth to scream again, but nothing came. The scream locked in her head, behind her eyes, swelled and burst. She wished she had righted the can, stood and touched him, tried to undo the noose. It was the first image she saw—that tongue—that she remembered, sugarplum purple and trapped between his teeth, with blood trickling to his neck. And hands, swollen as blueberries, hands that could repair anything, proper hands that never did more than hug and squeeze her, which had been enough, for them both.

She had no power, no self-assurance. At that moment in the barn when God tested her, she had failed. Maybe Edward was alive, barely, but she could have nursed him back. She sobbed and held her head and blubbered *why, why*. The next time she looked up through snivel and tears, his edges had softened and she thought he walked toward her, arms extended and playful.

She could not remember their neighbor Barney, first to appear because of Star, and how Barney carried her out of the barn. She could not remember Ben digging the grave, or Father Maloney at the burial. She did remember daylilies, pressed into her hands by Mama before the two women tossed them on Edward's pine box. She remembered Doc Rosen's head, shaking back and forth, how he insisted Edward was dead for hours when she found him, and Ben, working backwards about that fateful night, coming up with eleven o'clock as the time Edward left the men. Yup, Doc said, that put him up in heaven at least six hours by the time you found him. And Father Maloney chimed in with the one-size-fits-all, "May his soul rest in peace."

It was too long ago, those offerings of absolution. Father Maloney. Doc. Ben himself. Perspective. It takes a long time. So when Billy, one of Mary Clare's teenagers asked, "Grandma, what was the best part about being eighteen?" Agnes said, "Nothing stands out." She held fast to a belief there was no point in telling youth about your mistakes. They wouldn't learn from them. They'd be more apt to repeat them. Or, they'd fall back on your mistakes as some excuse for their own.

Billy insisted, "Aw, Grandma. There must have been *something* good about being eighteen."

"The best part of eighteen," Agnes said after some thought, "was turning nineteen. And then twenty." Because by age twenty, Mary Clare had come along. Still, neither Mary Clare nor three more babies after that plus decades of prayerful recitation helped when she pondered that small life with Edward, his sudden abandonment. The farther she got from him, the closer he came.

And now at Mary Clare's, with the day done and no breeze in the sitting room, she plopped in the rocking chair, then bent over to untie the sensible arch-supports. She sat back up, winded, and snugged toe to heel to winch off first one shoe, then the other. She bent forward once more and unpeeled the sock-like nylons so vigorously, they ripped. The effort spun her equilibrium. She leaned back, grasped the rocker's arms and closed her eyes. Her moist blue sausage toes wiggled against the maple flooring. She sat there for a long time as the evening cooled and she considered telling Mary Clare about Edward. But of course, it was only a consideration. It didn't hurt to consider.

Deadly

I had committed one of the seven deadly sins. Jealousy. Judge me if you will but you'd be jealous too if you saw that slip of a girl, lean everywhere, the plane of her face, slim thighs, the short-cropped hair, those calling hip bones, her obsessions with blue jeans, BMI, and BMWs. Recently, she had spent money to get permanent make-up. I asked why she did this.

"So when I wake up in the morning, I'm set to go," she said.

Her lips shined with robust sunset pink. Faint earthy eyeliner rimmed her eyelids. Even her cheeks glowed. It was all so natural, so necessary for a blonde (yes, *that* too) who ran a high-end resort, coached tennis, and wore clothes sold in the gift shop. Did her diet consist mostly of leafy greens? She walked with certainty, shoulders square that practiced charm. Oh, and she was married, a mother of two preschoolers.

We sat in her renovated dining room, sculpted by her sculpted husband, a carpenter who could take a rough-hewn piece of cedar and turn it into a cabinet or a bed. Their house, built in 1938, carried all the marks of modernism, including a sliding glass patio door, open now, the screen wafting in smells of white peonies. Late afternoon sunlight splashed off the hardwood floor that the husband had laid with diamond-shaped precision. No math-straight floorboards for him; this floor started in the middle like a star and reached to the very edge of happiness.

I was swept up in wishful thinking. My husband could not balance a checkbook and thought Amway was a pension plan.

"You are so lucky," I said. There, I had put it out there, my honest statement of jealousy, the rude sister, the bad twin, my sin both cardinal and venial.

She sipped her water laced with rosemary and mint. I followed suit. Silence suddenly arrived like the guest who didn't bathe.

"See that glass door?" she asked in a measured Midwestern tone.

"Yes."

"See that deck?"

"Yes."

"I'll never forget the day I came home from work and there he was, in just his shorts, silky tan, pencil behind his ear, tool belt and hammer swinging from his hips."

"Yes?"

"I loved him so much right then and there. I had come in through the front door, stripped, and then I threw myself against the glass door."

She was a liberated woman with some semblance of toughness. I could imagine her hipbones leading the way, how her rounded biceps stretched to heaven. That, and her flawless made-up lips and painted toenails, the palest of sea foam. I resisted the urge just then to look down at those nails. My ears buzzed while I took a sip, wondering where this was going.

"You think things are what they are," she said, catapulting to the punch line.

I set my glass down. It was sweating.

She continued, quietly, without inflection. "Garrett doesn't like sex."

"All this," she continued, gesturing. "He can make something out of nothing. He can turn a sow's ear—as they say—into gold."

"It's a silk purse," I said.

"Whatever." She looked at me, dabbing cloudy blue eyes. "It feels good to tell someone."

"I know," I said, though at that point I only knew my own behind-the-scenes story. And now I knew hers. And I knew why her make-up didn't run as she dabbed.

She rose and opened the patio door. "I have to check on the boys. Be right back."

I watched her move with the even keel of a runner, realizing how the body can take a lot and how, once aware of what is happening, can actually right itself.

Almond Joy

It's March. Clumps of dog fur begin to appear on the Berber carpet, the stone entryway, the red tiled bathroom floor. This is because the West Highland Terrier is shedding. This is because the dog thinks it is summer.

Beckman, her owner, thinks nothing. Not since that woman moved out—just like that—with three months left on the lease. Now the insouciant and daring Beckman can't paint. He can't draw or sketch. He squints at the easel, that woman's clavicles and toes and elbows on the stretched canvas, undone. He studies the mix of light and shadow, amazed by the strange and wild thing where bogs and shapes and coastlines formed. He bites his bottom lip, glares at the vacuum cleaner agog on the studio floor. Scents of oil, acrylic, and shaved charcoal swirl in the corners, but he cannot smell them. He cannot smell the savory in her homemade pasta lingering in the kitchen, above the antique trunk used as dinner table.

Instead, he smells dog hair clumped like dead protein, the DNA of seasons transformed like moldy towels and rancid socks. Other years when this annual shedding of dog hair began, Beckman left the vacuum out, plugged in and ready to attack on a daily basis. So this year he again leaves the vacuum out, vigilant for cottony strands in the entryway, the refrigerator's bottom grate, and fluff clinging to the Bose speakers. But, dear reader, just because he leaves the vacuum out does not mean he uses it. Even a clean freak must one day push the boundaries.

Yip yip yap the terrier named Almond Joy says.

I know Beckman replies, flicking a yarn-like ball from the chocolate-brown leather sofa. It is ten o'clock in the morning; he should be somewhere but can't remember where. Thin yellow light stains the blinds. Four stories below, squad cars and trucks cough and wheeze. He lifts the hairball to the light, noticing these hairs of the West Highland Terrier are not really white. They are champagne, winter mood, maybe baked Brie. He sits down on the sofa and beckons the dog.

In a flash, Almond Joy leaps onto the sofa and snuggles next to him.

Stay there Beckman says. Almond perks her pink-tinged ears and tilts her head. She stays. Beckman disappears down the hall. A hollow-core door opens, then closes, *plook, sphlook.* Almond whimpers but stays. Objects hit the wall: a tinny spoon, a running shoe, and a wooden wastebasket. Then, the heavy thudding of art books and newspapers tied with twine for the recycler. Almond whines and yips.

Yeah yeah Beckman yells. *I'll be right there.*

And he is, clutching a bottle of Elmer's glue. He sits on the sofa and Almond climbs into his lap. He strokes her back. He tickles the small inviting gullies behind her delicate ears. He takes her entire face in his hands and lifts her jaw. He rubs the jawbone like a massage therapist, which he is not, but had thought of becoming for rent money. Almond purrs and groans and moans, sounds of a creature loved for who she is, not for what she does.

From below, treble and bass pound the oak floor. *You fool* Beckman says. Almond lifts her head and perks up those ears. *Not you* Beckman says. The dog barks and the thump-dump music swells. The dog barks again, intently.

The rump-dump music suddenly stops, a blown speaker perhaps. Or a blown frontal lobe of the so-called listener.

At that, Beckman opens the Elmer's Glue. He separates fur on the dog's back until the petal pink scalp appears. He drops a dollop of glue. Almond shakes the way she does when coming out of a July lake, front to back, rhythmically, a wringer of wet going to dry. *Hold still* Beckman says. The dog holds. Now Beckman selects several fibers from shedded hairs on the sofa's arm. He attaches them to the dollop of glue. He spreads another area on the dog's back and drops another bead of viscous white goo. Again, more hair fibers meet the goo. For the next half-hour, he is gluing and pasting, carrying Almond around the apartment to find more shedded hair, grinning like a savant, a philosopher not with the right answer but with the right question. How can he stop time? How can he prevent seasons from changing? *She'll be back, full of devotion and ardor* he tells the dog, who produces a low, protracted, peevish sound.

Beckman pats her. *It's not about love,* he says, blending old hair with new. *It's about loyalty, about keeping promises.* The dog *grrrrs* and Beckman continues to glue and paste, talking in his head, talking out loud, and finally, not talking at all, lost in a frisson of pleasure that used to come from long hours of painting.

And so, time passed as Beckman scoured the apartment for more fur balls, emptying one bottle of Elmer's glue and scavenging for another until in the end he had affixed dust bunnies, several down feathers (discovered under what used to be the communal bed), and even cigarette ashes found on the bathroom floor, confirming that she had lied about that too. Soon even parchment paper and dried angel food graced the dog, by now loving this attention.

Stay there, Beckman said, finally. He rose, going directly to pillows on the fainting couch. He grabbed one velvety rich as caramel and began to cut it into strips. *Yes* he said to the dog. *This is it.* The dog watched, eyes soft, mouth open and panting. Beckman then returned to the sofa and tied one strip tastefully around the neck into a droopy bow. Then he took other strips and wrapped them around the dog's middle. *You are so beautiful* he said blissfully, unaware that the dog looked like an Almond Joy bar, his favorite, the very gift she gave him after they met on Match.com, before she moved into his space.

The Dresser

Light diffused through the bedroom window, the icy plum of winter dusk. Pete had never been bothered by December days when the sun went south. Now, he was gloomier than those depressives who saw shrinks and heard it was about motivation, how you had to be motivated to buck up, take charge of your life.

Well, yesterday, he had taken charge.

Yesterday he had worked in fits and starts, filling boxes with Ellie's personal effects while their freshman boy was in school. First he tackled the closet, starting with a floor-length lavender bathrobe. Next, the flower print blouses, T-shirts, Beatles and Beach Boys sweatshirts, chain link belts, and blue jean skirts. He had grinned at the fake suede coat with fake fur. Even Ellie couldn't bring herself to wear it, a recycled gift from some aunt. *Just keep busy* rang in his ears and so he accelerated the pace, clearing entire shelves of winter scarves, flannel pajamas, shoes in boxes, and straw hats with silk ribbons. He worked fast, staying ahead of any disturbance caused by strong feelings.

When he took down the wicker picnic basket, however, he felt a flutter of his pulse. He undid the leather straps of the suitcase-like basket. Inside, secured by more leather straps, were two stoneware cups with two matching plates, two knives, two forks, and two spoons. She had bought it for a winter picnic, expecting him to take a day off—actually put up a CLOSED sign on the shop window—to enjoy maple and birch forests, sandy dunes, and hemlock in the dead of winter at the State Park. You're kidding, he had told her. Now he realized what a disappointment he must have been with those cracked knuckles, grease in the cleft of his chin, and vapors of gasoline clinging to his hair. He ripped off the price tag and dumped the basket with the other disposables. Then he returned to the closet; he lowered a pile of jeans. Each pair had been meticulously folded. Smells of her steam iron still clung to the denim and made his pulse pound.

And that's when her terrible absence filled the room. He had slumped on the edge of the queen-sized bed and surveyed the wreckage. He considered Gabe, their only child—that when it came to the desk, the back hall items, and the gardening things—he ought to involve the boy. He was, after all, fourteen. So at supper last evening, Pete declared: *Guess there's no hurry.* Probably, he had meant the opposite. The sooner he cleaned out Ellie's personal effects, the sooner they could move on with their lives. Pete could *never* say what he meant, and over hot dogs and beans he had twisted what should have been simple and straightforward.

Gabe had panicked. "Hurry? What's to hurry?" He surveyed his father's gaunt face for a clue. Finally, he said, "Dad! Are we moving?"

"Move?" Pete replied. "Why would we move?" His placid expression stayed put when he added, "No, buddy, we're not going to move." Still, the weight of maturity was upon his shoulders and now he looked at the red-and-white checkered tablecloth. Move? Perhaps they should, he thought, and move big. Go all the way to Alaska or Nova Scotia or Paraguay.

The rest of that evening he felt urgent and nearly nauseous to get going. That night, he barely slept. The radiator in the room clanged and two floors down, the monster furnace chortled and spit. That too needed work, he thought. When morning came, he had a plan. First, he fortified himself by fasting. Maybe if he were hungry, close to the bone, he'd get closer to what he was feeling. Other people, mostly Catholics, thought calories cured sadness. After Gabe got on the bus, Pete walked the 300 feet to his repair shop. He flipped the OPEN sign on the shop door to CLOSED. Then he walked back to the house and found a Coke in the fridge. He set the kitchen radio to the local station and cranked up the volume the way the kid did, bulging spores of sound. Then, he went upstairs. He made it through the bedside stands and the medicine cabinet while Springsteen and the Grateful Dead played before and after the farm report, the obituaries, news of an impending oil crisis, Nixon's impeachment, and Solzhenitsyn being expelled from the Soviet Union. At one point he sprinted down the stairs, fetched a second Coke, downed it, and, wired, made it through the rest of the closet.

Her dresser was last. He opened the bottom drawer. There her turtlenecks lay, rolled up real tight, yellowing like outdated eggs. But instead of tossing them in a box, he slammed the drawer shut with his softball-pitching arm. Then he kicked the drawer, his steel-toed boot giving that dresser all he had. Two empty vases toppled over and it seemed the walls fell flat on all sides. And then he heard the bus pull up. Where had the day gone? Was he mad, his senses distorted as the potheads who hung out at the gas station? He tossed his head from side to side, cracking the bones in his neck, his thinking tangled in regret. He opened the bottom drawer again, telling himself *it's time*. The bus engine fired up and he thought perhaps it is not time. Maybe this zone he was in needed to continue because that's all there was to continue.

Meanwhile, downstairs, he heard Gabe come in, a slamming of doors followed by a riot of crashing glass. Perhaps the kid was hammering at the loss that expanded day by day. The sun was teasing the sky with a bolt of gold, and then the pallor of winter settled again. Pete flicked on the bedside lamp. Shadows in the room moved but not enough. So he walked over to the wall and, with a quick jerking movement, hit a switch. Artificial light from an overhead fixture flooded the room. In the luminosity, he approached the dresser with all the heft of a man with a sledgehammer taking down a cement silo. Lift, whack, slap. Chisel away at the silo 'til it tipped and then run like hell before it crashed. Now in one fell motion, he slapped everything from the bottom drawer into the big cardboard box destined for those less fortunate. Lift, whack, slap. The middle drawer of sweaters was taken out in a hissing of *why why* and *damn you, damn you.* By now Gabe lurked on the landing, spying and holding his breath like a small child, trying to turn blue and hoping, ultimately, to get attention. Gabe wondered if his father sensed he was there; Pete only had to lift his head to see the baffled kid straight on. But he did not, maybe because by now he was on a roll. He had made it to the top and final drawer.

He opened that drawer and padded, push-up mounds of flesh looked up at him. Or so it must have seemed to stare at Ellie's bras, lined up, spaghetti straps ready for when they danced the jitterbug. Gabe watched his father glance across rows of slips, the soft clothing bent over in an apparent bow to ecstasy. And her panties were compressed, too, thin rims of lace and elastic telescoped together. And then Gabe saw his mother with her green thumb and a blown aneurysm behind her green eyes. She had come back to life with these colors of rose-petal pink, ecru, and muted coral. He sagged against the hall wallpaper. What once was hush-hush now felt gruesome and creepy, especially since he had never seen that dresser drawer. Nor had he ever seen his mother naked. She was very pretty and very private. In his mind's eye, Gabe imagined her buying these secret things, then posing in the full-length mirror on the back of their bedroom door. All that *stuff.* What was it called? Lingerie, that's what it was, a smooth name for satin piping and curved wire, an entire drawer of feminine charm, waiting, just waiting. He felt sick.

Pete, meanwhile, was in a trance, immovable. He stared at the top drawer while outside, the wind picked up. In the still bedroom, changing light crossed over his face like a front moving in: the pressure drops and then, bam, the thunderstorm. He stood there and braced himself, his grease-stained fingers clutching the tilted, open drawer. The struggle ramped up. "Men don't cry," he said.

So, he knew Gabe was there all along. "Uh-huh," Gabe said, softly.

"They can't." He took his eyes off of Ellie's stuff and, without looking at the squirrely kid, yanked a farmer-blue handkerchief from his back pocket. With the swiftness of an arrow leaving a bow, he whisked the hanky across his nose. The shabby piece of cloth darkened like an oil slick. Gabe took two steps into the room and suddenly they both smelled Ellie's perfume rising from that top drawer. It was Estee Lauder; they had bought her some last Christmas. Now Pete made two more swipes across his substantial nose. Then he jutted out his left hip and rammed the hanky back in the pocket. "They can't," he said again. He pondered the drawer's dovetailed corner. He seemed dazed. He was scaring the kid, who feared that his father might crash to the floor, all those Marlboros. Just then, Pete gasped. "It's not right," he said.

"Sure," Tool chimed in, worried and confused. He felt that any minute lightning would strike his own chest. Count the number of seconds between the lightning and the thunder and you know how far away the storm is. Then Pete said something about that women do the crying. Tool nodded and began to count. By now Pete's face was red and wide as a ripe tomato, splitting seeds and phlegm into the drawer. Snot and drool glommed his chin. A trickle ran down his neck. And then, all of him imploded. His knees buckled.

He caught himself. His eyes, tiny veined and bloodshot, swelled shut.

When Pete began to dribble onto the underwear, Gabe looked away, gritting his teeth on the bizarre reality. The teenager stood there, hearing his father's growing helplessness. He was so embarrassed and disappointed that he willed himself to march away. He discovered he could not. His father's panting and slobbering had become hypnotic. He was trapped. He tried to think and drew a blank—or at best, a blur. Was his father letting loose just for himself? Or was it for a teenage boy, also? Had his father planned it, like the time he wanted to have a birds-and-the-bees talk but couldn't, so he just asked how the filmstrip went in health education class. It would take years for Tool to realize that what he had witnessed was a display of closeness, a commitment that had morphed into intimacy, the intangible dream of two as one. The concept was so beyond a fourteen-year-old brain, it rattled Gabe. At the moment, he feared his quiet and easy-going father had either wimped out or gone crazy. And he was certain that without his mother, they were both shattered, ruined.

Gabe looked back at his father. Pete was drenched. He looked like he had been beaten up, his forehead all red and his cheeks purple with bruises. "Dad," Tool said, going to him now. "Dad."

Pete gripped the kid's arm and let up on the bawling. Then he fetched the old blue hanky. He blew his nose, hard, snorting from one nostril to the other until it seemed he'd blown out the very air that held him up. Then he threw the sopping wet rag into the Goodwill box and crisscrossed its flaps into a kind of square knot. He caught his breath. Patting Tool on the shoulder, he pressed his lips into a strained, straight line. At that, he turned back to the dresser, put his hip on the open drawer, and with a sudden sharp single movement, whipped it shut. "Gimme a hand, buddy," he said. He lifted one side of the unwieldy box and Tool lifted the other. They angled it around the landing and down the stairs. They set it in the living room, careful not to obstruct the view of the television that nowadays lulled Pete to sleep.

The boy had hoped they'd deliver the box to the Goodwill store together, like when they drove to town, always together in search of auto parts or to stock up on five-gallon pails of Butter Brickle ice cream. But the box disappeared the next day when Tool was on a field trip to the Museum of Science and Industry in Chicago. That evening after the field trip, he returned late and lunged into the house, ready to spout off about the over-sized heart he had seen and actually walked through. "Hey, Dad," he said.

"There," Pete said from the La-Z-Boy. "You made it."

"I did. We walked through the chambers of a heart." Then he tracked his father's line of sight from the La-Z-Boy to the television and bounced on to the couch. He let the space between them settle and at the commercial, he spoke up. "Where's the box?" he asked.

"Oh, I took care of it," Pete said.

"I wanted to go with you," Tool said, releasing each word with precision.

"Tell me about those heart chambers," Pete replied.

They grew careful of each other from then on, skimming their bond off of life-sized thumping hearts, carburetor valves, and replays of first downs, interceptions. They avoided any mention of Ellie and her intimate apparel. If the boy had thought about it, he would have known his father loaded up the items like a farmer delivering heifers to market, the animals skittish and bellering, an aliveness to which the farmer feigned detachment as he drove the dreary landscape into town, chain-smoking and pushing passion to the edge of the flat world. For that's how the Singer sewing machine, clay pots, gardening supplies, and envelopes of saved seeds disappeared, too. Pete called it *man's work*, a way of sparing a boy he thought too adolescent, too abandoned, to load impossibility into a truck and deliver it to the Goodwill store. And yet, when Pete pulled up to that store, a high-school dropout unloaded the boxes while Pete sat in the cab with clenched jaw.

For years, Gabe wondered how long that top drawer kept its fullness. Maybe Pete never threw any of it out. Gabe never saw him rummage in there again and he never looked. Once, he dreamt his father put the slinky items in shoeboxes and tucked them up in the garage, in the rafters along with her Raleigh Retroglide Seven-AL bicycle. It was a three-speed with hand brakes and white-walled balloon tires. Over the years, a few collectors had offered Pete a pretty penny for it, but Pete's position was firm: the bike was not for sale. Last time Tool went home, the bike was still hanging upside down, same place for two decades. The two of them stood in the garage together, spring winds blowing grit and dust across the cement floor. And then Tool remembered how his mother had ridden the Raleigh while he pedaled his Schwinn.

"We used to take the gravel roads like we could fly," he laughed.

"Yeah," Pete said, "you two were going to beat the redwing blackbirds at their game."

The father and son jawed back and forth, recalling how the birds dive-bombed at the head of any bicyclist, screeching, determined to maintain territorial rights on the high wires. Gabe mentioned the first-cut alfalfa, how the scent filled the air, how Ellie would cheer, *Hurry up!*

"And I would," Gabe said, "my knees whirling around on those pedals while I whizzed down the road and she clapped and laughed and yelled, *That's it! That's it!*"

And it was, then.

France

In 1997, Wessel was found dead in a buckling white clap-board next door to St. Isidore's Church and School. It was ten below the day Father Nick discovered him. But let's back up a bit and see how Wessel came to finish there.

1. Raymond P. Wessel—the P stood for nothing—was born at home, the second of ten kids. That was 1923.

2. Raymond grew up with dairy cows, chickens, hogs, and lots of cats and dogs but never really took to animals. He did chores from the time he was five and Pa let him go to high school except when a cow was calving, pigs farrowed, or corn needed picking. He graduated from Greenwood High in 1941, didn't go to World War II because the draft board ruled he was needed on that Wisconsin farm.

3. When the war ended, he went down to Chester's and drank beer and smoked his first cigarette—and his tenth. He came home in the pickup at midnight, set on telling Pa everything he'd been meaning to tell him. Pa sat at the long threshing table with a whittling knife and stick of willow. "Shoulda gone to France," Raymond said.

"Not what the draft board said," Pa replied flatly.

"It's what I said." Raymond weaved to the table. "It's what *I* said," he repeated and whacked it.

"'Sides drinking, you been smoking," Pa said.

"Celebrating," Raymond said, "it's called celebrating."

4. Raymond became obsessed with France, though it took him awhile to realize it, what with falling milk prices. Farmers dumped milk in ditches rather than accept two cents per hundredweight from local cheese factory owners, the scoundrels. Someone needed to organize those farmers, but it wasn't Raymond. So he got a job in town. He worked at the feed mill for a year, then at Holden's Hardware where they said his smile was wide as a mile. Pa said, long as money comes in, okay then.

5. There was a barn fire one scorching August day. Gilson's place, out on Valley Road. Raymond raced out there like everyone else but it was too late. Old man Gilson died fighting the fire. Westerlies carried the stench of smoldering hay and burnt cows for days. Gilson's son Rudy tried (not too hard, it was said) to make a go of the farm. Finally Rudy let the whole shooting match—tools, machinery, even antiques—go to auction; he moved to what he called a flung away, flat, breezy place with opportunity aplenty. Florida.

6. Raymond had a needy thing with Joyce, whom he knew from high school. She got pregnant and, three months later, lost the baby so they agreed to call off the marriage.

7. At Chester's, someone said the weather in Florida was like France. Wes started acting like a scared rabbit and kept money from Pa even though Ma needed yard goods. He bought an RCA radio with the money.

8. *Gildersleeve and Molly* became his favorite show. He loved slapstick.

9. A Fuller Brush salesman nosed around Holden's Hardware. "Raymond P. Wessel at your service, sir," Raymond said with that smile.

"Wes," the guy said, "Mind if I call you Wes? Sounds more . . . *with it.*"

Soon the newly-named Wes was on the road with that guy. After every stop, Wes threw his suitcased samples in the trunk, sat in the passenger seat and paged through *LIFE* magazine.

After Wes got his own route, he stopped home every now and then, opened a *LIFE* and bragged he'd seen some of the places photographed. No one could be sure if he had, for Wes had become a bullshitter.

10. Wes found out about the Roaring Twenties. The rest of his life he said he'd been born too late.

11. His brother Hilbert was killed in a tractor accident. That was 1949. Hilbert was the first-born, Pa's favorite.

12. The next year, Wes bought a Nash Rambler and drove to a place he deserved, Florida. He rented a motel room in Tampa and set up his RCA radio. The rent emptied his pockets, but by week's end he had landed a sales job with R.J. Reynolds—thanks to Gilson's kid Rudy, proving it's not what you know, it's who.

13. When he cashed his paycheck, Wes insisted on crisp new bills. He indulged in shrimp, key lime pie, and odd colognes. At Rosa's watering hole, he learned to love gin and tonic while he heard how people fucked up their lives. He was a nice bachelor, what Rosa called a wooden ship in an age of steel. He even took up bird-watching for awhile. No one knew he bought light bulbs by the case because he feared the dark, didn't know why.

14. When Pa died in 1960, he and Chrissy drove home. At the funeral Ma's lanky brother Arno, a bachelor in his early seventies, asked, "How is it down there? You play much golf?" By then Wes was thirty-seven, a devoted golfer who played twice a week, had a handicap of four. Silver rings saturated his fingers and a silver chain glittered around his neck when he told Uncle Arno the driving range was five miles from his pad, which by the way overlooks a canal (more of a water ditch). Arno listened keenly, then said, "Man after my own heart."

15. Everyone at the funeral buzzed about Chrissy—cripes, she could pass for Marilyn Monroe. Chrissy told Wes over ham, scalloped potatoes, and Jell-O in the church basement that she thought he came from class. Have a homemade brownie, he said. Then on the way back to Florida his corn-colored Chevy convertible with white sidewall tires broke down in Mississippi. They walked two miles on a dusty road before finding a Standard station. Chrissy chipped a nail and cracked one of her new Lucite high-heels. After that, she stopped sleeping with him.

16. Which was no problem. With slicked-back hair and forever-tan skin (it was the Czech in him), dames loved him. Ritzy ones supported him. He let them. Inez took him to Paris. Bonjour, bon vivant and 5,000 other French ticklers (his words) rolled off her tongue. He was ashamed he couldn't speak French. Or the Queen's English.

17. He had many fantasy girls, but only one lit something in him. Suzanne Gorman, eyes like pearls, hair of bright sunshine. Daddy owned Pink Flamingo Golf & Tennis in Palm Beach. Suzanne said, "I know you know you're loved inside my mind." Cooing like that drove him bonkers.

18. In 1965, they got pregnant; she was exuberant, he, unsure. She was twenty-six with a fresh masters in philosophy from NYU. He was forty-two and balding—with a presence, however.

19. Daddy, who called Wes a poor provider, knew doctor types; one dusted and cleaned Suzanne. No back-alley business—she went high-rise with white roses afterward. She called from Second Avenue with the news, including a bumbled, jumbled goodbye. After that, his ribs sometimes ached like when a Holstein had kicked him. He slept with his watch on so if he awoke he knew the time.

20. Laugh-In made the country laugh; Vietnam made it crazy. Baby brother Steve enlisted and wrote home. *Hashish, pussy, jungle. Can't tell—am I in heaven? Or hell.* Steve's

casket arrived before his letter. Wes called home. "Raymond," Ma said.

"Ma," he replied and dropped to his knees, howling.

21. By 1974, Wes had been with R.J. Reynolds for twenty-four years, tangled up like traffic in the booming Mickey Mouse state. The new marketing director showed off pictures of her son. This upset Wes—women were always mixing business with pleasure, couldn't keep their mind on one thing if they tried.

22. Bartender Rutkowski at Pink Flamingo said there might be a connection between kid photos and Daddy's deed with Suzanne. That's bullshit, Wes said, and ordered another gin and tonic. "Sometimes you don't know what you want," Rutkowski said, "'till you can't have it." The next morning Wes went to a clinic. He thought he was having a heart attack.

23. Migrant workers of every color descended on Florida. So did geriatric Jaycees, Blacks, and hippies in headbands, loony from staring at the sun too long. The teeth in Wes's smile turned yellow as old ivory piano keys.

24. He began to play less golf, said sales kept him too busy. But his job wasn't sales, never was; it was service—of vending machines. He unlocked glassed boxes, counted rows of Salem, Kool, Kent, Marlboro Lights, and Tareyton, then refilled the stacks. At bigger accounts he had a drink or two with a smoke, told a damn good joke. He preferred Salems.

25. He was told he needed heart surgery. On Sunday afternoon he sat staring at his walls, bare except for two crocodile posters, now curling. He stood and counted his crocodilian collection of doorstops, pens, figures of all sizes in pewter, alabaster, and plastic. 157 pieces of shit.

26. Eastern religion was in, and at a psychedelic emporium Wes paid $150 for a meditative mantra. In a ceremony of running water and rags, he received *hareem-hareem-hareem* with parchment paper instructions on how to sit when he

repeated *hareem-hareem-hareem* three times a day. After six months, he rolled up the parchment and set it on fire with his Bic lighter.

27. About that time an attorney in Wisconsin tracked him down to say he had inherited a house. "Who'd leave a loser like me a house?" Wes asked.

"Your uncle. That old fart Arno."

"Sell it," Wes said, wondering what it would bring. He'd never been a homeowner. Besides, he couldn't go home like a dog with its tail between the legs.

"Sales must be bad down there," the attorney said.

"Alright," Wes said, "I'll think about it." This was new, to think serious. Mostly he thought about when to call the exterminator.

28. Florida's inland lakes were dying from development. Avocadoes lost their allure. Mosquitoes got worse. A trap door creaked open in Wes's forebrain and he joined AA, went dry. His new mantra became *day-at-a-time, day-at-a-time.*

29. Within a year, he left Florida's increasing drone of air conditioners, boats, and planes. He moved in to Uncle Arno's house. *My house,* he said, stomach queasy. He met an unlikely couple next door in St. Isidore's rectory: Father Nick and Gertie, his tomato-faced housekeeper.

30. Wes had heart surgery in Madison. Big wigs there said they extended his life ten years. Got that in writing, Wes joked, his handshake with a small tremor.

31. He became janitor for St. Isidore's Church and School. The only time he entered the church was to mop and dust it. He liked being in charge of lost and found: tassel caps, mittens, rosaries, holy cards, softballs, hankies, overcoats, rubbers (not what you think—another name for overshoe.) He even found a soggy purse on the playground with marijuana baggied in the lining.

32. He limited himself to two Salems a day, morning and evening, alone on his porch while he listened to wind stirring

wheat fields, wind stirring snow. At recess, the shouts and squeals prickled him less and less. Once a year he showed off his crocodile collection to the second-graders. Sometimes at night he dreamt he had a son. He named him Peter.

33. One day he coughed up the dream to Father Nick. Father listened at length, frowning. "Make the pain so worth it," Father said, and then shared his own secret: he himself had a flesh-and-blood son named Nicholas, off in boarding school. Father never knew about him until the mother Lois was dying of a brain tumor. Wes asked why they split to begin with. "She didn't know about Nicholas at the time," Father said. "Besides, mixed marriage was out." He scowled. "I would have made the rules different."

"I would have made no rules," Wes said. "Rules ruin everything."

34. When he died, Wes willed his house and surrounding acre to St. Isidore's. The acre came in handy for the grade school's expansion. Before bulldozers demolished the house, Father Nick and Gertie carried out a dozen odd crates plus hundreds of *LIFE* magazines discovered in the back bedroom, evenly stacked, protected.

The Trouble with Ellen

There were three things wrong with Ellen and by fourth grade, we all knew what they were. None of them alone nor all of them together, however, should have caused the bad thing that came into Ellen's life. Though we didn't know that at the time.

We Catholics saw cause and effect between bad thoughts and bad consequences. Like, if you dreamt of a fire and the next day the neighbor's house burned down, you knew it was your fault. And impure thoughts: if you had one of them and then broke out in a rash, well, it was easy to conclude how thoughts created reality.

And the reality in fourth grade was that Ellen was pretty, smart, and rich (not much to like there). So here's point number one: she got her hair curled—a "permanent," in a real hair salon. No one had ever done that. No mother had even attempted to apply a Toni Home Permanent to create poofiness. Ellen's perm brought out her high, round cheekbones and green eyes; green eyes that looked like jewels with her newly tanned skin, which was point number two.

No one had a tan in January, but Ellen did. From a Florida vacation. We got summer tans from picking beans and making hay. A perm plus a January tan? It was enough to keep her away from us at recess.

One day, the nun in our classroom left to fetch hand-outs from the mimeograph machine, and someone went nuts. Maybe it was a spitball, copied homework, or a love note read out loud. The exact nuttiness doesn't matter. What mattered was the tattling that followed, a code among classmates broken, by someone blurting to the woman in black with starched white cardboard framing her face. Sister Mary Francis had cheeks with red pores and buckshot for eyes: the face of a possum.

Beautiful, tanned, and permed Ellen tattled to Sister Mary Francis. Gave out four names of fellow students, two boys, two girls. And out came the ruler. Not on the hands. On the backside. Humiliation flamed up in the four, unjustly accused. So there was point number three that Ellen gave everyone in class—everyone—one more reason to hate her.

At recess, someone said to her, *Wish you were dead.* We all cheered but she held her ground. She was, after all, a doctor's daughter. That gave her executive privilege and pastoral protection (Daddy gave lots of money to the church and school)—this, in addition to the prettiness, perm, and tan.

We had an impromptu roller skating party that Friday night and Ellen wasn't invited. We couldn't wait to see her Monday face, see if a hair was out of place, for that was the thing about perms; they guaranteed to never have a bad hair day.

Monday came and Ellen wasn't in school.

Maybe she got sick of herself, someone said after Mass. We giggled, smug and out of range of the priest.

Back in the classroom, we settled into our lunchbox break-fasts—fasting was required for Communion, so we could swallow the host every school mass morning.

Then, Sister Mary Francis clapped her hands. "Class. Continue eating," she said solemnly, "and as you take in your meal, take in too the sorrow of Ellen and her family."

We stared at possum. Her eyes had sucked themselves farther into her head. She folded her hands. Looking out over the tops of our heads, she appeared to be in a trance. Then, in a near whisper, she said, "Ellen's father died of a heart attack this morning."

The room fell silent, even squiggly Eugene who ate white paste and staples and did anything to get attention. Now, the attention was on Ellen. And she wasn't even there with her beautiful, bright, tan, and newly permed self.

She would never be the same.

And neither would we—our hatred had caused her father's death.

In fact, it was the first time we learned of the power of hate. And we worried whether our sin could fit in the confessional box—and what penance could we possibly serve.

How to Make a Permanent and Wild Gesture

Ezra Cooke, small and birdlike with quick jumpy ways, was born in Holland during World War II, food shortages, the runt of the litter and any loud noise, especially at night, shot him out of bed and so, when he couldn't sleep after a gig, he brooded through the streets, fidgeting with a nervous stomach. One morning at daybreak, he found himself on Beacon Hill, which in those years smelled of fresh newsprint, flower stands, and fresh dog poop.

He passed a red telephone booth with clear window panes. It was empty.

Walloped by an incessant migraine, he entered the booth and lit a joint; it clouded the booth as he dialed the operator and shakily said that he needed to speak with Eleanor Schmidelkoffer in Wisconsin, could she find the number, please.

The operator said, "It's a big state, would you know the city?"

"If I knew that, I'd bloody well dial it myself." There was no Eleanor Schmidelkoffer.

"Try Ellie," he said.

"No, Sir, there is no Ellie."

He tapped his right temple: *think, you dumb sot, think*. And think he did, remembering in a flash the name Peter Myers, which he told the operator. She asked if he could spell it and he said P-e-t-e-r. The operator laughed.

"Glad to be of your amusement," Ezra said.

"The last name, Sir, would it be M-e-i-e-r, or M-e-y-e-r, or M-y-e-r?"

"All of them."

The operator said she could give two listings for free. Ezra chose the first and third listing. Reaching in his shirt pocket, he pulled out a book of matches, and wrote down the two numbers on the inside cover. Then, he hung up, waited a minute, and dialed the last number.

A new operator came on. "Please enter your payment code," she said.

This time, he went for his wallet, removing a paper that had been folded and refolded. He opened it, smoothing each fold with care lest the paper rip. On the paper had been written, *There is no end of things in the heart*. He was once someone else, someone with a home, good-looking, racy, a droopy left lid that rode his face like a permanent wink, something Ellie had loved. He turned the paper over. It held a list of numbers. He squinted at them like someone picking the winning horse of the day. The morning sun shifted and from behind a cloud, a beam struck the silver coin box, making it difficult to see.

"Please enter your payment code, Sir."

"Madam. You in a hurry?" He hunched forward to create a shadow, his nicotine-brown index finger tracking down a column of numbers as he cradled the receiver and tried to recall the last one used. He couldn't recall what time it was in Wisconsin, yet he usually knew the last number he had used.

"Sir. Do you have a credit card? A payment code?"

"Give a man some space." Just then, a guy in yellow hot pants rapped on the booth, patted his wristwatch, wiggled a finger at Ezra, and patted the watch again. Ezra flicked him off.

"I am trying to help you, Sir. Sir, do you have a card?"

"I have a card. Stop *sirring* me." He selected the seventh entry in the column, then punched the digits into the touch-tone keypad.

"Thank you, sir. Your call will now go through."

"Stop *sirring* me," he repeated just as someone answered. Ellie. Her tone was friendly as she said hello, hello. She sounded clear, voice rising from a lovely chest, not that nasal quality so many Americans had. But the pitch was lower than he recollected. He folded the dog-eared-paper, shivering in October wind blowing into the booth while by now a cigarette—the joint having consumed itself—dangled from his mouth. He inserted the paper in his wallet.

"Hello," Ellie repeated, less friendly. "Myers Residence. Or Pete's Repair. Who's calling, please."

"It's me."

There was a heavy, long pause and then, "So it is." Just like that, she turned nasal like she had a cold or her Midwestern twang had fallen into an echo chamber. Or one of them silos.

"Hey, chickee poo." He flicked his ashes at the glass. "It's been a while."

Ellie straightened her spine and looked at the maple losing its leaves. The school bus would be here soon. "What do you want," she said, releasing each word like a stone from a slingshot. She wondered if Pete had picked up the extension in the shop as she repeated, "What do you want."

It was not that Ezra wanted something. He had his Section 8, after arm-wrestling first with City Hall and then Social Service. Hell was other people: stamp this, authorize that, three signatures in triplicate, search out a notary to say he was who he was. Only minutes earlier, walking down Beacon, the wind had picked up in a way that reminded him, in spite of the warm temperature, it was nearly October. He had passed several Hare Krishnas. In bright orange, they whirled around like dervishes, chanting, barefooted and baldheaded, sounding out peace and love without the usual trappings of commitment.

He was who he was or who he had become; he needed her to understand. And make the kid understand. From inside the booth's smeary windows, he looked up at the clock tower on the Parker House Hotel. Then he remembered she had asked him what he wanted. "I'm trying to figure it out," he said, pausing. A tight cough stuck in his throat and he tried to suppress it and failed with a hack-hack-hack before he asked, "How's he doing?"

"He's doing."

"I wrote a letter." He ironed his moustache from the center out. He was sure he had written and nearly sure he had mailed it. With a stamp.

"Dream on." The bus would be here soon and she had an urge to hang up but the urge to hang on was there, too. Even after all those years, she did not know why. People said there was closure to events. Flash-bang, it wasn't true.

"Did you get it?" The guy with yellow hot pants came back, this time pounding on the glass. "Beat it," Ezra said.

"Beat it?"

"No, no. Some weirdo is bugging me."

"Sure."

"Anyway. Did you give him the letter?"

Ellie's nostrils flared. "You have no right."

As if he had not heard her, he went on and on about the letter, the kid, I wrote him, did he get it, did you open it. A hot ash dropped on his finger. "Ouch!" he yelled. He stuck the blistered finger in his mouth as a city garbage truck opened its jaws to trash and growled, compacting the refuse. "Listen, baby. I've been trying to figure . . ."

"Jerk. He doesn't need you and doesn't need to know you."

The operator came on. "Sir, the time on your passcode expires in two minutes. Do you wish to renew?"

Ezra fumbled for his wallet and pulled out the dog-eared paper. "Yes, yes," he said, scanning for a fresh number but by the time he entered it, the operator told him his party had hung up. He opened the booth door. There stood a young man with blistered skin and dirty bell-bottoms, telling Ezra he needed to call home.

"Bummer," Ezra said. He walked across the Boston Commons where the kid had been conceived on a summer night, jumped down the subway stairs near Filene's, stole on to the train, and hopped off at Copley Square. He walked several blocks south to his neighborhood where the bums never panhandled him. Up in his third-floor flat, the smell of cooked cabbage rose through the floorboards. As he laid down on his cot, his heart raced, knowing that phone call was the beginning of something or the end of something. For now, it was sure something.

Stones

Iwas sweating and drooling. It was April. I had almost made it through fifth grade. And now I was leaving the planet. Permanently. Until I heard, "Abigail, honey. Wake *up!*"

I couldn't.

"You have a fever," the voice said, panicky. It belonged to Jane, my mother, sliding her hand under me, her only child.

I squiggled. I squirmed. "Leave me alone," I moaned and meant it. Babies on TV were born kicking and screaming, but when I was born, I surely cried, *leave me alone.* That's what Jane and Lester (he's my father) did, anyway. Monday through Friday, they left me alone. A latchkey kid. Precious. Rare. Oh, precocious, too—been hearing that one since preschool. Like any of that mattered when Jane found me with my hands limp on a book I was reading about a girl ostracized because she was poor and Polish.

"Easy now," Jane said and peeled me off the futon. Just that morning she had certified me sick enough to miss school. She wanted to come home at lunch but Mr. Glander was donating a Rauschenberg and Jane *had* to be there. At noon, she called to see how the chicken noodle went down.

"I'm not hungry," I said.

"You have a different hunger, honey."

When she said stuff like that—after reading one more parenting book—I almost thought she cared. But my parents were in their own world. Lester was a Wilson and Wagner accountant, a number cruncher. Jane was a bigwig at the Madison Museum of Art and Foreign Objects. Foreign Objects wasn't in the title. I made that up. Lester and Jane worked together well. He was total brain, but quiet; I guess you can't shout at numbers. She was a drama queen, very outgoing, in high spirits and obnoxiously optimistic. I'd never be like Jane. She could convince someone to buy drawings of naked people. If you asked me (no one ever did), that was gross.

But back to that different hunger of mine. When Jane called at noon about the chicken noodle, I felt like a noodle. I didn't tell her that. She would have raced home, ranting about having to be in two places at once. She would have fawned over me or maybe she would have called Mrs. Davey three doors down to flop over in fluffy pink slippers and poufy blonde hair with dark roots. So naturally, I told Jane I'm okay, just sleepy.

"Good, good," she said in her everything-is-wonderful tone. "Take a nap."

"I don't want to nap. I want to read my book." I also wanted to report the words were getting fuzzy on the page, that maybe I needed stronger glasses, but before I could, Jane's tone shifted.

"Remember then . . . oh shoot . . . I'm late for a meeting." She smacked her lips, which meant she was applying fresh lipstick. "Keep the door locked. Oh, and don't answer the phone. I'll be home early. But you call, honey, if you need anything."

I didn't bother to say, *Roger, Jane,* because she had hung up. As for answering the phone and hearing a stranger? It was 1991 and we had caller ID, my parents guarded and careful.

I poured a glass of apple juice and sat at the dining room table, watching kids who went home for lunch walk past our house. The day was damp and misty. Daffodils were starting to come up in the front yard. Grandpa and I loved these days. I called them subdued. (It's from Latin *subducere*, to draw from below, in case you want to know.)

Grandpa saw these days differently. "Mother Earth needs a break from Old Man Sun." He winked. "And you, crabby Abby, need a break from those books."

Just between you and me, I liked it when he called me crabby Abby. It was not what he said, it was the way he said it. I was thinking about Grandpa when I saw a girl named Taylor skip by. Taylor was a PPRB. Pretty Perfect Rich Bitch. Whenever there was a gathering of three girls, Taylor was the one in charge, bossing the other two, who allowed it. Why? Girls did anything to be popular. The triangle changed, one or two moved in or out, but Taylor ruled.

Right then, I spied her ruling even the sidewalk. I yearned to know how she did it. I wanted to be in Taylor's crowd, wear laced-up boots with a denim jacket, and watch *Ferris Bueller's Day Off* at her house, instead of alone in my den. Right then, she sensed my wish; she sauntered up our walk and passed through our brick house, her tumbling hair and skinny hips turning into an airplane. She scooped me up and flew the two of us over the rooftops. We saw the mall and the Congregational Church with its white spire and the belt-line highway around Madison. We saw Luke's backyard with caged-in Dobermans, pacing and whipping saliva strings at the thick wire. We saw Ryan's mother unload groceries from her Toyota wagon.

Then, my head wobbled as if I had the outside seat on the Tilt-A-Whirl. Taylor gave me a you're-so-stupid shove. "At least, Taylor," I pleaded, "invite me to your birthday party. Please, please."

"Just because you wear aviator glasses?" The trill of her laughter pushed at me. I never got a chance to push back because the next thing I knew, Jane picked at my face as if a lint storm covered me. Pick, pick, pick. Later, I learned she was peeling strands of hair off my fevered face. She carried me upstairs to bed. Water ran in the bathroom. She slapped a wet cloth on my forehead. She ran downstairs, back up, and this time plopped an ice pack on my forehead. Then I heard her punch buttons on the hall phone and screech, "Nearly unconscious!"

"Ohh," I muttered. "Not so loud . . . ohh, ooh . . ." My neck pinched. My teeth pounded. Time reversed and I was on the playground with Taylor and Meredith. I had them under my spell. I told them I thought we could be friends and they started whispering and I said, stop whispering, and they did and then they said they liked my new powder blue sweater and I thought, should I believe them? By mistake I said, "Should I believe you?" Then I started to confuse myself and my mind went mumbo-jumbo. I stood on a swing and announced I would stop talking to myself because it showed what a fool I was. Suddenly, Jill buckled my knees from behind and I took a nosedive into the sawdust.

Then, whoosh, I was in the Sisters of Perpetual Guilt Hospital. It was over a hundred degrees. Jane answered some questions (birthdate, address, insurance) before exploding, "Is all this necessary? She's dyin'!"

A beefy woman with cigarette breath appeared and lifted my rag doll frame unto a stretcher. I puked. "Looks like meningitis," she said just as I underwent total transformation. My frizzy hair straightened into flowing corn silk. Birthday girls held helium-filled balloons around me and begged, choose me, choose me. The scene shifted and I morphed into an inchworm, hiding under rose bushes in Ravine Park to watch teenagers smoke and grovel each other while the meningitis germs drilled holes in the scene.

The germs entered my brain too, a maze of distorted thoughts and twisted feelings. It turned out I was in a hallucinatory state—which I had read about—though it's nothing like what I read. I can't describe it and this sounds crazy, but

I saw love and it is thin as light. Meanwhile, nurses wrapped me in a cooling blanket. It felt good, to tell you the truth, because I was hotter than melted wax.

I had trouble opening my eyes, too, yet I knew Grandpa was there, holding my hand, talking by touching. I had always been number one to Grandpa and overnight, I became number one on Lester's appointment tickler. And Jane? She fussed over me like when she dressed me in crimson velvet for an Opening. I was three, staring at stiletto heels and Guess-jeans, the wing-tipped men eating Chicken Oscar. Bored, I stuck my finger in the punch bowl and licked it, expecting sweetness, but the punch had a kick. My throat burned. My eyes watered. I wanted out of there, so I said, "What's the opposite of opening?"

"Not now, lover," Jane said, rushing to my side.

That was before she changed what she called me. Lester said he was her lover and so Jane called me honey, which in my mind was bee excrement. She never called me Abigail and I wondered why she named me that. Anyway, I knew the opposite of opening so I said, "Closing!"

"Why, yes it is," Jane said, petting my shoulders.

It was the same nervous pet she gave me in intensive care, only there she did not scan the gallery floor, ready with how-do-you-do. This time her eyes darted between the IV needle in my arm and my chest sucking air like a bad swimmer. Her eyeliner welled in bags under her eyes. I had her full attention and I knew why people got sick.

Well, the devotion from my parents lasted a week. It was replaced by attention from classmates—not during my days in the hospital—but after I returned home. Taylor brought a roll of freezer wrap paper. When she unrolled it, I saw it had been signed by 24 fifth graders at Xavier Academy.

"Miss Williams made everyone sign," Taylor sneered before Jane came out of the kitchen with bakery sugar cookies and milk. Taylor unloaded my geography and spelling books, plus two sheets of math homework. She put on a nice act for Jane, pretending I was not four-eyes-brace-face, or the last one picked for Keep Away.

"We miss Abigail," she said. "Especially at recess." Her hair caught the light and she looked like a model or movie star. I felt sicker.

"She missed you, too," Jane answered for me, a habit begun in pre-school when we carpooled and she clucked away with other kids while I sat there, amazed she could talk about nothing and make it seem something. Even then I liked numbers because in my mind they did not have personalities or secrets. They were what they were. Human beings, on the other hand, were unpredictable globs of Silly Putty mashed into shapes to trick me.

"The playground's not the same without Abigail," Taylor said.

"I bet," Jane chirped.

As if I would miss a playground where I neither kicked a ball nor caught one. A place where I once fell off the monkey bars, jammed my knee, and told no one. A place where kids called me spazzy Abby. I went on the slide only on Saturday morning when Lester was there to spot me. Listen, I was not one of those fat, creamy kids with cookies stashed in their lockers. I didn't crave Kit Kats or cheesy popcorn. I was just skinny and on the first day of fifth grade when we got our geography books, Josh paged through and promptly called me Ethiopian legs. I could not help being skinny. I had thin genes and Grandpa said they're the best because they're easy to haul around. But Grandpa wanted me to stop hauling around my pickiness.

It's not like I picked my pickiness, I told him. It picked me. Grandpa laughed at that. He was old but his laugh wasn't and he tried to help me with the Taylor terror. He wanted me to laugh her off, but he didn't know about all the trouble I endured. Like Eric, the football bruiser who slammed me into the lockers and gave me a black-and-blue elbow; I didn't tell Jane because somehow it would be my fault. Either she would say I was so dramatic or it would not happen if I were More Positive. I am Positive-Positive it was Matt who trapped my back foot, tripping me so I lunged forward, face flat on the floor. After that, I learned to walk with eyes in the back of my head, wondering why kids picked on me.

Once, I told Lester I was hen-pecked. (If you have studied chicken behavior, you know what I mean.) "I find that hard to believe," he said. He ran his finger up the side of his nose. "Unless you're different at school than you are at home."

"Yes, I am."

"I find that hard to believe." Then he pasted yellow smiley-faces on the foyer mirror, hoping something subliminal would happen to me. Soon, I filed these situations—they would come to be called bullying—like a column of numbers, unaware of what they are adding up to.

Back at the dining room table, Taylor and Jane twittered away like best friends while I counted signatures on the poster, most printed, a few in cursive. They were all there. I looked at Wiley's name, written left-handed in smeary blue ballpoint. I had a crush on Wiley and he had written, To Amazon, his nickname for me. Did he mean a river or a South American hummingbird? Maybe he meant a girl soldier, or worse, masculine woman. Amazons cut off their right breast to facilitate the use of the bow and javelin— like Wiley would know that. I was stupid to have a crush on someone like him, a square-faced bratty boy held back in first grade for dyslexia. Miss Williams said he was just lazy. Lazy or not, he was cute. He wore Jordans and sat on the bench, mostly. But off court, he was popular, dressing in early granola, baggy pants hanging off his hips, a Marky Mark slouch. He got some C's, mostly D's. He had already found the key to his father's porn videos. Everyone said he would hold the first beer party for the class, with marijuana for dessert.

I looked again at his slanted writing: *To Amazon. Wiley.* I imagined him hunched forward, nose at the paper, pen cramped in his left hand, crafting each letter from bottom up. If that handwriting had arrived on a get-well card, addressed just to me, it would have seemed dreamy. Instead, splayed on the poster, it mocked me. Right there in my own house, I felt like hitting someone. I had never felt like that before. Only the rehearsed poise of Jane kept me from sending Taylor to another dimension.

Other names marched at me. Ryan, who twisted my fingers until I gave up my math. Jody, who had more gums than teeth but her father was school board president with power over us all. There was Crystal Anne, a new girl I hoped to have a chance with. There was Beth, the only other girl not invited to birthday parties. And Taylor, who had drawn eyes but no mouth in the O of her name. She depicted herself correctly, a girl who last fall promised to include me in her sleepover if I carried her books for a week. That extended to two weeks, and then three, before I caught on. And now Jane offered one more cookie to the enemy who took it while I wished for more sickness. I wanted the sudden strangeness of fever, when there was nothing to understand or compete for, just eternal soaring and flying.

I stared at the cookie crumbs on the lace tablecloth. Taylor was already at the door. She said, "Well, see you in school."

"See you," Jane said, beaming.

I stuck my tongue out at Taylor and braced myself for four more weeks of school before summer vacation, when I would get a break from Taylor and her back-up band of mean girls.

That weekend, Grandpa came for dinner. He brought me a plant—one huge purple flower with stripes on it. "It's an amaryllis," he said. "It blooms indoors. Like you."

I put the plant on the mantel right next to my favorite photo of Grandpa and his stoneboat. The boat was a thick, flat plank. It was bent where a clunky chain hooked it to Grandpa's Ford tractor. Every spring, he picked stones and put them in the boat. That's pretty funny, if you think about it—no wonder that boat couldn't float. In the photo, Grandpa's arms were tanned and bulky like Hulk Hogan and he grinned ear to ear, like work made him happy while all I could think was, no wonder he took long naps.

I looked at the amaryllis; I looked again at the photo. I thought of him spring-toothing, then picking all those stones. Grandpa hobbled over to the bay window and sat on the silk cushion. He asked me to bring him the photo. He squinted. "There weren't a stone left when we finished." He sounded melancholic, which is a word for sad that actually sounds sad.

"Do you miss picking those stones, Grandpa?"

"I do and I don't."

I wriggled next to him. "Not a stone left when you finished? Not one?"

"You're smart. You are." He rubbed his bony knee. "You're right. The following year, there'd be more stones to pick."

Because of all the television I watched—Milwaukee's cannibal Jeffrey Dahmer had just been arrested, Rodney King's beating was captured on video, and *Unsolved Mysteries* intrigued me—I figured there was a dark motive at work. "Did someone unload their stoneboat on your field, Grandpa?"

"Nope."

"Then what?"

"They came out of the earth itself."

I had studied gravity. I did not think this was possible. Stones were supposed to sink, not swim to the surface. I told Grandpa this. I told him it was worthless, picking stones every spring if they were going to multiply. Grandpa laughed his laugh that rolled up from his belly and burst through his lips. He wasn't laughing at me, however. I knew when someone laughed at me. Grandpa wasn't doing that.

He simply said, "You and your curious side."

He liked the side of me that questioned everything. But I couldn't tell him about the things I questioned most, things that were my stones: the parade of mean kids, teachers who ignored the teasing, and his very own daughter, Jane. But mostly I couldn't tell him about my feelings. They were inside me and it took me a long time to find them. I was pulled to a life of the mind and often I wished for some clue from my body. I dreamed there might be a path between the body and mind that would tell me which feelings to share. And which ones to keep to myself. Like that thing with Wiley, calling me Amazon because he thought Amazon sounded like Abigail. Did he like me? How would I know?

"Abigail." Grandpa cleared his throat. I turned to see him reach in the pocket of his flannel shirt. He pulled out some well-worn red string, tied together at both ends. "How about a little Cat's Cradle?"

My heart opened as he looped the string around both his hands. Then he put the middle finger of one hand through a loop on the other and pulled. I took my thumb and forefinger and pinched the string, pulling my hands farther and farther apart until the string was taut (that means super tight). Then came the best part. I pointed my fingers down, scooped the string up through the middle, and there it was—Cat's Cradle, a simple set of swoops and loops for two people.

Besides the Cradle, Grandpa taught me Soldier's Bed, Diamonds, and Candles. The loopy red string weaved its way between Grandpa's fingers and mine, one formation after another. Grandpa was all smiles while I thought of going back to school and facing Taylor and Wiley. I thought, too, of how many spring times it must have taken before Grandpa finally picked that field clean.

I was not going to ask him, however. I knew it had to do with volcanoes and earthquakes and reversing gravity. Once I figured it out, I could figure out how to make a friend. Maybe I could even find a friend to take a ride on Grandpa's stoneboat.

The Fedora

Becca snuck down the farmhouse steps into a basement of cobwebs and bone-yellow light. Twenty years old and home on spring break, she needed another look at her earlier find. Her sneakers hit the scummy cement as she angled a flashlight to scan a row of cardboard boxes along the cistern wall. The boxes, with their tops cut off, had become trash bins. In each box, empty tin cans spilled over, their jagged lids clinging like a thread.

Earlier, she had tried to chuck more cans—Spam, Green Giant Corn, Campbell's tomato soup—into the boxes. It was that time of year for her Daddy to hitch the trailer, load the boxes, and then unload them in a dump hidden in a hollow on the back forty. She was moving cans to make room for more when Willie called long-distance and she raced up the stairs to talk, then scurried back to the basement.

Now the furnace, due for stoking, sputtered and above in the kitchen, doors slammed and her little brother groaned, "She always disappears when it's time for dishes." In haste, she rummaged through box after box, finding empty wine bottles carefully layered beneath the cans. Specifically, Muscatel wine. Later, she would learn it was made from Muscat grapes with high floral aromas making for a sweet wine sold in bottles small enough for Skid Row transients who found a few pennies. It was wine that gave a fast buzz, intended for a swig out of a bag by a derelict. Indeed, it may have led to the creation of the term *wino* as a reference to all alcoholics, even those who used grain alcohol, beer, or gin for their belt.

She stared at the nests of bottles, sugary smells swirling, the results of fermenting Muscat grapes and then adding brandy to stop the fermentation while residual sugar remained. She felt dizzy, disoriented, a cotton candy high. Maybe she already knew, the way children of divorce say they didn't have a clue, but they did. She had found Daddy's golden liquid with a kick, drained to the last drop. His breath often smelled complex, with a finish both edgy and lively. She imagined him with a bottle—not in the basement but on stage somewhere, he had done local theater in a town three miles away, in his twenties—reciting Arthur Miller: *Let you look sometimes for the goodness in me and judge me not.*

Greenish mold on the damp cement wall permeated the air. She gagged, feeling confined like a prisoner. For sure, she was confined in the middle of eight kids and oodles of cows, chickens, pigs, turkeys, dogs, cats, and a horse or two. Where did she belong, a college student discovering home was not what she thought it was. She remembered a photo of the parents, their embrace in 1942. Daddy wore a three-piece suit, plaid tie, starched white shirt. Atop his head, a fedora at a quintessential sexy angle. They held hands, Mama in a pale blue shirtwaist dress with white stripes, Mary Jane shoes, a leather bag clutched under her left arm, Daddy holding her hand like a lifeline. It was. They had met when he woke up from his appendectomy and saw her, a nurse tending to his post-op course. He thought he was seeing an angel, he said. Often.

In the photo, their eyes lock on one another, smiles wide and inviting, anticipating kisses, Becca always thought. And Daddy's arm ringed around Mama's waist, ready for the Big Bands that magnetized them and set their toes tapping. Becca idolized the photo, had seen it countless times, a sweet moment before they married. She had seen other photos, too. Bar scenes with Daddy's catchy grin, Chesterfield cigarette in one hand, cocktail glass in the other. Once in high school, finally able to ask the question, she said, "Were you tipsy?"

"I was happy," he winked. She never questioned his answer nor read into it, for Daddy was a man fortified with jokes and an easy, swaggering way with people.

Becca put the cans back in place like sod over a grave and went upstairs to dry the dishes and think about the fedora. Maybe it would channel Daddy. That night, while the Philco TV cast a ghoulish light on her sleeping brother, she opened the door to the guest closet. The guest it housed was Daddy: his fancy clothes, suits, hats, and starched white shirts hung there while the closet in my parents' bedroom held Mama's Swiss-dot dresses, plaid wool suit, and nurse's uniforms. She found the fedora, its patina of Old Spice and Dutch Masters cigars, the fold across the crown. Daddy would crease the felt hat before putting it on, a repeat of a fold already there, but it had to be just right like a woman's seams in her nylons.

Inside the hat was a grosgrain band, rippled, with smudges of darkness, Daddy's dancing sweat, a handsomeness not found in the barn, a lifestyle that drove him to escape as Fred Astaire on Saturday night. She put on the hat. Something about it confirmed her fear—Daddy got oiled every day. She simply had not paid attention. Every time he stoked the furnace or carried a can—one at a time—into the basement, he took a swig, a twenty percent alcohol swig. This, in addition to things he did not hide, cases of Kingsbury in the garage and Corby's brandy above the refrigerator.

She took off the hat and studied it more. It was pure 1950s, yet the brim was broader, flamboyant, dipped and rose like Daddy's personality. She was on to something, yet would avoid confrontation, learning much later in life why families like hers did not confront. They aimed to please.

Be polite. If you can't say anything nice, Mama said, don't say anything at all.

And so, she returned to school that spring with Don't-Say-Anything in her head, trying to forget her discovery, which is to say she ignored it, a wound that would never scab over if she picked at it. But it became harder and harder to ignore and finally, being *argumentative* as Mama claimed, she wrote a letter. Not to Daddy, to Mama—since she feared reprisal from Daddy. Thus, she put the burden of correction on Mama, who, after all, ran the household and made decisions; in Becca's mind, Mama was in charge of Daddy, too—fix him. In the letter, Becca detailed Muscatel nests in the basement and the lurid Listerine on his breath, but mostly she railed about deception, transparency, role models, and emotional honesty.

Mama did not write back. Mama did not call. It was months before Becca went home again to learn what had happened. When the letter addressed to Mama arrived, Daddy opened it. He read it and handed it to Mama. There was no discussion. For three days, Daddy gave Mama the silent treatment. Mama crumbled, not yet having been to assertiveness-training class at the hospital where she worked as a meek nurse. She was a caregiver. She took care of Daddy; that did not include confrontation.

And so, the *Little House on the Prairie* illusions continued, including a Thanksgiving Becca was put in charge to play mother at the first meal without parents, who had gone on a rare vacation, leaving Becca to make thanks with three brothers and two sisters, all younger than her. Two older sisters had already moved out.

Mama had bought a Swanson turkey roll for she guessed Becca couldn't handle a real bird. While the turkey roll (processed white and dark meat glued together with gelatin) warmed, Becca prepared the dining room table with a plastic lace tablecloth, candles the color of cornmeal, Noritake

China and Oneida flatware, the kind of show put on for company. She brought the food from the kitchen to the table, then all sat down and recited the prayer—*Bless us O Lord and these Thy gifts which we are about to receive from Thy bounty through Christ, Our Lord. Amen.* They were farm kids with scant bounty, dreams plowed under by daily chores, and a schizophrenic God: Daddy was a Lutheran who didn't attend church and Mama a Catholic zealot who sang in the choir, went to confession, and drove the kids to Sunday Mass and Catholic grade school.

At one end of the table, in Daddy's chair, sat the oldest brother ready to carve like Daddy. Gripping a knife and fork, he deadpanned, slow as Alfred Hitchcock, "Good e-e-e-evening."

"Where's the turkey?" the next brother moaned.

"I want a drumstick," demanded the next brother.

"I want a wing," one of the little girls begged, shouting to get attention, everyone whining at the same time, talking over one another as pieces of perfect round whorls of factory meat flopped on the platter.

At Becca's end of the table, she passed lumpy mashed potatoes and lime Jell-O loaded with bananas that soon melted into pale gravy on the China plates. They looked like orphans, though no one said so, having learned to mask feelings. After dinner, they fought about whose turn it was to do the dishes or sweep the floor or carry food to Scamp, their Dalmatian.

When Mama and Daddy returned, Becca gave a sanitized report, keeping secret about the yucky meal (most of which went to the dog), infighting over chores, and squabbles over TV. She returned to school with her agony growing over the primal question—*Where does it hurt, Daddy?*

That question would go unanswered, for it was never voiced.

Wild Turkey

Jonathan Cable labors his way to a finish in Olive Cable, not with aplomb, but sweaty and on edge. He then dresses, locates Olive's desk calendar, and circles that March Sunday in red before he's off to the kitchen to crack two eggs into a Le Crueset skillet, punch the microwave to wrinkle Nueske bacon, and sprinkle cinnamon sugar on sourdough toast. When all is ready, he slides bacon and eggs on a plate, laying the toast on a torn piece of paper toweling.

Meanwhile, Olive goes to the bathroom to wash off the drippage.

At the island bar, he inhales the food while reading the *Sunday Times*. As usual, he begins with Business Day and the stock market, then technology, movies, real estate, and autos. When done, he leaves the strewn newspaper, eggy plate, and sugary toweling for Olive. (Once, in the early years, she called him a slob.) He puts on his Red Wing leather boots and stomps out, slamming the door. The force tilts the hallway mirror sideways.

Later, she straightens it.

Outside, wind blows brisk, the spring equinox. If Olive desires, she could stand at the second-floor window of their Greek revival and watch him in his gentleman-farmer orchard. She does not. She knows how he grips the pruning shears—the strength in those hands. She can almost hear the sound of the blades as he clips the Golden Delicious, then the McIntosh. She knows how he will raise the iron hammer and drive a stake next to the leaning Mutsu, its trunk having been bent by winter winds. Many times, she has heard him set foot to sod, a hard-fall, a furious mark, before he stops to inspect a graft on the Cortland, his thighs locking like a wrestler looking for the pin. Over twenty years, she has seen his ears redden, starting with flesh of the lobe and creeping to the wired top.

She does not even want to stand on the balcony and view this heavily mortgaged land with its long gravel road winding back to the main road where life begins, traffic lights, courthouses, do-gooders in Rotary and Optimist Clubs, the gravel grinding like whorls in his ears that roll her words before his correction: What you mean to say is this.

She should have put on her walking shoes after it happened. Instead, she learned to pull stays from his dress shirts and pre-spot rings around collars, each ring advancing like a thin bruise. Which is what she does now, checking each pocket for gum and Pilot pens, finding his scribble on an index card: The law has nothing to do with justice. In another pocket, another scribbled card: Evil Angel Fashionistas. She slots them into a shoebox on the counter and continues, pre-spotting undershirts—the armpits smell of old fish and licorice—before mashing the undershirts atop the dress shirts. She pours in Seven Generation detergent and hits the start button. All the while, she thinks, is it too late? His plans for the barnlike big house had been set in stone—cathedral ceilings, five bathrooms, wine cellar, sauna—and the plans steamrolled on even after sweet, sparkly little Olive got run over and Jonathan drove himself to take on more surgical cases while she went numb.

Back in the kitchen, she gathers up the *Times* and sits at the island bar, reading about why people marry: legal, social, libidinal, emotional, financial, spiritual, professional, and religious. She cannot remember their reason or if they were the same. She recalls last evening at Marcello.

"We have a new surgical tech," he said, sipping Merlot.

"And?"

"Great ass."

She barely raised her new eyebrows. He took another sip, the pink of his rosacea cheeks pinker, yet his eyes blank as if he'd lost something he would never find. He pursed his lips. "Have you thought what life would be like if you were an hour hand?"

"An hour hand?" she asked, wondering what loin-rocking film he had watched last night.

"That's what I said. An hour hand. Did you not comprehend?"

She had swan-like features, though flesh had begun to fall from her neck and her hair sagged too like a bird matted in an oil spill. She looked at him and said, "I think . . ."

"I'm not so sure you do." Then, he looked at her with an old flash of himself that wavered between tenderness and affected humor. He tried a smile, then added, "Denial is my favorite state, remember?"

"I don't know or even remember if I knew." She folded her napkin and set it on the table.

He motioned to the waiter, who had been watching them closely. And that had been it, a public meal, a generous tip, 20-year Tawny Port for dessert, him overindulging because he had warned her that she would drive home and she had bit her tongue lest she relapse and see him back down the cement apron of their old house without looking, having forgotten to close the front door, in a rush, having taken time to confront the builder before a seven o'clock hip case. And she had come to the door to see him roar off while she stood there, screaming in silence.

She sits at the island bar, reading, perusing the help wanted, not much there, it's all online now. Besides, she is—was, a librarian—not an engineer or software designer.

She reads the book reviews, scans the theater, health, Sunday Magazine, Style Magazine, lingering on sundresses and open-toed shoes. Silver bracelets and watches are on sale. For her birthday last year, he gave her jewelry. Nipple clamps. Another year, it was a tube of lipstick that vibrated when she opened it. He said he thought it would help a problem he thought she had.

Problem, she thinks. From a stone mug, she chooses a mechanical pencil to focus on the crossword puzzle. Soon, stuck on a ten-letter word for the space between what you know and what you imagine, she looks up. He'll be in from the orchard soon. Making haste, she stacks the paper for recycling. The sports section lands on top and a large photo catches her eye. It is in full color, a hunting story with a picture of a woman in camouflage, though the way the sizeable body is dressed in jacket, pants, and cap—it could be a man. The caption, however, names the camouflaged woman Romelda Case. Romelda is gripping a rifle in one hand and a wild turkey in the other.

Olive feels weird pleasure. The turkey is dead, upsidedown, and the woman turned hunter grins like a savant as she squints into the camera. Her teeth are yellow stubs and her eyes wet and cloudy. Olive cannot say how old that camouflaged woman is nor how many hour hands she endured before coming to shoot a turkey.

Olive cannot say that. Not—yet.

Geraniums

Men don't cry. Believed that my whole life so imagine my surprise to learn it ain't so. I'm saying it ain't so because since something went zing in my head, I cry. Know what? Ain't no big deal—especially if you got something to cry about, which turns out I did. Let me say that other men here cry too and that includes screamers screaming *help hellp helllp* the livelong day. (Some, quite frankly, are beyond help.) Aides ignore the screamers, but try crying; they're over you like seagulls on a plowed field, picking and poking for grubs.

What's wrong, what's wrong, that's all I heard in the beginning. If I could talk, I'd have said ain't nothing wrong. If something's wrong enough times, starts to seem right, like Velma nagging. I gotta hand it to the aides, the way they lift and feed, scurry to check alarms on wanderers like Harold my roommate, then munch sweets and tug at creeping bloomers. (There'd be less tugging if they bought bigger bloomers.) Pill queens work hard too, pushing locked carts of syringes and pills every color. They're a little bitter (the pills, not queens or aides).

Patty's my favorite aide, too much thigh but good for the job. Goes about one ninety, probably has a sorry past, not abused or nothing—just misplaced, adrift. Maybe tried teaching but couldn't stand kids teasing her about her big butt, radar ears. Makes sense she'd fall in love with old folk.

We're like pets—faithful, devoted, dependent. When Velma and I visited Grandma Bev at the nursing home, I often saw Patty's kind, nosy nellies peeking inside heads of old farts, searching for a piece of the puzzle. Ain't no puzzle. The odds are against us: one in one go.

Anyway, Patty's a good shit. If I shudder at them horse pills, she wraps a hefty arm around me and says, take your time, swallow what you can. My daughter LuAnn tells me that, too. (Never mind what *I* want—a point we'll come back to.) LuAnn can't let me go. My son Stanley's not so emotional about all this. I'm ready for the end and Stanley knows. After Velma died, he worried about me being alone. He wanted me to give up my license; I won on that one, but gave in to power of attorney crap. I gave LuAnn power for finance; she's good at counting, especially husbands. Stanley's my health care agent. He's first-born and blessed with common sense. He'll speak for me when I can't, when two white coats declare me *incapacitated*.

"How will I know when incapacitated hits?" I asked Crinwald, my attorney.

"Don't need to know," Crinwald said. I sat between the kids at his big oak desk. "Long as Stanley here knows what you want."

"That's easy," I said. "If I'm a vegetable, let me go. Got that, Stanley?"

Stanley nodded like a sheepshead player with the queen of clubs and Crinwald's desk became a card table where we studied one another's face, laid each trick, counted trump. "I've lived my life," I said evenly.

"Daddy," LuAnn shrieked, "don't talk like that." She fiddled with the silver ring on her index finger, twisting it on and off. Everyone got real quiet. I scanned Currier and Ives prints on the wall. Stanley coughed. LuAnn worked the ring. A tick-tock behind us grew louder. Finally, Crinwald said, "Can't see you as a feeble old fart in diapers."

"You're creeping me out," LuAnn said. Her ring bounced on the terrazzo and she scrambled to fetch it.

Death and taxes, Crinwald said, that's all we're sure of. He rat-a-ta-tatted his cigarette creased fingers on the desk. He cleared his throat. Looking out the window, he said, "Myself, I wish for death by truck." Then he asked if there was more questions and I thought, only if you got answers, buster.

Stanley laid his big hand on my bony leg. His palm felt warm, strong. He squeezed my knee, then reached over to LuAnn and nudged her. We'll do Pops right, he said. When she didn't answer, he raised his voice and said, "Right, Louie?" Thinking wasn't LuAnn's strong suit. She sat like a brick. So Stanley cupped his hand and thwop, thwoped her on the shoulder. She sniffled. He pulled her in and set the three of us in a huddle before asking, "What did Pops say?"

"If I'm a vegetable," LuAnn said, gasping between words, "let me go."

"Okay then," Stanley said.

The huddle broke without any go-get-em cheer and Crinwald pushed papers my way. I checked *no* to CPR, feeding tube and breathing machine, and *yes* to organ donation (who'd want an old glue horse like me?) When I agreed to Riverwood Nursing Home, Crinwald lectured about Medicare, Medicaid, personal assets. He eyeballed LuAnn. "You'll be selling the house, writing checks." Her ring landed on the floor. I picked it up and slipped it in my pocket.

It was one thing to plan for the end in Crinwald's office. It's quite another here at Riverwood, making do with Patty, a workhorse born piss-poor and always picking up shifts, worried about house and car payments and God knows what else. And yet she's so goldarn cheerful—she must be on happy pills. As for Crinwald, he never mentioned blood thinners, heart-timers, or antibiotics. Pills have become my limbo, my goddamn limbo. It's not that easy to die; I been at it a year now, least I think it's that long. Wonder what Stanley's waiting for. Don't he remember *let me go?*

After my first dizzy spell that spring, Doc Fickett looked over his glasses at me. "You're getting old, Arnie," he said. "This one's a warning." I told him so is the tornado siren and our county's never seen a tornado. Doc ordered me pills, but I didn't take them.

The stroke leveled me in fall, judging by Hallmark cards with autumn leaves. Then there was high winds, frost on the panes I vaguely recall. I lost spring except for daffo-dils in foil, and a damn speech therapist who dug for my voice and when she couldn't find it, stopped bugging me. It's summer now. Air-conditioning, that's how I know it's summer. Summer used to be butterflies, honeybees, and songbirds. Summer was pokers in the raspberry patch and thistles, making hay and shocking grain. Summer was sweat. No one works like that anymore. Overalls aren't destiny anymore; now they're fashion.

Anyway, chillers hum day and night, blowing winds like November. My bones feel each blast and Patty can't seem to find my long johns. I give Stanley a *do something* glare when he comes. Mostly he looks away, but today his eyes bleed into mine when Doc explains the stroke was massive, there's a reason Arnie's confused. Doc rubs my shoulder and says, "The worst part is that a stroke cuts off emotion." Stanley sucks air through his teeth. Doc continues with a tone like when he announced Velma's Big C. "Your father can't *feel* his feelings," he says.

Doc's almost right. You can't feel if there ain't feelings to feel. "Imagine this," Doc says, grabbing a clipboard. He scribbles, then shows Stanley: *Strokes maek wurds difficlt tew rede.* Stanley's face falls, but I think pretty soon Doc won't be able to read his own writing. Doc puts the clipboard back, at a loss for words, which ain't like him. I shake my head, wondering who decided to condition air. I sweated every day—that's how I got to be seventy-five, or is it eighty-five? Everything worked fine 'til LuAnn found me on the kitchen floor.

Doc pumps Stanley's hand and says, let's see how it goes. Stanley tips his Ford hat and they both leave. I'm like the Ford 9-N, one tractor light out and the other one goin'. Never replaced them bulbs 'til they both went, always trying for a fresh start. These aides start fresh every day, armed with laundry bags and linen, pens and paper to make notes about us cripples. Down the hall they go, indoor people who don't know seasons, rainfall, or wet hay.

They don't even know about Ralph and Floyd's barn. When it caught fire, I floored the pickup down Horseshoe Road and saw the whole place ablaze. Wet hay can do that. Thirty guys pumped and scrambled while wind whipped with a vengeance, Pastor said. Flames leaped from one building to the next so fast, so high, it was like trying to hose down the sky. God wanted those barns down and that was that. Damned if we knew why God wanted Ralph, who died in that fire of hell, and left Floyd to batch it alone. Wonder if Floyd's cornflowers grew back, those purple beauties I see when they park me at the day room window. I can see lawn needs cutting. Crabapples could stand pruning. It's time to inspect the corn, go smell the earth, all warm and wet, lie in the grass with Velma, let the wind catch her skirt, her giggle. Or stand on that rope bridge when we was courting. The bridge swayed and she kissed me, a poppy-red battle, the start of a lifelong back-and-forth. What I'd give for those years when she worshipped me, when my stubbornness was *strong beliefs*. I'd like, too, a nickel beer, and to lock her in my arms for one more polka or schottische. That woman could make me dance when I wasn't, whether cleaning boxstalls, picking eggs, or carrying milk pails. But that's all done. Now I'd be content to listen to bullfrogs and grasshoppers, and watch fog roll over the river in shades of gray.

LuAnn's afraid of gray. She's thirty-five, hair streaked blue and skin the color orange. Didn't Velma include skin cancer when she wrote the Body Responsible Rules? Now I hear, "Hi Daddy!" There's my girl, shameless in black lycra. "You look so sad, Daddy, what's wrong?"

Not again! *What's wrong, what's wrong?* Where to start— that ice pick in my knee? Knots in my back? A wrist drooping like a sunflower and bursting in pain? Itches I can't scratch? Or eyes plastered to the ceiling 'til a queen of the night hands over a pill and I ride with

Paladin, keep them doggies rollin'. After a pill I'm in a deep sleep, and then they wake me up! For therapy. Every day, same damn thing—therapy. These places used to be Rest Homes. Now they're torture chambers with physical therapists and occupational therapists. Plus a hyper Activity Director determined to make merry. In spite of them, I sleep fourteen hours a day while reruns come and go in my head. Sometimes I see middles, no end. Other times, it's a beginning, no middle and then boom: The End. I'm in another world with Kingsbury and *Gunsmoke* when I hear LuAnn reading. *Hope you get better. Praying for you. Praying for your full recovery*—from nutty Cousin Ruby in California.

LuAnn's ex, James, sent some leaves and said I should I smell them. He's in California, too. Dried leaves have powers to heal, LuAnn says, reading, *You can't die cured, but you can die healed.* Cured, healed, don't much matter at my age. All I know is death is a big secret, and I'm soon to find out. If only LuAnn would leave me alone. "Daddy, wake up. Lisss-en." I wake up and gaze at her, pretty as her Mama. It's our wedding day and Velma's pregnant. And not happy. *It's not your body,* she said before the Grand March when her feet swelled and she didn't want to dance. I said *I do* and for decades, I did. I tried to do her right, new screen door, pasteurized the raw milk, hung more wash lines. New mailbox at the end of the lane. Jean Nate with fancy spritzer when I could. We had a little of everything with the rise and fall of wheat production and milk prices. She had herself a job at the five-and-dime until LuAnn came, ten years after Stanley. Our little girl wore hair bows and patent leather until Velma tacked *Biology is not destiny* to the fridge. When LuAnn turned sweet sixteen, Velma advised birth control. I said it was against nature and she said this girl will have a future, not like me. I said it's against nature and she said, "It's not your body." Even Doc couldn't argue with that. So Velma chose for LuAnn. And LuAnn chose men and travel and shopping. She never did choose any grandkids.

Now someone plants a kiss and I smell Jean Nate. It really is Velma, with a change of heart. She's run out of seminars, stopped biting her nails, lost two chins, the third one too. *Gimme a kiss,* she teases, breasts high in a new shirtwaist for card club, cheeks fever pink from cooking. She pours home-made fudge into flower molds and tells me to lick her fingers. I hold her close and lick and she says, *I'm mad about you.* Soon, card players are at the door and my Velma the prettiest of them all. I draw in her willingness; she slurps another kiss and says, "Don't give me that Goofy look, Daddy."

Daddy? Oh. It's LuAnn. I *must* be Goofy. I can't walk. Can't talk. Hell, I need round-the-clock babysitters. And Patty's the only sitter, I mean aide, who downright beams taking care of me as if I've got potential or something. Doesn't bother her that my pitching arm—God, I miss the Old Timers League—hangs at my side like frayed rope. When LuAnn was in grade school she lost her jump rope. Weeks later, after a couple of good thunderstorms, she came to me in the barn, crying and white-knuckling wooden handles with chipped red paint, white braids shrunk. I hugged her tight. *Fix it, Daddy,* she begged. Funny, now she wants to fix me, but I've been out in the rain too long. Back then, I said we'd buy another jump rope. She didn't want another one; she wanted *that one* because some shit (James) had carved "J" in the handle.

Years later, in a damn coinkidink, LuAnn came home on the Greyhound from Chicago and James was on the same bus.

Our green catalpa was white with blossoms when she called, asked if I'd pick her up. Not a year had passed since her and Lionel's wedding. I went down to Tessa's, had a shot and a beer, and waited. The Greyhound pulled up and whooshed its air brakes. I come out of the tavern to see her shuffling toward me while the driver ducked under the sideways door, found her suitcase. Where's Lionel, I asked. Had to work, she said. By the time we drove in the lane, she confessed what Lionel was working on. Another woman. "Promises are made to be kept," I said. "Forgive, go on."

Then she told her mother. "Some promises are made to be broken," Velma said, beet-red from whipping potatoes. "He broke his. Why shouldn't you?" Shows how times change, and not for the better. That Sunday she cried on James's shoulder; by summer they took off for California. That seems so long ago, long before LuAnn got bit by another bug—Possibility Thinking.

"You can think yourself to health," LuAnn insists, squinting now through cellophane on a package. She rips off the cellophane and reads, "Positive energy comes from positive thoughts. Wow. You can hemi-sync your brain, Daddy, with this tape." She believes in hemi sink but not in Doc who told her I would never walk or talk again. Doc had crossed, uncrossed his legs, leaned forward and told her she was *in denial.* From the way he pulled his lower lip, I figured there's no pills for that. Now she waves the tape at me. I point to the black box below the TV.

"The VCR, Daddy?" She strokes my sunflower hand. "No, this is a *cassette* tape, Daddy, not a videotape." So shoot me. I didn't wanna watch a sad sack movie anyway. Pretty soon the screamer starts up and roommate Harold (he's out of it) blasts a good one. LuAnn holds her nose, presses the call light, and reports Mister Harold needs help. Harold once ran Valley Bank. Now he can sit in his own problem and not know it. Broken hip brought him here. He used to click around on a computer until Alzheimer came for him. LuAnn and I wait for an aide to pooper-scoop Harold's problem. By the way, Patty told me aides do the poop, RNs do the pills, and when she told me that, her eyes became hard and cold, as if poop pissed her off. Well, maybe the RNs got pills for Harold's problem, which hopefully won't last long.

Sadness, however, lasts *very* long. It did in Velma. As we got older, she ranted, *I'll never forgive you for ruining my life.* She had talked herself into believing I *ruined* her life. With each rant I said, look, long as men and women fit together the way they do, there'll be more ruins. Her peeves went up against my drinking, her homemaker hen-pickings against my tractor time (only time I could think). On the tractor I came to understand the desire a woman wants—to be with her own kind. Women are too goddamn emotional, which is hard for living, worse for dying. That's why Stanley's in charge now, not LuAnn. The time her calico cat ran through the chopper, well, she'd a carried that blind, three-legged thing around forever. I put a hammer to its head and buried it behind the turkey shed.

Now LuAnn studies the cassette, says how music connects the brain, and sure enough, I hear bells jingle-jangle on workhorses when the plow cuts into red clay. LuAnn probably don't remember those bells. Stanley would; he helped harness the team for 4-H sleigh rides. He worked alongside me while Velma hauled LuAnn to dance, piano, and the library where they borrowed *The Feminine Mystique,* which by the way played no part in keeping the farm in the family. Stanley managed that. He converted my machinery shed into a fix-it shop. *Organic Mechanic,* LuAnn named it. Her workaholic brother makes money hand over fist without milking cows or battling aphids. That's why he don't visit often—too busy.

Now LuAnn pops in the cassette just as Patty shows up. "How are we today?" Patty says, whisking the curtain closed to clean up Harold, a skinny guy like me. And she means *we*—her and me, like we're one. She's middle-aged, well-scrubbed, big-boned and determined, a rare breed that never has a bad day. Patty's the best. Some don't know my favorite sleeping side. So I cry. They think I'm in pain, want an extra blanket. They're as baffled as LuAnn wanting *positive thoughts*, so I can go home with her. Pretty soon Patty whips open the curtain, done with Harold, and LuAnn corners her, asking how she knows what Daddy wants.

"How do I know?" Patty ogles me with a weird kind of joy. "Oh, sixth sense," she says.

"He needs to talk," LuAnn says, "I need him to talk."

Patty winks at me. She and I don't need talk, because she's in control, pure and simple. She knows when I want a nap, or one-armed bowling. So now I point at the closet, tell her get my jacket, I'm going to tip a few with Stanley. She pigeon-toes to the closet, grabs a diaper, and announces I need changing. I pound my fist on the bed and tell her—the jacket, I'm going to town. "Tell me again," she says and turns to LuAnn, "I have a compulsion to make people happy." Then she wraps her doughy hand around mine, "Say it again, Arnie." I open my mouth and scream—my jacket, the beige one with the zipper, and the Lions pin!

"Gobbledygook," LuAnn says, "talk, Daddy, talk." She tells Patty that she can't stand this anymore. Patty says she knows, slides one arm across my back, and scoots me up in bed. She smells of red potatoes. I stroke her buttery cheek. Aw Arnie, she says, propping my dead arm and leg with pillows. She says I'm a sweetie, that some here get belligerent. LuAnn sighs, asks Patty if her back kills by the end of the day.

"Sometimes," Patty says, "but not from Arnie or Harold. They're featherweights."

"Hey, Pops! What stinks in here?" It's Stanley, all six feet of him, in work clothes and a two-day beard. He marches in, sees Patty and halts. Patty reddens and rattles the closet door.

"Patty is Daddy's favorite," LuAnn says. Patty gives us her backside while she rummages in the closet. So LuAnn says, "This is Stanley, my brother."

"Hello again," Patty says, without turning around. LuAnn puckers her brow and says, you two know each other?

"Ford Bronco, burned-out clutch," Stanley says. "You *that* Patty?" Patty finally faces us and whips aerosol mist back and forth like a windshield washer on high. Stanley picks at the inside of his wrist. He comes over and shakes my hand. A buzzer goes off in our handshake. I pull back, befuddled.

"Stanley!" LuAnn sure sounds like Velma.

Stanley slides the buzzer into his pocket, another buzz. "Pops liked it," he laughs. "Bet he misses his exploding cigar and whoopee cushion, too." LuAnn tells him it's not funny anymore.

"Louie, Louie," he says, arms opening, "how would we know?" He hugs her, but his eyes red-line Patty and behind LuAnn's back, he rubs his thumb across his fingers, the moola sign. A moustache of sweat appears on Patty's upper lip. She clenches her teeth and bobs her head up and down. "Louie, Louie," he repeats, low and somber, then shows Patty a palm with all fingers and thumb stiff. Five. Five something. Purple creeps up Patty's neck. Her eyes narrow. She blinks several times, as if to say *yes*. Then Stanley releases his bear hug and Patty gets sweet, saying, "Let's get you up for dinner."

Five, I think. Five o'clock already? I'm dog-tired. I'd rather sleep than eat. Patty says, get up, otherwise the fever will win. She makes the kids wait in the hall while she wipes me down with pump water. She dresses me in one of LuAnn's finds, a Hawaiian number with parrots. I'm wobbly as a newborn calf, but she oomphs me into the wheelchair. Why does she do this work, with all those extra shifts? Is it worth it just to drive a big ass Ford Bronco? "You've suffered so," she whispers. "Your time will come." It damn better. My Ford 9N's idling, ready to bounce me to the back forty. Instead, I'm parked in a wheelchair, watching a cat fight in the hall.

"Nurse called," Stanley says. "Pneumonia."

"I *knew* he didn't look good," LuAnn says. (Not even in my Hawaiian number?)

A giant pause, then Stanley says, "Too many Chesterfields." LuAnn's pitch changes; she says I haven't smoked in years.

"He's breathing with rocks, Louie," Stanley says. "They want to give him antibiotics."

"So?"

"They want my approval."

LuAnn goes nuts. "What's to approve? What is WRONG with you?" She wallops him on the chest, pump, thud, a 12-gauge spraying birdshot. "You can't just let him dieeeeeee!"

Stanley doesn't budge. "Louie, Louie," he says. "Does Pop want to live like this?" I'm surprised to hear I'm living; thought I was dying. LuAnn whacks him harder, but he don't budge. "*If I'm a vegetable, let me go,*" Stanley says. "Remember?"

"What does that mean?" LuAnn steadies herself on the hall railing.

"It means, let him go. Let him go, Louie." Her ringed fingers clank the railing, stalling like Velma, looking for a comeback, but the only sound is silver rings, clanking. Then Stanley hardens. "Pop said *no feeding tube.* I know Pop. He'd say drugs are tubes *to keep him going.*" More silence, a touch LuAnn learned from Velma. Then Stanley begs, "Say something, Louie."

"I wish he'd been more specific. Ask him Stanley. Let's ask *him.*"

Stanley throws up his arms and does a three-sixty. I ain't heard such wrangling since he colored Barbie's hair purple.

They're hardly two peas in a pod. LuAnn's report cards said imaginative, persistent; Stanley's said logical, mechanical. They head toward me while the screamer winds up and Patty busts through, saying, duty calls. "Keep me posted," Stanley says, to Patty, holding up those FIVE fingers again. Patty grins like a Cheshire cat, and then gives a thumbs-up. Hrmmph. They're up to no good. I can tell. Then the kids start arguing again but the screamer drowns them out. The wheelchair gang lines up for dinner: crotch scratchers, head wigglers, couple of droolers. The screamer finally runs out of scream and my kids come to me, Stanley's arm around LuAnn, cheeks smudged with mascara. They wheel me back inside and close the door. LuAnn sits on my bed, dabbing her eyes." Tell me what you want, Daddy," she says, "give me a sign."

"Pops," Stanley says, jutting his jaw like when he studies a manual for Chevy's S-10 pickup. "You want antibiotics? Without 'em, you'll die." What does he mean? Crinwald didn't have a pill list to yay or nay. Asshole. The mattress rises against my hips. I'm clammy, short of breath. "Pills to breathe," Stanley says. He presses the ball of one foot to the floor, lifts the heel and quivers a leg up and down. My heart races. Something to breathe? What did I check about a breathing machine? I search for a feeling—fear, disgust, despair, anything. Nothing comes. I'm suspended, floating. "Pills to breathe," Stanley says, louder, "you got crap for lungs." Crap. I nod *yes* to Stanley. He's right. This is crap. The mattress is poking the hell out of me and now Stanley won't look me in the eye. His leg quivers faster. LuAnn hums and Stanley springs for the door, saying, "I'll figure it out, Pops. Promise." Then, he's gone.

LuAnn puts a cassette in the recorder and tells me to hum along with a guy named Mozart. I try but I'm tongue-tied. My eyelids droop and soon I'm at Tessa's, pot belly stove in winter, big floor fan in summer, playing sheepshead, a card game we adored, played for nickels. Five-handed. Call an ace. No double on the bump. Snacks washed down with bottles of Kingsbury while blue smoke hung in the air, incense. Tessa our minister preached on California, which she called The Land of Fruits & Nuts. Little wonder James and LuAnn eloped to San Francisco, sent us photos, flowers in their hair. I studied LuAnn's little girl smile, her squint into the sun. She was happy and young. They remind me of us, I told Velma; brings back the smell of gin, fresh sawdust on the floor. I could almost hear the concertina and the drummer. But Velma went in the pantry and wept. Isn't choice what women's libbers want, I said and sealed her in a long hug. She let me, but her arms hung like a rag doll, and she refused to hug back. She wouldn't talk to me for a week. Finally I wore my fake nose and moustache to supper and when she turned from the stove, my get-up caught her off guard. I realized then her silence was not anger, but jealousy. After supper I went to the woods, picked marsh marigolds and set them on the kitchen table to brighten up the room. Meanwhile, the object of Velma's jealousy, James, created more debt than income selling miracle fish oil, angel chimes and blue algae. (Those hemi-sink tapes are a James joke.) In time, LuAnn come home and found a job at the mall, selling jewelry. On every visit, she brings more mall to cure me.

I'm out like a light when someone rams a newfangled thermometer in my ear and chimes, fever's down. Days pass, maybe weeks. Pills and protein swim in milk shakes that curl my tongue. Three squares a day, all hog feed. One day LuAnn appears at lunch and sees I'm not eating. She screeches, pulls at her bird feather necklace and wants Doc called so he can *do something*. A new aide with four piercings in each ear looks up from feeding Harold and asks, "What should he do?"

"Exercise, something."

"Doc?"

"No, Daddy! He needs to work up an appetite."

"Arnie goes bowling," the pierced princess says, "with inflatable pins." Meatloaf falls out of Harold's mouth. She spoons it back in and says, "Arnie's got a mean left hook."

"I don't know how you do this work," LuAnn says, scanning the slump and drool in the room. "So-o depressing," she says, troubled, "but I can't just let Daddy *dieeee!*"

"Of course you can't," princess says, shoveling mash into Harold.

LuAnn stirs three scoops on my plate into one pile, asks if I'd eat beef roast if it didn't look like mush. "Squeeze my hand *yes*," she says. I squeeze and LuAnn looks away, peeved. When the princess says I could choke on beef roast, I raise my good arm, twirl and rotate my wrist: kay-ser-ra, ser-ra, what will be, will be. "Ohmygod," LuAnn says, "he doesn't know what he's saying."

It's LuAnn who don't know; she's young. Stanley, he has some age, readiness. Say there's a tranny and three ring jobs, all due tomorrow; he takes 'em one at a time, steady as she goes. Under that kind of pressure, LuAnn would squeal and dart, disorganized. Suddenly my nose drips and I sniffle. "What's wrong," LuAnn blurts, "Oh Daddy, don't *cry*."

What makes her think I'm crying? My emotions are flat as the lowland. There's no need for her hissy fit. I wave her away. She lays a Kleenex box in my lap—proof how either we're fussing over someone, or someone's fussing over us. My Velma fussed on the fridge with notices about second-hand smoke, size of women's brains (bigger than men's), financial independence, and evils of drinking. She found pleasure in her bitterness, I think, with me under her skin. I was a splinter she didn't want removed. Once she bent Doc's pity ear, asked how long I would live. And then she died first. Just goes to know 'ya.

Well, I'm not asking for pity, just to be done. No more trouble. But trouble rears up when the Angus bull breaks out of the box stall, and I lunge for his nose ring. He puts up a fight. I clock him, only it's Parks, the night nurse with pink scalp. "There, there," a woman says, call me Velma, cheeks flushed, strawberry mouth, arms around me to never let go. "There, there," she coos, only it's Parks again. Parks laughs; she must get decked a lot. Anyway, I'm grateful for reruns with of the good Velma, no matter how they come.

I'm settled in Riverwood with Harold for prid near a year; then one day they switch our beds. I move next to the window because they want Harold near the door, something about his *acuity*. It's temporary 'till a private opens for him. LuAnn approved the switch, though she wanted the beds in a North-South orientation *to enhance neuro-electrical flow*. That first night after the switch, I'm feeling upside down and sideways when someone slithers in like a fox in the chicken coop. Who in the Sam Hill is here? Harold don't smell, his alarm didn't go off, and he's not moaning in pain. The fox halts at Harold's bed and starts humming *swing low, sweet chariot*. Must be that Mozart guy, I think, cocking my ear. But no, it's a woman, a scratchy alto. Harold produces a choking snore and then gasps, *Uhhhhh*. At that, the foxy woman skitters out.

I try to count Harold's snores so I can get back to sleep. But it's quiet, way too quiet. Son of a biscuit. Well, I'll be damned. Can it be? I don't need Patty to tell me that Harold's done. I want to think he's a lucky bastard, that he got called back, went home, gave Alzheimer a kick in the keester. But then the hair on the back of my neck rises. An eerie sense comes over me when I realize that Harold wasn't called back—he was pushed! Oh, Harold, you old wheeling and dealing banker. How in blazes did you manage this one?

Before I know it, it's Sunday. LuAnn's here, Stanley too—ain't seen him in a coon's age. Stanley rubs the inside of his wrist and wants to know when I got the window seat. And where's Harold? LuAnn's shrill as a killdeer protecting just laid eggs. "He's dead!" Big surprise, Stanley says, and LuAnn tells him if he'd crawl out from underneath those cars and trucks, he'd know that Harold was snuffed out. Stanley's two eyebrows meet. He looks dog-tired. "There's an angel of death here, Stanley," LuAnn says.

"Impossible," Stanley says. He lies down on Harold's bed, one leg twitching. "That happens on TV, not real life."

"Real video. Of Patty."

"Patty?" Stanley bolts up, white as a ghost. "She eliminated . . . Harold?"

"Miss Sugar and Spice. Why do you think she worked here? You ever believe that personal satisfaction crap?" Meanwhile, Stanley rubs the inside of his wrist, harder, faster.

"Lethal injection of morphine," LuAnn says, "and poe . . . poe something." She picks up my ivy, sets it back down. Stanley thrusts his hand in a rear pocket, grinding his mouth like someone who chews. Poe, he says, potassium? He has that look that says *brilliant.* Then LuAnn gives the cop report, how a night nurse reported pain medicines weren't working. So they installed cameras, caught Patty emptying narcotic syringes, substituting water. How mean to inject water to suffering souls instead of morphine. They thought Patty needed morphine for a drug habit, not to kill poor Harold. They think she had more victims—make that customers—lined up.

Stanley wipes his forehead. Acne scars pickle his face. His cheekbones look like half-axles. God, he's getting old. "It's mercy killing, Louie."

LuAnn grits her teeth. "It's business in America, Stanley. Her bank thought she was a drug dealer when she deposited five thousand." She held up five fingers. "Five thousand," she said. "Cash! No wonder the bank called the cops."

"Come up for air, Louie."

LuAnn goes hysterical. From the gist of it, she thinks Patty snuffed out Harold. Bullcrap. My Patty? But wait, let's see here. #1. Me and Harold appreciate Patty; #2. Love-starved Patty thinks appreciation is love; #3. Patty holds us at the moment we pass and bottles our love forever. My head pounds to even think this. LuAnn collapses in the chair, spilling plant dirt and bawling that the angel of death could have struck Daddy.

Stanley heaves the sigh of a man who just lifted more than he should. "Someday an angel *will* come for Pops. Right, Pops? The angel of mercy." LuAnn twists hair around her finger. I recall when we put Scamp to sleep because he was deaf, lame, and couldn't herd cows no more. Stanley cried himself to sleep that night. He must have been six. Now he tells Louie to go water her plant. LuAnn takes the plant into the bathroom. Water runs. Stanley rises, leans over my bed. I see myself lean over Pa's deathbed, remember the terror of being him. "I almost had it figured out, Pops." He drops his head. I don't know what he's figuring, but whatever it is, he'll keep at it. He raises his head, goes soft around the eyes. "You used to say, if you want something done right, do it yourself." He pulls at his neck. "This one's up to you, Pops. You and The Man upstairs." I frown. "I don't know what you're waiting for," he says, cracking his neck on each side, "but I'll wait. I can't stand it, but I'll wait. Seems that's what you want." Then he kisses me on the forehead, something he hasn't done since we came home with a cast on his arm after he went headfirst over the handlebars.

LuAnn emerges from the bathroom and sets the plant on the windowsill. She don't have a green thumb and when this one drowns, she'll buy another. "We have to *do* something," she says, "Daddy needs a safer place."

"Ah, Louie, he's okay." But LuAnn's spooked. Before I know it, she moves me out of Riverwood into Harbor Lights. She hauls in chimes, crystals, dried leaves. One day she shows up with a bulky woman with chapped hands and a foreign accent. "Jackie, my new friend," she says, eyes dancing. Them two check on me every day, regular as deputies with donuts. They parade in eucalyptus soaps, lavender-scented pillows and essential oils. (Where's the non-essential ones?)

The last time I see Stanley he comes when I'm bedded down for the night. He shows me a perfect sheepshead hand—four queens and two black jacks. "You gotta play this hand alone, Pops," he says, sliding the cards under my pillow. Then he sits next to me, palm on my leg, a squeeze every now and then, deep in thought. We sit there a spell. I pretend I'm talking; it feels good. After he leaves I wish I'd told him I saw his Mama yesterday, wrote my name on her dance card, every single line.

A couple weeks later, LuAnn plunks down a small glass jar. "Earth from the farm," she says, "Stanley sent it." She unscrews the lid. Suddenly I'm at the creek with bullfrogs, water tinkling over stones. I take a break from cutting alfalfa to smoke a Chesterfield. Spider webs glisten in the setting sun. I think of The Man upstairs who made them and shake The Man's hand, but it's a bearded fat guy in wrinkled trousers who LuAnn found in the yellow pages. He sticks needles in my hands and feet and tells me to not move (which ain't a problem). I don't feel a single needle, so I must really be slipping.

Not much changes, including LuAnn. She hangs a sun catcher in my window for angel rays. She sticks magnets around the room to pick up the earth's polarity. But my lungs are still crap. I got fungus for toenails, straw for legs, and shoestrings for arms. LuAnn likes the staff here, says they respect her wishes. So she don't bug them much. Probably because since Doc doubled the dose in my painkiller patch, I'm out of it more than in it, which ain't necessarily a bad thing. Doc ordered happy pills too, to make me stop crying. Now no one asks, *what's wrong?* Frankly, ain't much wrong, except my daffodils are done blooming. LuAnn will probably bring geraniums on her next visit—they last longer.

The Odds Against Somet

hing

Gabe intended to keep the hijinks of Skeeter to himself, yet something nagged at him about secrets. About responsibility. Over the weekend, he mulled the solution over in his head and then it was Monday and he was back on the school bus in spring, a season of meltdown and change, the view on the twenty-mile ride changed too. Barn doors were flung open. Chickens poked their heads out for the first time in months and barn cats slithered from indoor haymows to sawdust under fence posts. A workhorse whinnied, kicking up its heels.

Spring fever revved up Sally (Sal for short), too. She bounded on to the bus and landed next to Gabe. Hey, she said. What's up?

Not much, he said a bit too rapidly.

What's wrong?

He pursed his lips. There must be something more than . . . *this,* he said, warily.

Than what? What's going *on?*

Spring, he said. Spring is going on. Geese are back. Cardinals. Robins.

What's *wrong.* It was no longer a question from a feisty freshman girl. It was a demand.

He rolled his shoulder. Bart Starr, he said.

She elbowed him. Nice try. Moisture clung to the bus window and she drew a smiley-face in the mist. The bus slowed. They were at Skeeter's driveway. The driver Irv Stone put on the flashers, stopped, and waited the required minute. No one got on. Gif stared at Skeeter's front yard: a rope swing hung cock-eyed from one rope, a cement bird bath lay in broken chunks, there were scattered twigs and matted feathers.

Where's Skeeter? Sal asked.

How should I know, Gabe replied. As the bus pulled away, he heard clattering cymbals in the engine. Or, in his head. It was hard to say which.

Nice try, Sal said, removing lip balm from her pocket. She slathered her lips. You know something, she said, clicking the cover back on the balm.

I know nothing.

She leaned over and tongued his ear. He recoiled. The shape of Skeeter in the barn appeared in his mind. He tried to push it away along with its sounds but it replayed at a visceral level. His stomach pitched. Never mind, he said.

This egged her on. Did his old man hit him? Did he run away? I think he's . . .

He's what.

He's . . . not . . . right.

So what! His fluster over his childhood friend made him feel wobbly as a newborn calf. Hootenkack, he said.

Hooten who?

Hootenkack. My mom says that. It means to try and talk someone into doing what he doesn't want to do.

Immm-pressive. She stifled for all of eighteen seconds before whispering, I'm thinking of going on the pill.

He barely heard her for it has just occurred to him Skeeter could be lying in the cow trough, drowned. Then it occurred to him old man Ronnie could have found him right after Gabe did and beat the crap out of him. Maybe Skeeter had a mental illness. Maybe he had one. I'm thinking of getting a mental illness, he said.

Don't be silly. Mental illness. Is that a thing, there's no test for it like a blood test or x-ray.

I think it's just something people *do* when they don't have a playbook. You know, a game plan.

Shut up! His heartbeat rattled his ribs. He had an urge to bang her tight little ass—was that desire or rage?—but after watching Skeeter, he felt paralyzed, the urge confused him. How did it work with people? One of the seniors said a guy felt his body only when he was having an orgasm, that's why guys did it in oil rags or torn T-shirts, a lot of desperate work, packing and unpacking. And then, ten minutes later, there'd be an urge to start over. Once, around age ten, Gabe heard his parents above the background of The Moody Blues. Gabe could not imagine what was going on. It was quiet, then not, then huffing and puffing. He waited. Then, his Mom said sex is a spiritual rite and his Dad replied, consider me converted. Gabe had moved away from the door and in the years since, puzzled over The Act: gross and peculiar. And now, mind-boggling.

Sal put her arm around Gabe, captivated by his shyness. He could almost hear the motor in her bones, drumming, her purple hip huggers and skinny paisley tie making music. What do you think about Planned Parenthood, she asked.

Parenthood? Are you gonna carry around a sack of flour, pretend it's a baby?

Better than a sack of doo-doo, she laughed.

He laughed, a little, in return. He could never tell if she mocked him or liked him. As freshmen, they had a lot to navigate. With no road map. My mother can close her eyes and see every flower in the garden, he said. She knows when each one will bloom. He paused. She can even visualize the height and colors

Immm-pressive. Now, spill.

He didn't know if he liked her or hated her. She was cocksure—for a girl—and pushed against his evasion. She had no evasion in a glove, basketball, or relay baton unless she used it incorrectly, at which point she ate her own error. Title IX had given equal access to girls in all sports and Sal was a coach's dream, asking them, have you seen improvement, I'm working hard, what else can I do. You can give it a rest, he thought, reaching the point where he said, Time out. He wiped her drippy smiley face off the window and saw a clutch of wild turkeys step through furrowed fields, cautious. In nine minutes they'd be at school. He could ignore her for nine minutes.

The bus rattled on gravel roads past more open fields, woods, and pasturelands.

You can tell *me*, she said once more. Then twice. Then three times. Trust, she added as a last resort, punching it home with feeling. He scowled, avoiding eye contact and noticing an eruption on the border of her bottom lip. Another cold sore, her inner fury festering. He rubbed his forehead. If he told, would Skeeter go to the nut house? Or, to jail? Had Skeeter broken a law of some sort? Farm boy and farm animal. Could a thing like that—what did you even *call* that?—be helped? And if he did decide to tell, who would it be? His parents? Not Sal, for sure. How about the burly phy ed teacher who was always saying, boys will be boys. Well, he was a boy and he had no desire for *that*.

Maybe Skeeter's missing a screw, he said at last, laughing at his own joke.

Her breath sped up. Come on. Spill!

He felt himself yielding. I remember the time Skeeter . . . he . . . he enhanced himself.

He what?

Grew a bigger dick.

Yeow.

He tied a Johnsonville sausage to his leg. I saw it in the locker room.

She had a laughing fit that wouldn't quit. More interested in sports than school, she remembered useless facts and now blurted one: male ducks have penises shaped like corkscrews.

The scene in Skeeter's barn returned. It pushed and shoved as he recalled walking the country road to Skeeter to eat Butter Brickle ice cream and potato chips, their Saturday night routine as kids. When Skeeter wasn't there, he had turned to walk home when he heard a noise in the barn. He thought it was a possum or fox scaring up the chickens. So he walked closer, only to hear commotion from the south end of the barn where the pigpens were. He had wished he brought his BB gun. At least he could scare the critter off.

Rather than open the big barn door, he went in through the milk house. Three noiseless doors and he stood at the end of the murky, long alley. Some cows were still upright, their stanchions clinking as they chewed their cuds. Other cows had laid down and were asleep. With catlike steps, he stole his way to the south end of the barn. A few bats zipped overhead and he stood stock-still, held his breath. The sound he heard was a pig alright, but not the pitch of one giving birth or a sow in heat fighting the boar. No, this sound was like one being rounded up for bacon, a 300-pounder climbing up a wooden gangway into the livestock truck. There was no truck in sight, though. And Skeeter's dad wasn't out there herding anything.

The sound had continued, low, grunting. It became a moan, more a sheep in distress. The fiery grunts spurted faster and faster, but in the dead air between them, Gabe heard something else. It was a human, breathing, growling, groaning, and squealing. Gabe's breath had frozen when he discovered Skeeter, pants down, pumping away.

Gabe's mind locked. What good would it serve, telling a story that could not be told, a story where you had to be there to believe it. He had been there and he couldn't believe it. Maybe he should tell his parents. No, he couldn't tell them. He felt Sal's heat. She was fun. She was pure game. Maybe one day he'd tell her—after he figured it out for himself.

Sal finally shut up. She probably knew this game was lost. Or maybe she was thinking about Planned Parenthood and how far her birthday money would stretch.

The bus hummed along, no longer stopping for passengers. The morning fog burned off and the sun began to grow. As the bus pulled into the schoolyard, Gabe opened his window. Beneath the melting snow, he saw winged seeds of maple trees that had come whirling down last fall. Thousands of them would compete to start a new tree. Most of them, his mother had taught him, would fail.

The bus driver parked the bus and opened the folding door. Sal hoisted her backpack and marched ahead of him. He arrived at his locker, hung up his coat, and headed to Mr. Roemer's history class, sliding into the third seat from the back, second row. His crotch itched. He poked at it, then opened his workbook and placed a Bic pen in the little channel on the desk. He rolled a spitball and considered delivering it to Thumper's neck. Didn't. Once, he heard Sherry call him silent but sexy. Would her mood change if she knew how a silent scream grew in him? He studied the back of Donald's head. Dandruff. Across the aisle, Glen was hunched over, taking notes as if the Foreign Service depended on him. All this high school competition, he didn't chase it, not like Sal. He was a stone skipping along the water while Mr. Roemer raved on about how lucky we are to travel and find people who speak English, no matter where you are in the world. How a Korean would rely on someone in Latin America or a Finn might cross East Asia. He didn't care. Every day he walked the same halls, sat in the same desks, observed tight jeans and tight Tees and Randy's coated shitkickers. For the first time, he felt pressed to veer off the path. Do something different. Stand up. Be the maple seed that grows into a tree. Was that tattling on Skeeter?

He looked at the large wall clock, then read about an old president named Nixon. What did Tricky Dick have to do with him? In one minute, the buzzer would sound and he would close his workbook, rise, and roll along to the next class, English, to be bored with predicate nouns and active verbs. Soon the buzzer sounded again and he landed in Spanish: declensions are to nouns and adjectives what conjugations are to verbs. *Senor, Senorita.* He endured thirty-eight minutes of this and finally entered the study hall, knowing teachers did not call him out because he was a good kid. He overheard senior guys uttering, joints and beers, Friday night in Foster's field. Bring some flashlights. They made catcalls in study hall, bragged how they stayed up drinking and jiving, smoked cigars, too. Was that what he had to look forward to?

From several seats over, Sal rolled a marble across the sloping floor. It hit his boot and zigzagged, a hollow ricochet across the maple floor.

Miss Sally. The study hall teacher hissed her name in a roaring whisper.

That's me, Sal grinned.

That's it, you get a yellow slip.

Gabe caught Sal's eye. She gave him a cold stare but there was hotness in it, too. Maybe he'd tell her after all. She was gutsy, brave, shrewd. She might know what to do. But then his silent scream started up again. He was clearly stuck between wanting to please and wanting to break out. Like a brain dropped in formaldehyde in the biology lab. Wanting to be with Sal and wanting to ignore her. Wanting to report Skeeter and wanting to shield him; which way would reset someone 'not right'? Wanting the shelter of parents and wanting to run away. He used to think he was adopted until he found out other kids felt the same. Then he thought he was a foster kid, taken in like a stray dog and loved, but not loved enough to be legally claimed. Who was he? And where was the person he could trust to tell and not be terrified?

He took a beef jerky out of his backpack. Chewing on it, he opened his math book. Math made sense of the world. It organized the chaos and described it. Square root. Nonzero. Indirect Proof. And especially, Venn Diagrams. He whizzed through the solution sets. And then he started thinking about the odds against something: $m:n$. You could expect an event will not occur m times for every n times it will occur. He set to work, calculating the odds. Of telling. The truth.

Corduroy

People who are lucky simply pay more attention to their surroundings. An accident is something that is not planned. Michael knew these two solemn truths. He also knew dark facts about a barking dog.

He had learned all this while teaching eighth-graders in Rock Island, those fat kids and phat kids, soccer monsters and songwriters, Gap look-alikes, overachievers, and a future drug dealer or two. He liked them all and they for the most part liked him. Maybe it was his shaved head and solitary silver loop earring. That crooked front tooth. Or, the scruffy jeans and black T-shirt, an air of adolescent impulsivity even before showing off a ripped bicep with the tattoo, *Ruby*. Ruby was his life support when the students got squirrelly, his wife of ten years—ten wonderful years, until lately.

They had met at Road America. He and Jake packed camping gear, coolers, and a grill, then drove six hours from Iowa to watch 400 drivers compete for the Triple Crown of Racing. They arrived at grounds rimmed by sagging snow fences. Many fans hurdled the fences; they paid, and in between *hey ders* and *what's up, you what* and *how cool is that*, they pitched a tent.

The afternoon was taxicab yellow, the grass jewel green. Westerly winds throttled in vapors of exhaust, weed, cigar, and cigarettes. They headed toward Hurry Downs, one of fourteen turns where drivers lived on the edge. A pack of cars roared by, enough supercharged engines to stop a man's heart. They toasted one another with 20-oz. Buds and scanned the female hips that just kept coming and coming. Soon Jake went on a Bud run and Michael looked up at the grandstand.

There she was. A strawberry-blonde with a camera strapped around her neck. She raised the 35-mm at the beer-guzzling, bratwurst-eating crowd of noses, sun pink and peeling. His legs began to move. He took the bleachers two at a time and sidled next to her. She lowered the camera and released her ponytail. The hair bubbled around a small chin and straight-nosed face rated, at best, a six. (He was done with pretty but bitchy nines.) At breakneck speed, he blabbed about Iowa State, his English degree, garage band, joblessness, how he thought of going to Russia. She herself worked for the *Chicago Tribune*. A Loyola grad. Her father demanded abstinence, an odd detail, but maybe not: she had enormous breasts. The back of his head vibrated. He handed her the almost empty beer cup. She finished it off, handed it back, and put the cap on her lens.

"Looks like you're done," he said. "Want to hang out?"

Her hands fluttered as she packed up several lenses and cords. She put on her sunglasses. "Go slow," she said.

"Isn't this a race track?" She grinned. He grinned back. He became hard. "I'm not much on cars, honestly," he said.

"Me either. There must be something else to do." And there was, under the grandstand where they melded, super-charged by rising fumes and balls of dust. And those breasts were not tittys, jugs, or cheesecake. They were enormous pillows. They were hers. And now, his too.

Within six months, they eloped. He found a teacher job in Rock Island. She opened a photography studio. And then, out shooting one day, she discovered the Dutch colonial, available for one dollar. The city's requirement was to live in the colonial during renovation and endure until trashy rentals became pricey restorations. The Victorian next door was vacant; surely someone would buy it, get to work on the yard of chicken wire and cordwood.

"You'll see," Ruby insisted.

"It's a risk."

"A calculated risk, a no-interest loan! Housing is hot. Gains are exceeding the stock market. This is a no-brainer, don't you see?"

He looked at her framed photos. There was an old man with pigeons, a leaf with dew, and a child mid-air on a trampoline. Clearly, she saw things he did not. And through her, he saw his way to a dollar house with a jumbo renovation loan.

A year later, she became pregnant. He argued for abortion. She considered it, but the idea rattled her. So did the idea of becoming a parent. Distressed, she practiced Zen and yoga. She thought of a body within a body. She thought of chance and of luck. Then she read how bones, blood cells, and oxygen came from ancient stars. The stars either exploded as supernovae or died slowly, releasing matter into space. She sensed a celestial body was within her. "A new star will be born," she said. "It's amazing good luck."

"Luck?" he replied. "Isn't a *falling* star lucky?"

To which Ruby returned a smile stiff with violins, silence, and some violence.

The baby came along, nicely. They named her Taylor. Oak trees tossed their shadows against the Dutch colonial that came along, nicely. Semesters came along nicely, too. And before they knew it, Taylor turned three and Michael turned Daddy-do-good, giving horsey rides, eating at the Dairy Queen, and paying for Montessori. His computer held a gigabyte of *My Ruby. My house. My Taylor.* Ruby became the coordinator of playgroup, story hour, car pool for Suzuki. She even had Taylor on a Mandarin waiting list.

"Hey, Mr. Mike." Brayden thumped a rubber-soled tennie. The shoe was untied, the lace worn and shabby. Michael looked up from his laptop. Kids in jerseys and oversized cargo pants jostled in while Michael took a long breath and, unperturbed, looked at Brayden. Brayden rocked forward and back, foot still busy, and asked, "You play pool?"

"I play upright bass and piano," Michael said. He smiled at Brayden's rhythm, incessant and unbridled. "Do you play pool?"

"I play you," Brayden said, shoulders jiggling. Behind him, Carter imitated Brayden and blurted, *Like dude, chill.*

"I play drums, too," Michael said. He rose, tapping the wall with his fingertips. "I bet you'd be good on drums." Then Brayden da-dummed the desk and Michael threw Carter a stare strong enough to set cement.

But enough about Michael's day life. It was nightlife that was killing him. And not the way you hope. You see, Michael needed sleep and he wasn't getting it. The lack of sleep made him feel drunk; he could only wish to be drunk—it might have been simpler. Which brings us to the barking dog. A barking dog in early evening is not the same as a bloody hound barking at midnight. And that is under a ho-hum script of everyday niceness.

Michael's life was not ho-hum anything, not since the November afternoon Ruby was sideswiped by an 80-ton semi doing 80 out on I-80. And no, the driver wasn't eighty. Worse: twenty-eight, weightlifter, three months on the job, divorced. Ruby was Flight for Life to University of Iowa Hospitals and there Michael was, SOL. Still, he was smart enough (master's in education) to shift gears: he dropped chess on Tuesday, band on Friday. He bustled Taylor to Suzuki and felt a subtle and nameless change as she lifted the bow and drew it across the strings. He thought of his father, an Atlanta dermatologist who often told him to lighten up and, ha-ha, not with ultraviolet or pot. God, he couldn't stand the man. Too bad; the old doc could offer advice about Ruby, especially the plastic surgery.

In any case, after three weeks with Taylor boarding at Ms. Brenda, he was ready to bounce between ICU and school, between Ms. Brenda and the basement flooring. But the day he returned to school, a hopped-up hound named Elgar appeared at the Victorian next door, collared to a wash line, oozing drool.

That night, Elgar revved up. Ip-yip-yip, yip-ip-yyip. Taylor called the dog "Big Bad." She thought Big Bad morphed to slime. It slipped into the room. Its shadow hung from the ceiling just like the bat Mommy caught one time. The barking increased. She bunched up her *banky*, the fragment of cloth that gave her security. Her eyes burned. Her tummy hurt. "Mommmmy," she screamed and then peed in her Big Girl Panties.

The overhead light went on. "It's o-kay," Michael said, thinking, fuckin' A.

"Mommy!" She looked at Michael suspiciously. Her nose dripped snot. She sucked her thumb and stroked the banky's fraying edge.

"Mommy isn't here." A tendon snapped in his back.

Taylor bit her lips. Tears piddled down her cheeks. Then, unable to breathe through the stuffy nose, she removed her thumb and sniveled. "Mommy?"

"Mommy isn't here," he said, punching out each word. Behind his forehead, blood throbbed. He knelt on the floor at the edge of her bed. She felt feverish. He ringed his steely arms around her. He thought of Elgar's feckless and mopey owner, how he once saw him kick the mongrel. Taylor gulped air. He should have left her with pudgy Brenda. Spying a box of tissues, he blotted the mucus streaming from her nostrils. "Blow." Instead of blowing, her jaws sprung open and she released a scream. "Blow." She did. He milked the nose and gathered the spillage. Then while she settled against his chest, he stared at the powder gray ceiling, recalling how after gutting the house, they hired contractors to restore Prairie School influences: hardwood floors, antique leaded-glass windows, and a claw-footed bathtub. A skylight crowned Ruby's office in the maid's quarters. *Rare Prints by Ruby* were selling and the one-dollar house had appreciated $48,000. Once the neighborhood turned over, they'd make a killing.

In the meantime, however, there were morons. And morons with dogs. Bullshit. He clenched his jaw and carried Taylor to the Subaru, buckled her in, and drove around town until two a.m. When he finally tucked her in, the coil of his ribs tightened. He wanted a smoke. Ruby would say, take a shower or get some Zen. Then she'd play strings along his spine, flexing his hips into sweet release. Had he ever thanked her enough? Is this why this happened? He lit a joint. In the liquid smoke, he considered his options.

As did Ruby, miles away in University of Iowa Hospitals. A baritone voice commanded she open her eyes. The voice intrigued her, and she tried but could not. Her lids were puffballs, immense and spongy, rheumy and itchy. *Ruby*, the voice said. *It's Dan. I'm back. You and me on night shift.* He smelled of cedar with a hint of clove. *Open your eyes, Ruby.* She wanted to see him; instead she saw dust—rubble dust, sheetrock dust, sanding dust—in the air, on walls, halls, stairs. Has she tripped on a workman's cord and fallen, paralyzed? *Open your eyes, Ruby.* He sounded gentle, kind. But she could not obey. *Okay, then,* he said. *How about you squeeze my hand?* His fingers were fleshy, damp. Suddenly, someone stabbed her thumbnail. *Press the proximal side of the nail bed. If she responds, it's a two.* Needle-like pain zinged into her wrist. She tried to cry *Michael*, but only *Mmmmm* came out. *You can also apply pressure to the suborbital ridge.* He mumbled something else before Ruby faded out.

The following morning, Taylor stood at the foot of Mommy and Daddy's bed, her hair tangled in knots. One hand clutched her banky, the other, Barney. "Sleepy head," she said to Barney. She bobbed Barney up and down on the bed. "Mommy?" she said. But no Mommy sat up, arms open. Mommy must be *on an overnight*. "No Mommy," she frowned to Barney. Then, she saw hills of Daddy's toes beneath the covers. She snuck Barney toward the hills. Daddy didn't move. Barney took a giant leap and landed on his chest. Taylor bent forward. "No more sleepies," she said. Daddy groaned. She crawled onto the bed and made schmoozing sounds while Barney kissed Daddy's cheek.

"Oh, honey," Michael said. For a stellar moment, he imagined his old life back.

Taylor jumped on the bed. "I'm thirsty," she said, pulling his arm.

He looked at the clock. Shit. Overslept again. He came to and in the slant light, saw Ruby's cheekbones in Taylor. "Let's go see Mommy," he said. He knew it was ill advised, not with Ruby intubated, maybe not even until plastic surgery.

"Goodie," Taylor said. "Now?"

"Not now," Michael said. "After work."

"Promise?"

"Promise."

For now, they hustled. He placed her in the car seat without the buckles and backed out of the drive. Next door, Elgar lapped at the water dish, tongue long and gray. Rabid, Michael thought, what if that thing is rabid? Soon he dropped Taylor at Brenda's and rushed to Wilson School, arriving as the second bell rang. "Settle down," he yelled, his shoulder seizing up. *Like wow, ease up, Mr. Mike*, Brayden said. Others said *ohmygod* and *hooah-hooah*. He made a few announcements, then popped in a DVD of *To Kill A Mockingbird*, hoping the new principal wouldn't visit today.

In the darkened classroom, he counted. One, two, three, four. It *was* his fourth day of being at odds with himself. A nerve-jangling dissonance peppered his mind, though his thoughts weren't on Ruby—her fate rested with doctors and nurses. They weren't on Taylor either—Brenda would play surrogate long as needed. They were, for reasons unknown to him, fixated on Elgar.

Meanwhile, in the ICU, the same deep baritone voice spoke. *She's had some ST changes.* The man lifted the muslin gown from her chest and pressed a metal disc against her ribs. At first, Ruby couldn't tell if it was super cold or super hot. She gasped. It was flaming hot! She called for help and then faded away.

At Brenda's that same day, one play station included markers, crayons, finger paints, and chalk. Another included a water table. Another was the Stratosphere, a playground of ladders, tubes, and pipes. Taylor hooked her legs on the Stratosphere and hung upside down, blood rushing to her head. While others finger-painted or water played, she swung upright and downright. By the time Brenda urged her to try the markers, everything looked like laughing mirrors at the circus.

"You look lost," Brenda said.

"No, Miss Brenda. I mean, yes." But that wasn't right either. Because she sensed she wasn't lost, so much as abandoned.

As the first period wound down, Michael forced himself to reality. During the video, he counted four kids dozing and two playing with themselves. Normally, he would have counseled all six. Instead, he turned up the lights and explained point-of-view. Then, the assignment.

> Pretend you are Scout. Only you are living in October
> 2001. Write what Scout would say. Get inside her
> head, her heart. Be specific. Write wide. Write wild.

Carter said *get real.* Brayden said *get Carter.* Josh said *you gotta be kidding.* "Yeah," Michael replied. "Even you guys.

Be Scout." Libby, neurotic over grade point, asked what Be Scout *meant.* So Michael re-explained, his fuse shortening. In the next three class periods he gave the same assignment and heard, *Dude, you're serious?* When the last bell rang, he booked it to Taylor and drove in a trance. He knew the gurgling tube in Ruby's nose was temporary. He knew her dull, searching eyes were temporary. He knew this staccato schedule with Taylor was temporary. And he definitely knew Elgar was temporary.

As for Ruby, Dan had come back. He spread her vaginal lips, draping plums and peaches across her abdomen. Cool water ran down her perineum. *So you don't get an infection,* Dan said, lifting her buttocks. Suddenly, more hands were on her. *This way,* a warble-throated female sang. *Turn this way.* But Ruby couldn't turn anything. So Dan and the birdsong woman bent her to one side, then the other. All the while, Ruby lay in twilight. She felt a purity of being. Nothing hurt, but nothing felt good either. It was nothing, the emptiness of being. Was this Zen?

The car ride took forever, giving Michael time to mull over Brenda's report. Taylor had spent the day climbing and played in the sandbox but refused anything else. Brenda wondered if Taylor was acting out. He mulled over that fact and realized how stupid it was to visit Ruby. He turned around.

Once home, he said, "How about some juice?"

"No!"

"Ice cream," he said, cheerfully, opening the fridge. "Peanut butter chip!"

"Yuck." Taylor squeezed her banky. "I want Mommy."

"Mommy is sick."

"Mommies don't get sick."

"Sometimes they do."

"They don't."

"They do. Sometimes."

"When?"

"Today. Yesterday. And all the days before that." A vessel in his temple throbbed. He felt fresh annoyance toward Ruby. Was she speeding? Fiddling with her cell?

"Mommy," Taylor said. "I want my Mommy."

He lifted her agitation, trying to control his own. He sang, "Hush little baby . . ."

"I'm not a baby. I want Mommy."

"Mommy isn't here." *Calculated risk. A star.* He looked at the lowering sky. Rain was in the forecast. He sat down with Taylor on his lap so they faced one another. She shoved the banky to her mouth, bug-eyed. "Mommy isn't here," he said again. Taylor worked the cloth, vigorously, *numm-numm.* "And if she were, she couldn't talk." Taylor's sucking quickened.

Michael stood and carried her upstairs to the bathroom, pausing in front of the medicine chest. "Open," he said. She grasped the porcelain knob on the distressed-teak cabinet and tugged. "Good girl." He reached for an amber-colored glass bottle on the top shelf. "Now, close," he said. Taylor closed the cabinet. "Mommy said this would help." Her jaws chop-chopped the banky.

In her bedroom, he lowered her to the bed, poured a spoonful from the bottle, and said, "Now you and Mommy *both* take medicine." Sticky red splattered the chenille bedspread. "Oh, oh," he said. "Let's not tell Mommy." Taylor lowered the sloppy, wet cloth. She opened her mouth like a bird and swallowed the cherry liquid, licking the spoon. Michael eased her to the pillow and waited. In no time, she zonked out.

He went downstairs, obsessing over fatherhood, the lawsuit, ungraded papers, Ruby's *oxidative stress,* and the dubious, half-done house. With sleep, he might manage; without it, he walked a minefield. He shuffled into his music room. Dust covered the piano; the upright bass leaned like a question mark. He located *Pink Floyd,* set it to repeat in the player, and poured a mug of Merlot. Then he lit a joint and flopped on the sofa. He soon fell asleep, squeezing an enormously soft velvet pillow.

Elsewhere, in a sliver of consciousness, Ruby saw a favorite photo: a left hand, female, with the glint of a gold wedding band and French manicured fingernails wrapped around a steamy mug. It was her self-portrait, a tight shot with the handle of a spoon resting between index and middle fingers. She had labeled it *Stop Time*. And now, someone had. She wanted to think WHY. But she could not think.

Michael awoke to Taylor shaking him. "Daddy, I'm thirsty." He rolled over.

His head felt split in two. "Daddy. I'm thirsty."

Michael shivered. Mid-morning sun streamed through the music room's mini-blinds. He cricked his head and looked at the clock. "Shit," he said.

"Daddy!" Taylor said. "Bad word." At that, the doorbell rang. Michael straightened his wire rims, hitched up his sweatpants, and scooped up Taylor. He opened the heavy oak door. A tall, skinny man stood there chewing on a cigarette. He extended a greasy hand toward Michael. "Name's Larry," the man said. Michael said he was Michael and then Larry said the muffler would be fixed in a few days; he didn't need cops after his ass.

"Bad word," Taylor whispered.

The stranger spun on his boots and tromped down the stairs. Then, spying the brooding Elgar, he said, "Besides. I can't be the only moment of stress in your life."

"Hey, wait," Michael cried, easing Taylor to the porch floor.

Larry flicked the ashes into bare lilac limbs. "Whadya need?"

"Oh, nothing," Michael said. "Thanks for letting us know about the muffler."

"Whatever, man." Larry looked up at the new, second-story dormers, then again at Elgar lying among tires, boots, and buckets. "Thanks for moving in, for trying."

"What day is it?"

"Might be Saturday," Larry said. "Just got off nights." He looked at Elgar again. "That thing deserves a bullet."

"You sure?"

"About the bullet?"

"No," Michael said. "Saturday. You sure it's Saturday?"

Larry drew his lips over his teeth. "Didn't mean to wake you." Then, smoke curling around him, he nodded to Taylor, asked her name.

"Taylor," Michael said.

"I had a little girl once," Larry said. "You take good care of her." He dragged his sadness down the stairs and Taylor hugged Michael's thigh with all her might.

Michael studied the sky. The pale day promised dry roads and good visibility. He said they should visit Mommy, bring Barney, too.

After half an hour in the car, Taylor asked, "Are we there yet?"

"Fifteen more minutes."

Taylor wondered how far fifteen was, but she didn't ask. Daddy didn't know things like that. Daddy would say *almost* or *pretty soon* or *did you see that big orange semi?* Ask Mommy how far is fifteen and she would say, *I'm not sure—let's find out together.* So instead, Taylor asked if Mommy knew they were coming.

"Yes," he said, though Mommy didn't even know that every minute she was supposedly falling apart and being rebuilt. *Billions of stem cells,* the Indian doctor said, adding, *The body has an amazing regenerative capacity.*

He looked at his watch as they went up the elevator. "Fifteen minutes," he said, clutching Taylor's hand. "Didn't I say? Fifteen minutes!" When they got to the nurses' station, a nurse welcomed him but scowled when she saw Taylor, mentioning a groove of scars. Did that mean Taylor or Ruby? Or him? An aide lured Taylor to the lounge with graham crackers; she helped her play Dora the Explorer and draw figures with flat heads and no mouths while Michael fidgeted at Ruby's bedside. It seemed there were fewer machines. Was that progress? Yet how could it be, when more flesh had collapsed from her cheeks?

He took Ruby's hand and ranted. "There's a barking, jumping, insane midnight monster, a Lab-chow mix—I swear he's part wolf—next door in the Victorian next door, you know, the one with an offer except the buyers got cold feet and this half-breed named Elgar moved in with a renter who could be homeless. It jumps five feet in the air, the mutt, not the renter, banging his paws against the door. And then at midnight, yip-dip-dip. It's driving me crazy; you *know* how I am without sleep."

Ruby gave a left-cornered smile. It could have been a reflex. Michael stared at the dripping IVs. He felt the walls contract. His chest tightened. He heard his father say, *miracle workers* and knew he should pretend to believe, in case Ruby felt his karma. So he planted his feet and leaned over her. He kissed her chapped lips and veiny, purply eyelids. He kissed her alongside a plastic pipe taped to her cheeks, a pipe connected to a ventilator opening and closing her lungs like baffles. He rested his hand on her shaved head and kissed her again.

She didn't smile. Yet, on a basal and visceral level, she knew he was there. The ventilator alarm went off and the nurse came in, saying it happens all the time. It was a seminal moment for Ruby. He was there. Their promises to one other were inviolable. He would always be there, Ruby felt, no matter what.

As for Taylor, the hospital reeked. Dora was dumb. The aide gave her bad apple juice and now her tummy hurt. And the aide put a Band-Aid on Barney. She said Barney would get better and so would Mommy. But Mommy wasn't sick. She had just disappeared. And Barney wasn't sick. And he didn't need a stupid Band-Aid.

On the way home, Michael navigated I-80 with podcasts blasting. He hummed and swerved on the straightaway, and if Taylor said *Daddy, Daddy,* he did not hear. And she, having been to Manners Class, did not cry or kick. Now and then in the rear-view mirror, he saw her taking in the landscape with the eye of a photographer.

They soon entered the Delft-blue kitchen cluttered with pizza boxes, chip bags, and Bud cans.

"Look, Daddy, I shut the door."

"Good job," he said, flatly. Then, forcing cheer, he announced it was naptime.

"No-o-o."

He rested his tongue between his teeth and exhaled. He made two fists, pushed them into the flat of his hips. "I said, naptime."

"No-o-o." She ran in circles around the cobalt blue island. Silently, he opened the freezer and seized Ben & Jerry's. He found two wooden bowls and filled them with Chocolate Razzle Dazzle.

"Mommy's okay," he said to no one in particular. "Mommy's okay. She just has a *really* big owie."

"A really big owie," Taylor repeated while Michael thought of Ruby's eyes popped out like a frog, a zipper of stitches that crossed her forehead and swung into her temple, holding her brains together, barely. Meanwhile, Taylor ate greedily and his ice cream melted while he imagined Ruby's dinner flowing through a tube. Taylor finished and he wiped off her chocolate moustache. "Naptime," he said. But she insisted on a horsie ride. His head went koosh, a deployment of fast-firing neurons, but he got down on all fours. She straddled atop him and he whinnied into the living room. "Hang on," he said, climbing the stairs while she squealed with joy. Upstairs, he fetched the cough syrup. "You're a good girl," he said.

And she was, swallowing two teaspoons worth.

Outside, it thundered, loud as blame. Over in Iowa City, the same storm kicked out the hospital's electricity. Ruby's ventilator coughed, but the emergency generator restored the kilowatts to pump air to her lungs. And the discharge planner, desk again fluorescent bright, reviewed the order for Ruby: *long-term placement*. It seemed premature, but everyone was under pressure nowadays from the bean counters. Who would tell that husband?

When Taylor awakened from her nap, the house was quiet. She clambered down the stairs and found Daddy at his desk, *in another world* as Mommy would say. Taylor hoped he was in this world, too. She needed him. Now.

Michael's world was that of homework. The first *Be Scout* paper belonged to Mason: *Hey dude, Jem saw a guy with a camera filming the towers.* Michael scribbled, point-of-view problem, get into Scout's head, not Jem's. He set the paper on the DONE pile. The next was Eben's: *I don't know why people need religion.* Michael wrote, what is religion's role? He thought of each student's destiny: a Radio Shack clerk, corporate bigwig, another ruthless Hillary, dozens of waiters. Eben might be the next John Cheever; should Michael push him to consider religion on the battlefield?

"Gotta go poopies, Daddy."

"Okay," he said, without looking up.

"Gotta go poopies, Daddy." Michael wrote furiously. "Now," Taylor demanded.

"One second," he said, but by the time he put down his pen, Taylor had regressed from age three to barely two, soiled and helpless. He felt a stab of sourness as he peeled off her pink Oshkosh B'Gosh overalls. He ran the bath water, dumped in bubble bath, and conned her with a lollipop to get into the damn tub.

At the same time, Ruby lolled beneath a goose-feather quilt, freed of parenting worries. She felt herself floating between white, the color of now, and black, the color of If Only. She was thinking *If only* the semi behind her would slow down when someone sprung open her lids and blinded her with a flashlight. Then her lids snapped shut and the semi exploded.

For supper, Daddy made macaroni with rubbery cheese. Then they watched *Finding Nemo* and Daddy even laughed. At bedtime, he read *Goodnight Moon* and carried her around the house, reciting goodnight to the banister, hatrack, chandeliers, and the wilted ficus. He tucked her in and stayed at bedside. As she fell asleep, he considered that fateful day when Ruby surely sped to pick up Taylor because he was at chess club. He felt enormous guilt, unaware that guilt came from anger, that anger deranged love, and that derangement sought revenge.

He tiptoed downstairs and dropped into the wingback, convinced that any resolution was impossible. He took a breath, inhaling this truth till it hurt, and exhaling to seek the detached mind of Zen. Ruby had encouraged Zen for his pervasive anxiety, his escape to dope. He had to transform himself. Again, he inhaled, exhaled. He closed his eyes; purplish mini-dots streaked into a vortex. He forced the breath once more and felt motion and stillness at the same time. *Oh, Ruby,* he murmured, *Ruby, Ruby.*

In the middle of his lament, he heard Elgar. He rushed to the window. The barrel-chested mutt strained at the washline, probably gone nuts over a rabbit. Or maybe the dog had seen Boo Radley for he sounded vile, ready-to-go. Michael hurried to the hutch and reached into a clay bowl. He pulled out a key. With the key, he unlocked a cabinet mounted high on the wall. Carefully, he brought down a shellacked case with a brass plate that read Atlanta Gun Club.

He opened the case. A Smith & Wesson .38 caliber lay on plush, red velvet. It was from his father, *to make you a man.* Michael picked up the gun and pointed it at the chandelier. He felt a weird pleasure. At that moment, Larry revved his engine, popped the clutch, and rock-topped into the street. Michael opened the double-hung window. By now, Elgar's growl was low and insistent. He heard his father say, *Finding your natural point of aim minimizes muscular tension needed to hold the gun on target.* He saw the man squared away in khakis, wearing parachute and diver pins from his Marine days: *If you have the eyes of a hawk, reflexes of a mongoose, and nervous system of a lizard, you can pick up a gun and hit what you shoot at.* Michael raised the gun. He pointed the .38 at Elgar. Sweet.

He breathed, exhaling completely: *shoot from empty lungs.* Fretful and on edge, he attempted to retrieve Zen precepts of moral control. They were nowhere. Perturbed, he tried again and in trying, spun to the *Be Scout* paper where Trevor recommended Scout carry a gun. Suddenly, he shouted, "Elgar! I have a gun!" The dog did not answer. Assured, he closed the window, put the gun in the case and the case in the cabinet, unlocked.

He sat down at his desk and fingered the next paper. It was Brayden's, amply smudged. *The guy's head was the size of a cactus.* Michael pulled at his neck. He looked at the cabinet. Please, Ruby, please, he said. He groaned; to Brayden, everything was prickly. 'Brayden,' he wrote, 'what does a cactus have to do with Scout?' He considered writing more, but best to deal with Brayden in person. He felt strange but pressed on to bubble-like printing from Kendall, a walking exclamation point. *If you're worried about something, you wouldn't tell someone, would you? It would only make it worse, especially if you told a girl.* 'Are you OK?' Michael wrote, adding, 'see me.'

He picked up Madison's paper: *there are things that shouldn't have too much meaning.* 'Interesting,' he wrote, 'list what those things are to Scout.' And lastly, there was Sully: *Very small things cast very large shadows to someone who is depressed.*

He stopped, drained. The house creaked. A mouse scratched the rafters. Outside, Elgar most assuredly lay in wait. He whisked up to check on Taylor, asleep with banky crumpled in her hand. Then he moseyed downstairs and stretched out in the La-Z-Boy. In twilight sleep, he saw Ruby's hairless head and marble eyes advance toward him.

Sunday evaporated and he floated through Monday. After school, he dialed the lawyer about the 18-wheeler slam. Someone was responding to someone; these things take time. He went in the basement and lifted weights, then went to pick up Taylor. They ate peanut butter sandwiches and then watched *The Lion King* until Taylor slumped into slumber. He tossed an afghan over her and placed *Zen Mastery* in the CD player, working to detach himself from negativity, to change viewpoint.

Michael worked until the mantel clock read 10:10 p.m. Then he rose with some ancestral gesture and opened the window, sensing the pathetic Elgar. He drew brisk night air into his lungs and exhaled, emptying himself of calculated risks, miracle workers, and lazy lawyers. Then, he retrieved the .38. He returned to the window. He took the full breath in, the full breath out, thinking *hawk, mongoose, lizard.*

At precisely 10:15 p.m., Larry's hole-in-the-exhaust popped into the street. Michael pulled the trigger. His palm smarted. Elgar produced a brief howl. And then, Larry's rabble racket faded and it was dead quiet. Michael couldn't believe it. Was it that easy? Mind control. Self-mastery. Viewpoint. Ruby would laugh—she would. And wait till he told Larry.

And now he knew another sober truth. Luck was more than being in the right place at the right time. It was being prepared.

From the couch, Taylor hollered. Michael hustled to her, transformed. But her face was pinched and startled. "It's okay, honey," he said. "We're going to make it. And we're starting with some goddamn sleep."

"Daddy!"

"Let's read!" He rummaged through a slew of picture books on the coffee table. "What'll it be?"

Taylor pointed to a book she knew by heart, about an English bear named Corduroy. "Good enough," he said, sitting down next to her. She snuggled in, sucking the banky. He felt deeply comforted, safe. He was on the way. They would be okay.

Then he hesitated, cocked his ear. Elgar whimpered, still alive and now suffering. He listened again as Taylor melted into him. The mongrel sounded weak and plaintive, begging. Michael had an overwhelming feeling of claustrophobia. He couldn't get a deep breath. He felt sick, suffocated.

Taylor nudged him as if to say *Read, Daddy.*

He tried, but words collided on the page. She nudged him again.

And when he didn't respond, she took the raggled, damp cloth from her mouth and began to recite. "Corduroy is a bear," she said, slowly, "who once lived in the toy department. He . . ."

They Said a Woman

We would have been friends on the outside. We would have been mothers full of heartache and achievement. We would have been there for one another, supporting one another. I was drawn to you because we're both good moms and because everyone else here are liars, drug addicts, manipulators, and well, the bottom of the barrel. (Go figure, it's prison.) And so here we are—with me figuring out in my head how to help you because you asked how to do it, how to get out of here.

I'll never forget when you opened up to me. All I wanted was to hold you and shush you and tell you it will be okay. Because it will. Because I will help you.

First, you must focus solely on the end result, be committed to your desire to be with your baby, which we know is where you belong. If you have a single doubt that day, wait. Wait until you can't stand it anymore. Wait until air feels like acid in your lungs because when you do it, that's how it will feel. If you have the smallest speck of hope in you, your soul will kick and scream and fight like a demon is upon you.

I know you panic just thinking about it. This means you are not ready. Yet. You must think how this journey will be like putting on your favorite cashmere sweater. Beautiful, soft, inviting. You feel amazing and everyone knows it when they see you. You have to know this is right, how this is your only option, a chosen path you were meant to travel. He is waiting. This needs to happen.

Start by being really calm. Let me emphasize: if you have a speck of doubt—DON'T DO IT. You will not succeed. Practice getting familiar with it like you do with a favorite book you read over and over. Feel the cover. Smell the pages. Run your fingers over the words. Let the story engulf you and take you to him. This is what needs to happen.

Okay, when you have your head straight—when you are there completely—I will give you the bags and you can practice putting them over your head, smoothing them down over the front of your face—feel how the plastic clings to you, how static draws it against you. Keep them on as long as you can. This is practice. When you actually do it, you will put panties in your mouth and earplugs I'll give you in your nostrils. The panties will let you get breath in. However, they will muffle your cries for help, if you can't help yourself. Do the panties first, then the earplugs, and then put the bags over your head.

Keep calm.

Do not panic.

I'll give you my Benadryl and Melatonin. Take your Ativan beforehand. Smooth the bags over your head, pushing out all air in the bags. Then take the tape and tape off the bottom so air can't get in. Continue taping around your neck. Over and over around your neck. Then tape your face and back of your head. This will occupy your mind for a time.

You can also tie your bathrobe belt around your neck, focusing on the lower part of your windpipe (it's most vulnerable there). It takes about three minutes to pass out—that's how long it takes when I tie off. We nurses know the brain can go six minutes without oxygen before brain death. When you are set up, get under your blankets. Let me know ahead of time when you are going to do it. I can check and make sure they're not coming around. I will knock three times if you're good to go, six times if not. It might help knowing I am there (for that brief moment), that I am with you, supporting your decision, pushing you to go. We don't know what happened to us to make us commit our crimes. I keep thinking, if only. If only I had reached out. Everything was so dark, I couldn't think straight, I felt trapped in a tunnel. How I want to go back, please, please let me go back and have my life again. I know we would both do anything to be given a second chance.

But here we are. You have spent years pushed to the brink of hopelessness and now you know what you need. I will help you make this work.

Figure out how to keep calm while you lay there—imagine holding him, seeing his chubby cheeks and big, beautiful eyes—think about how much you love him and how you are going to him. You will be together, where you belong, the only place you will find peace. This 'prison family' crap is crap. This isn't family. A family formed from broken parts breaks again.

Anyway, remember this—your body will fight. Your hands will claw the tape. Tape it so tight, your fingers can't get under. Have something for your hands to hold, like a towel. Wring it in frustration. Or pull it hard as you can.

You will pass out. And then, it's over.

It will be hard. But you can do it. You will find strength as he draws you to him. Let him. Give up on the will to fight. Go limp. Let yourself slip away.

There is nothing here but razor wire, mattresses of sand, and twenty years without a hug. Just think, no more scrubbing your cell with maxi pads. Or shaving your head or shitting your pants when food rots your gut. Repeat over and over, Mama is coming home. Let your mind fill with memories of when you were on the outside. Biking, swimming, carving pumpkins, lemon chicken in Little Italy. Let each one bring calm. Fight your primal side. *You* are in control. You can reorganize your mind, recode the subconscious. I hope this helps. We can talk more. I want you to die. I want this torture for you to end. Because I don't think there's any way to explain "why." Like you, I ask myself over and over—why didn't I ask for help?

Yesterday, after I figured all this out, I wanted to have supper with you and then walk in the yard. The lockdown put a kibosh on that. So I'm writing it down. First, to tell you I think you're a really cool chick. I wanted to give you a big hug at rec when you were so angry, even if it would land me in the hole. But I chickened out. I wish I could have held you and let you cry. Cry for your loss, cry for him, cry for being locked in this place away from everything and everyone you love. Cry because there's not a time machine and we can't go back. When you do it, you will feel nothing because you are prepared. Numb yourself to the people you love—if you hold on to feelings of love and acceptance, it will stop you from your goal. Be selfish. Don't care about them—it will be easier. You've been a good friend to me in here. But fuck me and fuck everyone else. I'm telling you this because you asked me for help. I'm trying to help you get to where you want to be.

I understand the need to end suffering, to stop shame and guilt because what we each did is grotesque, inhumane, despicable, and a whole myriad of other terrible adjectives— the list could go on for pages. The only other way is to ask for forgiveness. I can't, I don't know how. And neither do you.

Listen. Put on your armor and become a soldier, protect yourself. When I was in Iraq, I couldn't think of my family because it got in the way of what I needed to be—a soldier willing and able to kill. They said a woman couldn't do it. But I did. Now you're a soldier, too, willing and able to kill yourself. Be strong. Focus on the finish line. I'm here to help you however I can. That's how I show my love for you.

Two warnings won't make a fucking difference to me. In the military, I learned cold, hard persuasion. I'll use it to report how officers ignored you, therapy dumped you, rec dismissed you. Plus, I'll add how other inmates treated you like shit because you were educated, and even a teacher called you arrogant. I will be loyal to you. I could give two shits about any repercussions—they've taken everything they can from me. When the Captain took away photos of my girls and said I can't see them for eighteen years, I lost it. It hurt the most—no, more than the most—and I can't focus on it too much or I become extremely suicidal. So I must escape to my mind. They can't get in there. My mind is mine.

Today in meditation I was trying to mediate, but all I could focus on was how empty I feel. I couldn't get the thought out of my head of looking across the hallway at count—and not seeing you stand there. I don't know what I am going to do without you. I know you have to do this and I know you know I understand or I wouldn't have gone to the lengths I have for you. I meditated and, eventually, I saw you with him. And I felt peace. I hope when I look across the hall and there's an empty space you used to fill, I will still feel peace. That I won't feel incredible grief, loss, anger, or wishing I had not helped you. It's weird—I love you enough to help you kill yourself. I know you need to be with him; you're drawn to one another like magnets. I could tell from your photos. Just give me a sign you made it, that you're okay, that all this wasn't in vain. I envy you having someone to go to, but once you're there, I will have someone to go to.

When you asked if we'd be friends—if not for prison—I had to stop and think. I really do think we would have and our lives would have been wonderful. We have a lot in common, except our taste in men—wait, that's the same too. They are both pretty much straight up assholes, so we got that, too. Mostly I want to say I love you so much. And I will pray for you. Praying opens the heart to someone else's pain. So does love. I honestly feel more connected to you than my "friends" on the outside. They found me odd and tolerated me. You, on the other hand, complement my oddity and at times encourage it. I will watch *Modern Family* and *Grey's* for you when you're gone, but more importantly, I will recall how you made me feel: validated, loved, accepted. You never judged me or my crime. There is evil in us all. I simply recognize and accept it. You found the good in me. There is good in you. I've seen it.

I will think of your goodness when I meet a new person and decide if they are worthy of my friendship. I promise to stop telling others about my crime and start protecting myself.

Be brave, my lovely soldier, my mama friend. You know the way, the map is in your hands, and you have all your supplies. Don't look back for ONE SECOND. No one here is worth it, not me, not your mother, father, brothers, friends—no one. Go forward with blinders on. Suffer a short time, suffer the fate that was his so you can be reunited. I am with you every step of the way, sending strength and courage.

Failure is not an option. You know what will happen if you fail—we won't even go there. I promise I'll keep my composure. I promise to honor your wishes and not intervene or freak out. If I could do it for you, I would. But honestly, it's better this way; you will be absolved because you are doing to yourself what you did to him. You want this so desperately and I get it. I've been there and I will be there again. Picture me for strength. Picture him for fortitude.

I adore you more than all the stars in the all the galaxies. Keep your head up. I'll be there soon and we'll go from there, together.

Dancer

After Carson Miller hugged the dance hall bar the whole evening, drinking, chuckling behind designer sunglasses, he took my hand. "What a dancer," he said, "a really good dancer. I watched *you* the whole night." I replied to a.m. radio's popular slow talker with a polite thank-you. Then he repeated himself and I repeated myself and there we paused, hands cocooned, smiles frozen as overhead halogens came up and a disc jockey dismantled amplifiers and stacks of CDs.

Five hours earlier Carson had spoken on *Trying Times in Therapy* for our Communication Disorders Benefit. He retold how he overcame stuttering. He exaggerated unusual body movements with prolongations (llllllike this). Then he clinked away the rest of the evening with bourbon on ice, fielding questions from other bar flies about MILLER AFTER MIDNITE, his statewide show for third-shifters and insomniacs.

He had nodded to me earlier in the evening when I snatched some napkins from the bar, blotted my face and neck, caught my breath and raced back to a vast maple floor. At first I thought he wanted to dance with me. That nod, the way he rolled one shoulder, keyed me up. I was a heavyweight, a size 16 despite diet pills, counseling, and calorie counts. Cha-cha, fox trot, or mambo transformed me to a lightweight, though, a dancing queen reveling to *Mony, Mony* and *Scarborough Fair.* Whether jitterbugging or waltzing, I forgot I preserved fat as a national treasure, fat as so-called protective coating. On the dance floor I forgot I was thirty-five and single, a childless speech therapist with a way with kids. When dancing I said screw it to biological clocks, research papers, and my refrigerator magnet—*you can teach your body to think thin.* I was old enough to know I could teach someone else easier than myself.

Now in pearly blue light Carson studied my stationary body, a plumpkin in an era of gaunt cheeks and protruding collar bones. Embarrassed, I wanted to be far from him, content with his electrifying praise. I knew how these things went, how they played out or didn't play out. I had a fifteen-year history with cool guys like him; they liked my dimples but saw sister material, not girlfriend material. A haze of smoke and dust hung in the air. There were whiffs of spilled beer and sweat, and for the chosen few, an aura of sex. The crowd wandered out, chattering and backslapping. One kid stammered, for real, not forever, I hoped. Carson continued to hold my hand even though several parents approached him, saying things like thanks for coming up from Milwaukee, you're a great success story. My hand pulsated in his as he wooed his admirers, and said things like, my pleasure, it was grand, nice little town. On the radio dial his voice overlapped hard-edged cynicism with the little boy he must have been—intent, happy, lost in play. Now I noticed how that voice belied his physical self: mid-forties, five feet ten, an oval face with acne scars. He appeared shy and boyish in wrinkled khakis, white polo, and a Norwegian fisherman's hat. The last admiring stragglers filtered by and finally he released my hand, took a step back.

A nimbus of light fell on his canvas sneakers, messy and chic. Out of the corner of my eye, I saw my crazy friend Roxie give a thumbs-up. Roxie was always having a sense, looking for a sign. Evidently the spirits had moved her again. Later, she would calculate where my sun and moon were that night and which sign of the zodiac was rising as explanation for what happened. Carson cocked his head toward me, breaking my line of sight to Roxie. "W-w-what's your n-name?"

I liked his ability to poke fun at himself. "Sarah," I said, "with an H." The need to mention "H" should have been a major clue to my self-deception. He absorbed my answer, analyzed it. His body was lean, soft—both willing and asking—but tired, mostly tired. I grasped my tank top and waffled it. "Sorry, I'm boiling over." Deodorant goo stuck to my armpits and my underwire dug in.

He removed his hat with aplomb, revealing a sun-blotched forehead with deep lines and thinning hair the color of sand. He jiggled his cocktail glass, downed the last bourbon. "Boiling? How about a stroll?" he asked with stammer, "a cool-down stroll?"

I didn't answer. My '92 Honda with 125,000 miles on it was in the parking lot. It was one a.m. I taught Sunday School tomorrow morning, then services, then a parish council meeting. He put up his fists. "You gonna make me fight for it?" I recognized the reference; he'd fist-fought kids who teased him. I myself had withdrawn to reading—with a double chocolate blizzard. Not only was I a bookworm; I was a fat bookworm. I had learned to read people in books, not real life, and so I hesitated to check my list of fictional characters, see what they'd do. Before I could answer, he said, "What do you say, Miss Sarah with an H."

"It's Mrs.," I said and didn't know why. It was a lie. I seemed to raise one palm in a stop motion while waving him in with the other.

"Missus? You here alone?" His face was plain, unfettered, and his swagger off-balance. He buttoned his tatty sport coat. Lining sagged below the hem. "Tell mister you got carried away," he said, ironing his lips to flatten a decided smile.

And that was it. A decision. I walked next to him out of Wayside Inn's big dance hall into a foyer with fifties wood-paneled walls, yellow with thick wax and old smoke. A neon Budweiser sign buzzed on one wall while Hamms the Beer Refreshing lit up another. He opened the solid oak door to the outside, followed me across the parking lot where he spotted a car with TERAPY vanity plates. "Look at that," he said, tipping his hat at my Honda. "Someone can't say their t-h's." He laughed, laughter that jumbled sweetness and sadness, like Ferris wheel music that swells at the bottom and fades at the top. "Where to?" he said.

I pointed toward the dimly lit sky above Stangelville where I owned a small home, a small garden, a bicycle, and my grandmother's set of dishes. We were half a mile from town. We could have driven, then strolled. Driving would have been the sensible thing to do. But that night I did not want *sensible*. That night I did not want a life defined by a license plate. I wanted something, but what?

We walked. He sauntered beside me, then broke into long, wild strides for thirty yards and stopped. "Come on, slow-poke," he yelled. Gravel jabbed my white tennies. After a night of dancing, my legs were drunk, moving the way a roller-skater's do after the skates come off. He circled back, hands in his pockets, shuffling the balls of his feet. An owl hooted. Behind us at Wayside, car doors slammed.

"Smell that clover and quack grass," he said, tugging air into his lungs. "I usually smell asphalt and cement. Foundry dirt. Unless the wind shifts, then the Red Star Yeast factory makes us all believe Mama's home, baking bread."

"I remember that," I said intently, now thinking about his palate, tongue, jaw, and lips. "It blew over Marquette's campus." Airborne calories surely compounded my freshman fifteen, I thought, recalling the nauseous mix of yeast and city bus exhaust. "Yes," I fibbed, "what a homey smell."

Minutes of silence settled in except for June bugs and an occasional croaking frog. Dewy air swished around us. I wondered where he grew up and thought that might be the next icebreaker when he raised his elbows and posed, awkwardly, in a forward-twinkle dance position. He said, "How'd you learn ballroom?"

"Classes. At community college."

"What's that? Gym class for grown-ups?"

I glanced at him, a sense growing he wanted to know me. "It was okay," I said. "Better with a regular partner."

His gait went floppy. "You didn't take the mister?"

"Lenny?" The name of my father fell out of my mouth.

"Yeah, Lenny. That your husband's name?"

"Lenny doesn't dance."

"What *does* he do?"

"Construction. He works construction." My mind darted to Peter, my oldest brother who worked construction. Carson better not ask any more. Not only was my family not that big, there was nothing wrong with them. No dysfunction, no trouble. Nothing for good stories on night walks with a man. My usual man talk involved fundraisers, an ice-sculpture committee, or careful conversations with a father of a child with a lateral lisp, or a dad heartbroken over his son's verbal apraxia.

"So who *was* your dance partner?"

"Other singles, a mixture of doozers and dorks. Even husbands required to take turns because Brian, our instructor, said it benefited everyone."

"Brian was right. It worked on you." He patted his back pocket, like he couldn't remember where he put his wallet or keys. Or, address book. "I never learned to dance," he said. "That's why I'm glued on good dancers like you." Glued. I could feel it, a sturdy, long-lasting bond. A little voice inside me said: from now on go for the banana, skip the caramel corn. Yet another voice said: food is safer than being dumped again.

We walked with a dense, slow wind behind us. We came up to the lily-white sign that read Stangelville. And underneath that, in smaller letters, Population 1183. "How'd the name get this town?" He smiled at himself. His radio success came from a silver tongue and quick thinking, though he surely used that line before. I responded with a polite *exactly*. We walked another eight hundred feet to the first sidewalk, with old-fashioned molded lampposts. Honey pot light radiated from carved, glass bowls. The streets were deserted except for the one cop predictably parked at the edge of town to snare an OWI or two after the dance. Sweat crystallized between my breasts.

I relaxed, ran my fingers through my hair. "I'm a mess," I said. He was supposed to say something, something complimentary. Instead he rattled night air into his nostrils with exaggeration. He held that breath and then blew out a throaty treble. He took off his Howard Stern sunglasses and tucked them in the sport coat. Removing the sport coat, he flung it over his shoulder. Without the glasses and padded shoulders, he almost lost his status. He smelled of Giorgio Armani and cool mints and Wayside's fried chicken, cigarettes, and cigars.

"Talk to me, Sarah. About Stangelville. About yourself. *Really* about yourself."

I didn't tell him about my biological clock or boxes of Oprah Magazine. I told him about four brothers, a 100-acre dairy farm with a long gravel driveway, how I grew up playing outfield and swishing hockey sticks, how I drove a tractor and baled hay. I told him now I traveled the entire rural district from school to school, the same route every week. I told him I loved kids. I didn't tell him my bathroom curtains and towels were color-coordinated beige. He listened attentively, then said, "And Lenny?"

I balled up my hands and dug my knuckles into my hips. Then I twisted my head toward him and hunched one shoulder. "Do *you* have any lies?"

He imitated a fisherman sizing up the fish that got away. "The lies no one catches get bigger. Look, let's not let Lenny or other ghosts ruin this night. My whole life, all I ever wanted besides sluts and whores was . . ." He paused.

"Yes?" My eyelid twitched, an involuntary tic that appeared when I got excited.

"Funny. I can't even finish that sentence." He scooped up a few pieces of gravel. "In my business, it's mostly loose women who come on to me. Bitchy ones with fake boobs, all ages. They give. I take." He pitched a pebble. "Here I am, baring my soul."

To a *real* woman, I wanted to say. I imagined his address book scribbled with Nicoles and Tanyas, svelte women with sharp yellow hair and flawless faces, area codes in California or the Carolinas, women who wanted him but couldn't keep him like I would, simply and honestly, no feminist agendas. He would fondle me at the stove, goulash would simmer while we made love on the table or window seat or on the stairs. Afterward he would wolf down the meal and then do me again.

Despite my musings, we seemed disparate, though. I craved closeness; he favored aloofness. He seemed worldly; I was small-town. Still, we might balance. We entered Orchard Road where white picket fences bordered both small clapboards and large Victorians. The night smelled of peonies and roses. "Small towns make me realize," he said, "even here, I belong to the public."

"Of course you do. You talk public all night long. The public *loves* you."

"No," he said. "I belong to the public because I've never belonged to anyone else. I'm adopted, always lived with someone else's ideas about myself. I'm anonymous. It's all

I know." We walked past a neat little clapboard with wrap-around porch and suspended wicker swing. At the sight of it he meandered up the front walk, perhaps reminded of some place. "Let's swing," he said.

"Jitterbug or Lindy?"

"Can't dance, remember?"

Of course I remembered. It was just that the swing he wanted to swing on belonged to my Granny Elsa who at this hour slept, hearing aids on her bedside table. Many childhood evenings I sat on Granny's porch swing in jammies, eating homemade peanut butter cookies before bed. I spent two weeks with her every summer, played hopscotch and roller-skated on sidewalks, bicycled on paved village streets. It was a *sign* that he had picked Granny's swing. A sign, Roxie would affirm.

I wanted to teach him to dance. I wanted a regular dance partner, a companion. We climbed ten porch steps. A floorboard creaked. Subtle lamplight fell on the white wicker swing. We sat down. He pushed off. We lifted our feet and swayed behind a see-through hedge of Japanese yew trees at the porch's edge. A car of teenagers crawled by, flicking red-tipped cigarettes to the beat of a thumping bass, or the beat of their groins. A harried man walked a black Labrador who bucked the leash. Across the street, widowed Mrs. Schmidt clicked on her bathroom light. We watched her shadow advance and recede about the room until the light went out, her entire two-story brick Georgian went dark, and the huge elm in her front yard was no longer back-lit. And then it was true night, luminous and unchained. When the swing slowed, he pumped it. "I feel eighteen," I said.

"Me too." He lifted his hand and traced a vein. "Rivers of *life* or *rivers* of life?"

"Accents and punctuation are easy," I said. "Trouble starts with metabolic breathing and emotional vocalization." I tagged on a nervous little laugh, my signature. Right now

I didn't give a damn about fricatives, labiodentals, or sibilants. Unless he had kids who needed me. Unless *he* needed me. Had he been married? How many times? He seemed ungrounded, wounded. I waited, but he didn't put a move on me.

"Why talk radio?" I said.

"Why speech therapy? Why dance? Why anything?" He pumped the swing.

"Right. The sooner you realize life's an act, the better you get along," I said, surprised by my own bitterness. We seemed to be on an airplane, buckled into time for emotional truths. I leaned forward and pressed my cheek to his. There was a tingling sensation from his four o'clock shadow.

"You're sweet," he said and placed his palm on my Stove Top thigh. Warmth seeped through my moody blue skirt. Granny's swing swung, allowing a huge lapse of silence. Clouds fingered their way across the moon's surface and disappeared, leaving a shiny, white saucer alone in the dark wide sky. I pushed my nose into the hollow of his neck.

"That's nice," he said. I ran my lips up and down his neck. I smelled him in a heady, close breeze, a hint of clove and sandalwood. He slowed the swing, fondled one breast. "Stop me," he said bashfully. I stood up and he paused the swing. I angled between his legs and laced my fingers with his. Streetlight drizzled over him and when he lifted his face to look at me, I saw his eyes, bluebird-blue. I pulled him off the swing and led him to the other side of the porch where I picked up Granny's homemade lap quilt. Without a word, we went down the stairs into the side yard of poplars, lilacs, and roses. I opened the quilt and tossed it on the damp grass. He took off his hat, placed it on my head and bent to untie my tennies. Then, he rose. He rested his right hand on his hip, held his left hand up to hold an imaginary partner. "Something easy," he beamed. He shuffled a bit and kicked off his sneakers.

Waltz, I thought, tremulous. I formed my right hand into oath position and with three fingers tapped *daa*-da-da, *daa*-da-da on his polo shirt. "You need to feel the rhythm," I said. "Count *one*-two-three, *one*-two-three." I pressed myself to him. Our arms butterflied open. I continued to count *one*-two-three, *one*-two-three and took him with me into the forward box step. With calm regard, he followed me in the soundless dance. Each barefoot step glided, airborne and unbroken, until we dropped to the quilt, beaming.

"That *was* easy," he laughed. That same jumbled laugh.

"Like learning love, Brian says, all you need is desire."

"Maybe." His tone was tragic, revealing. He expected little. That made me feel bawdy, courageous. Wanton. He lay on his back and looked up at the moon. Smoke-gray clouds scudded before it, behind it. He lay there quietly while I nibbled his cheeks and ears, ran my hand down his leg. He blossomed into response, his scent earthy and primal. He rolled on his side, kissed me on the top lip, the bottom lip, lifted my skirt and fingered me. I undid his belt and zipper, tugged down his pants. A hot summer rain began to fall, a light mist the sound of angel wings. He unhooked my bra and rolled my nipples. I slid atop him, dropping one breast in his mouth. He drank lazily. We had all night for his tongue, warm and gentle, to lap and lick. Puffiness around his eyes fell away, his craggy cheek lines lengthened. And then I lost myself, opened him, rode him while he pushed my breasts together and gulped, frenetic. My nipples elongated, goose bumps peppered my thighs. We played a long time before his mouth dropped open in a muffled roar and I made noises too, louder than he. He squeezed me and then we separated, two halves of a walnut shell, side by side, holding hands.

Automobile tires slapped along Orchard Road, a mingling of car fumes and wet grass with the peonies, perfumed and eternal. I looked up at Granny's bedroom window with the broken shutter. Time passed. Finally I said I'd walk him to Wayside, to the room reserved under Communication Disorders Society. He didn't answer. We tucked ourselves back together. I wore his hat on the walk to Wayside, his sport coat our umbrella in the soft rain. By the time we got there, rain had let up and an orange sun climbed the horizon. My tennies were soaked and my skirt of rainwater clung to my thighs.

He opened my car door. "You left it unlocked?"

"You're in Stangelville."

He reached into the inside pocket of his sport coat, pulled out his Howard Sterns, and put them on. "Don't take anything for granted," he said. "Not even here." I felt woozy and betrayed but my meticulously polite self gave a wink—in hopes he'd lower the glasses and let me see his eyes. "Time to go," he said quietly and hustled me behind the driver's seat. He touched the nosepiece of his shades to press them firmly in place, ducked his head, then turned away so I couldn't see his face. I closed the door and he stood there while I started the car. I powered down my window and he leaned in, for a final kiss, I thought. But his air was insouciant, distant, and I could not connect the dots. His hands gripped the window frame. "You needn't worry," he said, businesslike, "not that you would. But, *Lenny* m-m-m-might." The sound of his voice passed through his throat and into his nose with a prolonged nasal *m*. "Anyway, I'm negative. *And*, I've had a vasectomy."

My mouth opened in a small, astonished gap. "*Fine*," I said. I powered the window back up and he jumped, rescuing fingers just in time. *Fine*, my mind hammered, we're both negative, and you've had a vasectomy while *I'm* married. Our lies were different, yet alike. Both covered deep loss. We were connected; I wasn't sure just how.

The next day after plodding through *Where is God When It Hurts*, after telling Mrs. Moore I *personally* saw Timmy punch Allyson, after two dousings of Visine, after excusing myself early from the parish council meeting, after running a stop sign, and after placing the same wrong key in my back door twice, I thought only of sleep. I made the mistake of eyeing the answering machine. It blinked with four messages. All from Roxie. Sleep would wait. I dialed her. She *had* to come over.

"Divine," she said. "When's his birthday?"

"We didn't get *that* far, Rox."

"Get day *and* time. I need exact time and the longitude and latitude of his birth to judge whether or not the Sun changed signs at that hour." I told her the moon seemed more interesting and told her everything. She drew an astrological pie chart, eager to fill it in. "Think he'll call?"

"Dubious." But I was lying.

"Call *him*," she said. "If I do his chart, we'll know his commitment level. We need birth date to crack his code."

I wanted to call him, but for what? To pull him into my small, exacting life? To live his public life, forever behind sunglasses? No, I'd be content with one fine night I shed my Gummi Bear image. And if I wanted my big butt a smaller size—to attract another lover—I'd stop consuming bags of Cheetos, rectangular cartons of ice cream.

Weeks passed. I replayed the night, how he started it, how I took over. How he let me, like he wanted it that way. If that were so, why didn't he call? My confusion replicated itself. I couldn't sleep. And I lived too far from Milwaukee to draw in his radio signal unless I drove south, which I did one Friday at midnight, my radio dial set to his station. Bubbly static scoured my mind into nothingness while I drove darkened back roads. I began to hear rhythms like when the vacuum cleaner runs a long time and I relaxed, a can of Pringles at my side. Somewhere outside Howards Grove a deer crossed the road and I slammed on the brakes, barely avoiding it. And then his station came in: classical guitar, agile hot sounds, feel-good music while Carson said if you're just tuning in, thanks for spending the night with me and Peggy in Waukesha whose husband prefers woodworking to lovemaking. I turned off at the next crossroad and parked just as Carson said, talk to me, Peggy. Peggy complained, a guitar hummed and then Carson told Peggy, love takes many forms. Peggy bragged she was a cosmetics manager; she worked out, lifted weights. Carson replied, like I said, Peggy, many forms. I opened the Pringles. For the next three hours, I loved him and hated him, this voice I had slept with, his ease and wit, intensity and slickness in talking about baseball, raw food, Mom, the English language, cremation, people who slept with dogs, garage bands, affairs. All over southern Wisconsin women were having orgasms just listening to him resonate about desire and longing. I polished off the Twinkies, Cheez-Its, and Animal Crackers and at four a.m. drove home, wiser and re-magnetized, convinced this man and I had a future.

That week Krispy Kremes went down readily, then sat in my belly like a rock. I caught a cold, lost five pounds. If that's what it takes, I thought, give me flu. My love of food changed: I ate half a Snickers' bar, half the platter of spaghetti. I lost another five pounds and considered calling him, my voice lighter. I imagined what I'd wear when I saw him, how he'd *Wow* me. Not my blue jean jumper with short-sleeve T-shirt sprinkled with daisies. I'd wear skin-tight pants, black, and a titty-tight top with plunging neckline, especially if we did the pubs on Milwaukee's Brady Street. But I knew how I'd look; I'd never be Cream City girl. So my rational, boring, common sense side won: I did not call. Yet all week my moods swung. My stomach hurt constantly. It hurt if I fed it; it hurt if I didn't. The thought of a Pop-Tart nauseated me. I had heartburn, big time, the kind Tums couldn't handle.

Acidic, thick haze hung at the top of buildings when I got off I-43 and made my way downtown to Doctor Henley who examined me, inside and out. She wanted to know what I ate, when, and if I had traveled anywhere *exotic*—nice of her to ask. When she poked at my Pillsbury Dough belly, I braced for the weight loss speech. But she skipped it, as if my shedding pounds meant shedding personality. Then she took a ballerina step, handed me a slip, and waved me off to the lab.

The next day she called when I was between Jackson and Ryerson Middle Schools, stuck in a construction zone. She wanted more tests, just a follow-up.

"Follow-up to *what*?"

"You're pregnant. Ultrasound will confirm it."

Pregnant? My orderly life and day-planner collided. A flagman waved to stop. I floated past him. He slapped my hood and yelled, "Cram the cell phone, lady."

My mind filled with sand and I pulled into City Park, hyperventilating. I opened the sunroof and said, "Say that again?"

"Ultrasound next week," she replied. "Eleven a.m."

"Sure," I said, "eleven a.m."

I immediately called Roxie at her restaurant; she insisted that when I call him, I should get his birth date.

"I'm not calling," I replied. He's a jerk."

"A father deserves to know."

"The father with the vasectomy?"

"So a man lied. Since when is that news? *He* had sex with a married woman."

"He knew better."

"No, he wanted you married. Forbidden is better. Look, you've nothing to lose. Whoops, the gaggle of Rotarians are here for their noon feeding. Call you later."

Roxie was right. Some kids were planned, even demanded. Others were unintended, the new word for illegitimate. I'd seen all kinds, wanted and over-wanted and unwanted. My child was *wanted,* on a pre-destined, primordial level.

I didn't want marriage, well, I did, marriage *and* a child—with Carson.

Over the weekend Roxie and I talked Carson and baby non-stop. They were two miracles in my life. I wasn't some teenage rebel who got herself pregnant. I was an educated woman, keen, ready. To celebrate, Roxie brought my first baby gift—a cast-iron antique music box. On Monday I called WGJC and a way too cheery secretary patched me through to his voice mail. I unwrapped an Eskimo Pie and Carson's recorded voice came on: *Miller here. Talk to me.* His voice, his message, god, everything, threw me. I recovered enough to say: *Hi. This is Sarah Reimer. Stangelville, remember? I'm calling to complete details on our benefit dance.* I left my home number.

He called four days later. I blurted to him that love takes many forms, that surely our night felt real to him too, that I was pregnant. "A baby," he said. He sounded calm and tentative. I heard him shuffle papers, probably psychological tips for the troubled or literary quotes on relationships, fillers for dead air space. "Sarah with an H," he said, "I've had a vasectomy." He paused, then added wistfully, "Stangelville's nice."

I looked at the music box, intent to ask birthdate, mention he could discover himself with a child, get over the adopted thing. Instead I whimpered, "Vasectomy. Reeel-eee?" I sounded like a first-grader.

"I wouldn't lie about that. Sorry. Gotta run. Good luck finding Daddy."

But I had found Daddy. This was his big lie. Blood tests would prove it. Once again, I felt a connection with him and all of life. I had let myself go and discovered that you ended up where you wanted to be by doing an about-face. The reversal got you there, not a lesson plan but a willingness to let life *happen.* Then I wavered, psychotic; was the pregnancy in my head? Psychogenic pregnancy—Roxie knew a cuckoo waitress who had one of those, a complete psycho invention. But wait. The urine test said *pregnant*. It was ten p.m. I dialed the clinic and got an on-call doctor, who told me one in six hundred vasectomies fail. "Reeel-eee?" I said.

"Clinical, scientific, evidence-based fact," he said. "You need something else?"

The phone slipped from my hand. I schlepped to the kitchen and poured a glass of Chambord, liqueur for special occasions and nightcaps. I filled a wine glass and drank; it went down like milk. Another couldn't hurt. Ah, better. I poured a third and wandered to the living room sofa where I spread an afghan over my cataplectic legs. One by one, folds in my brain collapsed until I couldn't think, not even of tomorrow's ultrasound.

Roxie picked me up at noon the next day and drove me to the medical center, to the same strange, non-pile carpet of Henley's office. Iceberg blue fluorescents flickered. We took the elevator up to ultrasound, then down to Henley's waiting room. Women of all ages came and went while Billy Joel played. A twentysomething strutted in, her billowy shirt emblazoned in rhinestones with BABY. When they called my name, Roxie got up with me. Oh good, the assistant said, you're not alone. She placed us in an overheated room with a desk and soon Henley came in, carrying a painting-size envelope. Roxie quipped about a penis, with or without, but I trembled with uncontrollable wild emotion, knowing intuitively that whichever grew inside me made sense—the sense of my body as vessel, a vessel to finally fill. I was part of mother earth, the human genome, the miracle of children and grandchildren that came from crabbiness and cramps. And, okay, one-night stands.

Henley opened the envelope and spread huge gray negatives across the desk, right side up to us. She extended a hand to Roxie, who introduced herself and raved she was not family, but would be the spinster Aunt. Then Henley sat down, wove her fingers together. A wisp of unruly hair hung from the bun atop her head. She deliberated. Then her eyes turned into bottomless puddles, the darkest gray. "I am sorry," she said, her delicate fingers pointing to a blob in the middle, a blurry black-and-white daguerreotype amidst shades of gray. She called it "a nebula." I leaned forward as if that would help me understand. "A blighted ovum," she said gently. I frowned, unsure of what she was trying to tell me. "I am sorry," she said, "but there is *no* baby." I stared at the heartless white space on a blackened background. I opened my mouth in a rant but nothing came and Roxie too went mute while Henley retreated into science—how it happened, what it meant, what now, what next, but I grasped little of it, only *blight*, the parasite that destroyed my green beans last summer.

Roxie drove home, weaving between lanes, cutting off other drivers. "False positive," she said, "what the hell is that?" My urine test had scored a FALSE positive. I stared across the gentle swell of fields along I-43 to the horizon with Lake Michigan, bluer and colder. I alternated sobbing with cursing, my mind a sieve, riddled and useless as my two-ton self.

Roxie and I got to my house around five and started drinking. I wished I smoked. I wished I weren't about to devour countless Oreos. I wished for more Chambord and Roxie, still on her first, poured me number I-don't-know-what.

"Birthdate," she said. "We'll never know his birthdate."

"Yes we will," I laughed nervously, then dialed his station.

Roxie grabbed the phone and said tomorrow, call him tomorrow. And that's the last thing I recall her saying before I passed out to fight nightmares of two-headed babies, babies with missing fingers, babies without brains. I awakened in late morning, my mattress a bed of nails. In the bathroom I examined the damage: a purple onion face, scarecrow hair, eyelids puffy with trapped tears. I tromped downstairs to the kitchen and found Mr. Coffee with a post-it in Roxie's handwriting that said *Press button to start.* A single red rose lay on the counter next to a white box wrapped with white butcher string. There were long johns and éclairs inside that box. I could smell them, my favorites, but I couldn't even push the start button.

My tears dammed up and I reached in my bathrobe pocket for tissues. Instead, I discovered Carson's number on a crumpled napkin. I smoothed it out and clenched my jaw. He was part of me now, his failed vasectomy, my failed pregnancy. Last night I knew I must call him, call him Daddy, see what he says. Roxie had advised *tomorrow, call him tomorrow.* In my tomorrow I imagined I still had him. I dialed the number with a ploy: apologize for my accusation that he had lied, tell him my *new* news, garner an opportunity for us to meet. The same cheery secretary answered, "Miller After Midnight, only it's daytime." She probably wore a size four, fake nails, and thong underwear. Her low-slung denims probably played peek-a-boo with a flat little midriff. She probably slept with Carson.

I set the phone back in its cradle, then trudged into the living room and fell sideways onto the sofa, cramming my face into velveteen corduroy. The pulpy fabric scratched at my cheeks. This wasn't about Carson. It was about me—and my baby. Tomorrow I will call Henley, ask what she meant when she said *what next.* This thought consumed me as I tugged the afghan around me, tight as a papoose, and felt my heart drop to my belly, pounding, pounding.

A Phone Call Away

Since Julia lured him to those Tennessee Hills, Billy had made one friend. It was Stockton, a fellow lab technologist who watched Billy's riot grow as the two of them handled stool specimens, cross-matched blood, and listened to the whining centrifuge at Mercy Hospital. There Billy was, hands meant for a sax, now fingering pipettes and Petri dishes. Even whiffs of formaldehyde reminded him of cocktail bars with dry smoke and leftover perfume, scenes of men hawking women, women snaring men. He missed his sax, that long golden fish on his chest, the jamming, hanging out.

Mostly, though, Billy missed the original Julia, a centerfold kind of girl who could throw a glance and reel him in, a girl who now muttered, you're too good for me, I'm worthless, I don't deserve you. Her discordant remarks upset Billy. Lucky bastard Stockton, a heavyset single guy, went home to play bass clarinet, and every weekend, had a gig. Stockton had peace. And music.

It was a principle of music that compression followed by expansion created the real interest. And the genius of jazz was that it improvised as it went along. So Billy thought, improvise, be patient because the shrink promised Julia's pills would kick in and her crying jags would die down any day now. But today wasn't that day. Even Billy had the blues, impatiently patient, nothing more than usual, nothing he could put his finger on when he observed Julia's black-eyed Susan eyes, now end-of-summer Susans—withered and spent. She sat in wrinkled cut-offs and a Miles Davis Tee, barefoot, baby Victoria tucked into the crook of her arm while in the high chair, two-year-old Stoney drummed his chubby little palms against the high chair tray, da-da, da-dum.

On a hunch Billy offered to call in sick, let Julia get some rest, but Julia responded, "You're sweet, Billy. That's you to a fault." She gave Stoney a bowl of grits and a silver baby spoon. Stoney pitched the spoon, then scooped up a handful of grits and licked away. Julia calmly tsk-tsked the toddler, then turned to Billy and said, "I'll call if I need something." She lifted Victoria for a burp; yellow run-off cascaded down. Billy fidgeted. "Go," Julia insisted. When he didn't move, she knotted up a smile and said, "I'm *fine*. I'll call. Promise."

So Billy kissed her and the kids and off he went, a phone call away and worried, quite frankly, he'd get fired if he called in once more. He drove to work, Max Roach keeping him alive until all this passed, which it would. At the hospital he parked the van, patted the dashboard and said later, brother.

Stockton was hard at it when Billy stepped into the lab and put on his lab coat. Stockton pointed at red- and purple-top tubes and said *stat*. Billy uncorked them, glad to have something simple to do. Run a test, get a result. Stockton asked how his sorry ass was today and Billy, sick of grumbling, said one of these nights he'd unpack the sax, find his groove again, you know? Billy had just tubed the stat results when the phone rang. It was Julia, sooner than expected. "You should come home now," she said. It was a command, smooth on top and underneath, a countermelody that jarred him. Her words detached from one another, each held in atonal misery. Her breaths were short, labored, like someone frightened or winded.

"Are you okay?" Billy said. His heart raced. "Answer me. Are you okay?"

In the same flat tone, Julia slowly pushed out the same flat words *you should come home now*. Then, she hung up.

Billy grasped the employee ID around his neck and looked over at Stockton, in another world with colonies of staphylococci, squinting through the microscope's beady eyes and moving the carefully prepared slide to count microbes under his breath. Stockton sat upright, found his glasses in the jumble of requisitions and said, "Julia?" Billy nodded, his hands tremulous, pressure building between his temples. "Bill-leee," Stockton drawled in a nasal, lazy way, enough to drive an outsider like Billy crazy.

"Billy the lamb," Billy replied, a dolt eager to please both in the lab and at home. But his mask of normalcy cracked and his mind, jittery and anxious, flitted to his mortgaged house in the woods. Was Julia safe? And the kids, too? He looked helplessly to Stockton.

Stockton touched the nosepiece of his black-rimmed monsters, pressed them in place and spun toward the monitor screen. He clicked on the mouse and said, "Go. She's top space. Go." He shrugged. "Back by ten?"

"Ten?" It came out raspy.

"An hour, man." Stockton sounded genial, friendly. "Need more?"

"Don't know," Billy said, brooding over how he'd come to this moment: *Love is blind. Bad luck, buddy. You get what you ask for. Did I ask for the right thing?* He had examined each possibility many times, running from day to night, lab to home, wanting truth and at the same time, afraid to find it. "Don't know," he said, not sure if he had already said that. Then, feet frozen in place, he said, "I don't know anything anymore."

"Who does," Stockton replied, "until sickness. Leave it to germs or haywire cells to give focus." He lifted a tube and told Billy-boy he'd best get going.

Billy lugged one leg before the other, a man in a white coat counting paces past micro and chemistry, out into the hospital's busy main corridor. He found a door that led to the parking lot and pushed. It wouldn't yield. He pushed harder. The miserable door still wouldn't open. Oh, he said, it says *Pull*. He pulled the door open and moved to a staccato beat, counting, counting. The counting filled his brain; all he could do was count. Three hallways, four doorways. More stairs. One hundred twenty-five paces to the Dodge minivan. Almost there. He found the Dodge fifth row, twenty-seven down, and worked the key in the lock. It wouldn't go. He added pressure, heard a click, and popped the door open.

Canned heat fizzed out. In the back seat lay a windshield protector with half-notes and quarter-notes resembling Tennessee Hills, a gift from Julia. He never forgot to put it in that heat. *It's not the heat, it's the humanity*, a bartender at Sweet Orchid used to quip, and Billy thought of him now as he opened the van windows and turned on the AC full-blast. Outside it was 99 degrees. Inside, it was hotter than hell.

It was hot that day too, three years ago, when Streetmen, Billy's scrappy combo, played in Boston's Back Bay. Shop windows with trendy clothes beckoned students with genetic bankrolls. Thin bodies were in. So were out-of-towners who left a life behind when they funneled down a treacherously angled stairwell into Sweet Orchid, a natty room where musicians left their ego at the door, and jammed. Logan, Streetmen's drummer, was first to notice Julia. Logan ba-bammed, chattered cymbals and swished brushes while the band set up and crazy Eddie on trumpet told the one about a guy who walked into a bar and asked for a bloody virgin.

Billy fingered the sax and tootled around while the crowd draped scarves and sweaters on bar stools. Embossed cigarette cases flashed. Talky guys in turtlenecks and too-tight sport coats called for more drinks; Orchid didn't accept credit cards so customers forked out cash for a Black Russian, Birdland, or Porkpie Plenty. And Streetmen got paid a living wage, as they said back then. A life, Billy would say in the future.

"Gentlemen." Logan's brushes fell silent. "Tonight we play to an angel." He swished the snare drum, a bridge to the girl at the bar. She sat on a stool, long legs crossed at the knees, sandal dangling from a tanned foot. She caught Logan's smile, cocked her head, ran her fingers through hair the color of coconut, and looked at the band. The hair fell where it was, free.

Billy studied her. He would never have a ghost of a chance with a girl like that. It was 1985. He was a white guy in a mixed racial band experimenting with Latin Salsa, sounds of South African black townships, and messages from Bulgaria. Music business was in a slump despite large sums to launch Bruce Springsteen, Billy Jackson, U2. Streetmen hoped to advance from clubs to festivals and concerts. Billy didn't worry. He had the back-up plan, a med tech degree. He was young. He played sax. He was good. And he searched, like anyone else, for luck in long nights.

He played until a tipsy angel from the Tennessee Hills came to Boston, to this street, this club and gave *him* a fuck-me stare. Make no mistake about it: only liquored chicks did this to a guy with half-axle cheeks and a chicken-bone chest. Women did not fight for Billy's delight, Logan said. Billy watched her work the bartender, watched him light a cigarette and leave it burning in her ashtray to hustle back for a drag, vapid talk. How, when he opened tonight, he was short on maraschinos. Or how, when he saw her, he knew she'd survived a loss—that one a dead ringer to show a guy's sensitive side. Openers, come-ons, lines most guys did well. Not Billy.

Between sets, Billy stood beneath the red EXIT sign, sipping white soda. He watched her as the weasel bartender darted about.

She lifted the long, windswept hair and when he saw her delicate face, his shoulder twitched, an involuntary tic. The soda bubbled on his tongue as she lifted the hair once more and across the bar said, "Nice solo, pretty boy." When people talked, Billy went on the notes of what's played out of the vocals. He needed to hear only ten notes to know whether or not they were going to do something. So when she spoke, he took her for serious. He smiled back, nervously. She continued to gaze at him and he toasted her, then tripped back to the sax, playing harder, weirder, the rest of the night.

At two a.m. the bartender walked a red-cheeked drunk to the door. On the way back, he approached Billy. Billy, packing his horn, ignored the weasel until the guy said, "Would you escort her outta here? Name's Julia, plays piano. One too many Wallbangers. Your chance, man. That solo did something."

Billy looked to the bar but she was gone.

"Little girl's room," the bartender said. "Chick she came with left. Whadya say?"

Billy thought of the worn videos he went home to, doing himself night after night to a steady stream of big headlights and bumpers, awful hungers. He wondered about the small of her back, about sunshine hair draped just so. He was replaying *nice solo, pretty boy* when the bartender said "Okay fella, all yours."

Yours, Billy thought, and he piloted her up the stairs, down the street, 110 pounds guided through a hotel lobby, up to room 321. But he did not take advantage of a girl with runway legs and little hooks for hips that sent a shiver through him; he wanted her untainted and clear, so she could feel every nerve ending, every neuron beginning. He hit the floor and slept there, in fits. In late morning she stirred and when he brushed the hair off her face, she vice-gripped his arm, hanging on to a nightmare. Sorry, he said, I thought you were awake and then, over-anxious, asked about the pretty-boy business.

She relaxed her hand and intoned, "You're pretty where you can't see."

"I am?"

Her waking-up eyes, caked with mascara, looked piercing, out of control and exotically pensive. She pushed her pale honey eyebrows together, sweetening her *yes Billy, you am.*

Billy felt his ears redden. His cheeks were on fire. That stupid involuntary tic in his right shoulder started before he knew it. Here she was, sober and still liking him, and what did she mean by *you am.* Her fierce wanting magnetized him, called him into place in her world. There was something here, but he didn't know what, or how to develop it. So he grinned, asked if she wanted to go for coffee. He waited in the hall until she emerged in blue jeans, a white Tee, and fresh lip gloss. She was twenty and he twenty-three when they walked hand in hand down Newbury Street, gusts of wind catching their chatter while pretty-boy Billy floated with good luck. It seemed like she needed him, that was the thing, needed him more than he could know that Saturday morning.

And now he was needed again, Julia's personal rescue squad responding with thrill and chill, only this time with growing dread because she hung up, for chrissake. It was probably nothing. The washing machine flooded or Stoney found her acrylics and was blue-faced as a blueberry. Inconveniences, nothing to qualify as emergency unless, the shrink said, you crept inside Julia's mind where skies rained broken glass while a different mind, say, like yours Billy, saw a shower of confetti, messy but manageable.

What else could it be, that hang-up, he thought, flooring it through a yellow light. Did Victoria aspirate or Stoney fall down the stairs? He had warned Julia to keep the gate in place.

During the brief call he hadn't heard *Mah-meee* or his little man plinking piano. He punched the van into overdrive. Did Stoney lock himself in the bathroom? Billy intended to replace that piece-of-shit lock tonight. He stomped the accelerator, keeping time until he entered the kitchen, this time without an opening statement. He would not be agitated or panicked. He would show calm and reserve. He regretted his short-fused *now what* from last week when he left in the middle of cross-matching blood (go man, Stockton had said evenly) and got home to find Stoney's hair spiked with Desitin, iridescent white grease smeared all over the recent pack of Kodaks. He had chuckled, then snapped a photo for Stoney's high school yearbook while Julia refused to turn her mask from tragedy to comedy.

Within two months after the Sweet Orchid night plus a weekend in the flesh to follow, Billy landed in Tennessee, a scrim over the afternoon sun. Julia packed a wicker basket with civilized food (fried chicken, potato salad, homemade cornbread), no moldy baloney or crushed Cheerios that would dot the TV room too soon. They strolled down to Shakerag Hollow's poplars, tulip trees and cottonwoods, the land rolling, Julia sashaying from hip to hip. Billy said she seemed to be from Athens, and she laughed, Georgia? Billy, a Northern boy, never heard of Athens, Georgia. But he wanted to hear everything: why mist drifted like billowing smoke in the hollow; why Confederate flags flew from backyards on thin poles stuck in circles of cement; did foggy mountain tops have tips?

He learned that Daddy called Julia *my summer.* He bought her a piano when she was six and a month later, died of a heart attack (so she was told). She remembered the ambulance in the dead of night, swirling red and white, her mother Ginger screaming to stay at the top of the stairs, stay out of the way. I still have nightmares, she said, adding, where'd he go? She slipped into the hereafter, then told Billy he was good to talk with.

That was understatement for a guy who spoke through a saxophone. A guy who couldn't pay attention to all this family history, though if he had, his life would not have gone as it did. Because, he might have said: If it wasn't a heart attack, what was it? But he didn't say that. He actually thought to ask: Why *my summer?* But he didn't. Instead he ringed his arm around her waist and nudged her closer. His palm rounded her buttock and he got hard, realizing she wore no panties. She rambled on about Daddy and finally, Billy said, "That was then, this is now." So she pulled him down to the soil, damp with moss and soft twigs, and he lifted her skirt to kiss-kiss her from her knees up, moving slowly, deliberately. She gasped as he traveled her thighs, arriving at her mound, droplets forming like musical notes. Her fingers danced on his cheeks and her voice seemed half a measure from melancholy when she said, *you love me, you do.* Then she tugged him up, her mouth to his, kissing and talking, saying it was good to find a nice guy to open up to. And open she did, drawing Billy out, giving head to make every drop come. She teased *don't* and he *did.* They played for hours and she produced muscle actions he never felt before. "You're my toy," she said, "my secret toy." And he shook, speechless.

Secret toy, Billy thought and zoomed toward Running Knob Woods, the AC spitting out sticky, fungal air. He pumped up Ellington and gripped the steering wheel, jamming past the strip mall, Fresh Fire Worship Center, Church of Jesus Crucified, and a Quonset hut for Abundant Life Followers. Boston had the Old North Church and King's Chapel, dignified places. Down there, storefront religion boomed and he hoped the offer at Mass General came through before he fell down Julia's spiral, too. Boston had been the plan all along. He'd been making the rent at his Clarendon Street walk-up. Julia would move in, waitress at Sweet Orchid, and enroll at the Art Institute. Crazy Eddie could get her in at Ginn and Company with an art illustration degree. The idea seemed clear and simple: up all night, love all day, a rhythm unlike the cacophony that kids brought to a relationship. Add to that Julia's ridiculous refrain, I wish Daddy could see the kids.

After lovemaking that day at Shakerag Hollow, it became clear the only degree Julia would ever attain was 98.6. "Conceived?" he said, his shoulder seizing. "You're kidding." A wet sun washed her face. She was radiant, animated. She took his hand, placed it on her little belly, and said, feel it. The earth convulsed beneath him and he snapped back his hand, saying, how could you?

"Could what?"

"Forget the pill."

She ran her fingers through that hair, lofted it high, and let fall. She crossed her arms and held her breath. Her eyes were small. "It wasn't supposed to be like this."

"No shit," Billy said. A couple walked by with a rottweiler chafing at its leash. A crow cawed. There was a heavy yellow cream in the sky—and Billy was falling into it.

"The baby is meant to be," Julia said. "Your reaction is *not.*" And then her tears came. Billy jumped up and ran to the nearest sycamore, ready to throw her southern fried chicken to the dogs and barrel out of that backwater state with the clothes on his back, and his sax. She looked down at her hands and sobbed, "You love me, you love me."

Perhaps he did. Perhaps he didn't. He hadn't gotten that far yet. "Love is one thing," Billy said, heaving a groan of despair, "but a baby?" Then she informed him that not only was the baby meant to be, but Billy was meant to be the father. That's when it hit him: she had *stopped* the pill, trapped him.

"I was never on it," Julia replied, blowing her nose.

Of course. An au naturel girl, from free-style hair to food, from bare feet to bare buttocks. He had never asked if she was on the pill; he had assumed. It *was* the eighties after all. She rambled: *You think you were my first?* (Well, no.) *Was I yours?* (Well, yes.) But here was the clincher: *God wouldn't put a baby in me with just anybody.* So God was in it, too. How could He not be? Astride billboards and storefronts, inside rivers and radio waves, God had cornered Tennessee. And not Billy's kind of God—jazz, an everyday atheism, adequate and enough. Billy braced himself against the sycamore and told her flat out: she was mistaken, this was an error.

"How could Stoney ever be an error?" She tilted her head and patted her stomach. "His urge to be born is so-o big." She asked Billy to put an ear on her stomach, listen, and Billy, caught in the vortex of her logic, shook his head, no, no, no. Her eyes flared. She swept up the plastic flatware and paper plates, rammed them in the basket, and pitched the celebratory bluebells. Then she curled her lips in simulated ecstasy, somehow revived, and said, "Don't you love it when things go together that aren't supposed to, but it all makes perfect sense?"

Moisture covered his body. She wasn't even a churchgoer, that God in prayer books and choirs. Her God was a sin-gular private vision called fate. He whisked up the picnic basket and marched out of Shakerag Hollow, head throbbing and buzzing. The space between them grew as they drove in silence until Julia brought out one of her mesmerizing corkscrews. The best we can hope for, she said, is an oppor-tunity to play it out. She sounded like a plaintive trumpet, totally off-key, but she snagged his curiosity, and worse, his conscience.

Billy couldn't relocate a pregnant Southerner to Yankee country, especially after Julia's cousin finagled the lab job, guaranteed income, benefits. All that after he couldn't bring himself to suggest she eliminate the rapidly multiplying cells. It wasn't his body where they grew, so he couldn't tell her what to do, though part of what was inside her was him, inextricably tangled. It took him forever to dignify the exploding mitosis with a civil ceremony at five months, Julia's dreamy eyes, those baby magazines. He would play it out, like she said. When she whimpered about a house, he folded on that, too, because expectation had grown on him, the promise of parenthood, a tiny head in a small bed.

Soon he no longer felt tricked, he felt blessed, especially after Julia was right: the baby *was* a boy. He *looked* like a Stoney, with Billy's cheekbones and saxophone fingers. Yet who could predict her dark tones, first heard on the ride home with Stoney safely strapped in the back seat. "I should be happy," she said, "then why am I sad?"

It had to do with hormones and stress, that much Billy knew. So he waited, a believer who believed there was a hidden track, a cure for everything, even her *shoulds*: what Stoney should listen to, her lace teddy should fit, Daddy should see Stoney. Her milk dried up and while she slept, Billy got up for nighttime feedings. He took a leave until Julia got her balance. Even after he went back, if Julia said *can you come home,* he went, thanks to Stockton. Each time he went with hope. He hoped while Madonna sang Material Girl and people stitched an AIDS quilt. He hoped while the Berlin Wall came down and the Vietnam Wall went up. He carried hope home at lunch, Happy Meals to replace rubbery macaroni or burned potpies. Finally the blues lifted and her swoop through the underworld faded, what with mandatory overtime, landscaping the house, time stolen for each other. They made love and gave love—earlobes, toes, dipping wells around the navel, their skin hungers satisfied while Stoney babbled in his crib or slept to the tempo of his parents' movements.

Then Grandma Ginger delivered Daddy's piano, yanking Julia into questions about his sudden departure. On the front walk Ginger whispered to Billy that Daddy died from depression, not a heart attack. Then, quite loudly, she said, "There's no room in my new condo. Julia will love playing." And she did. It proved a good thing. At Stoney's first birthday, she played piano, Billy played sax and Stoney pounded on his new Playskool drum. Then, spellbound, Billy said Stoney needs a sister. And Julia, full of fate, said if it's meant to be, it's meant to be.

Back in the van Billy swerved onto the soft shoulder— once, twice, regaining control each time, his mind on the tiny, squalling bundle placed in Julia's arms while he beamed, Victoria, our sweet serendipity. Julia, drenched from long labor, refused to hold her. Billy took the baby, whose little fingers curled around his pinkie. "Look, Julia," he said, "she's got your nose, my eyes."

Julia looked at him blankly. "You have no idea," she said.

The following weeks suffocated with Julia's blank face. Billy practiced Zen-like calm, focused on the six-week marker when her blues would fade. Six weeks came and went. Her poor appetite and guilty feelings continued. She was a bad mother; Victoria's colic was her fault; Stoney watched too much TV. Billy hugged her, mentioned the secret toy. She bit her lip and looked at the floor. She wore pajamas to dinner, complained of MSG when Billy brought home Chinese. He once surprised her with Chick Corea sheet music, but her reaction was unreadable.

Nights turned into days, Billy counting each one as Kreuzer (shrinkhead found by Stockton) experimented with meds, see how she responds to this one. And Billy remained the love drug: faithful, reliable, passing one pick-up, then another, to get to her, flashing back to night number eighty-nine—how she sat on the floor while he loaded the washing machine, poured in Tide and dropped the lid. Come, he had said, tucking her tangled riddle of hair, messages from outer space, behind her ears. He checked doors and windows and set the thermostat, then coaxed her up to the bedroom, now strictly a sleeping room. After he clicked off the light, she said impassively, the kids are better off without me.

And he lay there in the dark, haunted, her small back to his, thinking she was right—he should divorce her. Then he thought of Kreuzer saying this can't last forever, most self-correct and Julia's lucky to have a man like you, hang in there. In the dark, Billy realized divorce would create more problems—childcare, whether he stayed here or moved them back to Boston. He thought of adoption too, briefly and not seriously. The very idea repulsed him—he would never give up Stoney and Victoria.

He was finally asleep when Victoria wailed, high and reedy. He rolled over in the queen-sized bed. *Where* was Julia? He got up and heard katydid love songs and locust noise, thousands of insects rasping out a kind of radio-dial static, insistent, unnerving. He fumbled down the hall, stubbed his toe on a cracked water gun and hissed God*damn*. He found Victoria beet-red, snot all over her face. He picked her up, changed her from head to toe, and while she crabbed in his arms, warmed her bottle. She drank and swallowed while Billy quivered *Hush little baby, don't say a word, Papa's gonna buy you a mockingbird.* Without a job, Papa can't buy a damn thing, he thought. It was past four. He felt like shit. He tucked her in, tiptoed back to bed.

Just then the front door opened and closed. Julia's hands tapped the railing as she made her way in the dark, patting the wall until she reached the doorjamb. Billy clicked on the bedside lamp and Julia said oh. Yeah, oh, Billy replied. "Can't sleep," she said, folding her arms, one palm quivering against her bicep. Then the volley began. Where were you? Went for a walk. You shouldn't be out.

"You have no idea," Julia said.

"I'm sure not," Billy replied, something ripping inside. "Come to bed."

"For what." When Billy said for sleep, Julia asked what's that. Light from the top circle of the lampshade threw ghoulish gray on her face. Her nostrils swelled. Billy said he couldn't quibble with her; in two hours his day begins. Mine never ends, she said. Please Julia, he begged, please.

"Please, please." She spiraled down. "You have no idea."

Which wasn't true. He had two ideas: get some shut eye; count the number of pills in her bottle in the morning. He turned off the lamp and dozed, ear cocked for her downstairs, rustling from room to room. In the morning he found her asleep on the sofa. "Don't worry," she said, spiraling up, "I'll figure it out." So will I, Billy thought, though he was at a loss where to begin. He made it through the workday with only one argument: a request for jazz on the lab radio. The secretary checked her enameled nails with snowy-white tips, popped her gum and deadeyed him. She asked what it was worth, then blew a bubble of Bubblicious at him, arching her back so her breasts rose. She was new. Billy used mnemonics to remember names, but hers escaped him. "Forget it bitch," he said.

The following night brought another round of where-have-you-been. Julia wasn't sure, but she was mad at him for sleeping when *she* couldn't. Please, Julia, please, he said, feeling her sleep disturbances were contagious. She was taking Kreuzer's pills—he had counted—but now in the five a.m. fog he hesitated: was she supposed to take two or three a day? The number kept upping. So he planned to call Kreuzer that very day, take her back in.

Take yourself in too, Stockton laughed and Billy blurted, what? It's a joke, man, Stockton said and added, be cool Billy-boy, be cool. And then Kreuzer called that very hour. Stockton handed Billy the phone. "No more pills?" Billy said. "Wow, Doc, I was going to call you . . ." Kreuzer shouted something and Billy shifted the phone to the other ear.

"I can't give a haircut over the phone," Kreuzer said. "She missed two appointments. No refills without seeing the patient." Then Kreuzer lost it, screaming, "No more pills." Billy raked his scalp like a man at the races with a dark horse, nervous, incredulous. She missed her appointments? Twice? Maybe she wasn't taking her pills, or taking enough pills, or feeling enough support from Billy. Often Billy pushed Victoria in the carriage while Stoney rode his Big Wheel, giving her a break. Upon return, he'd hear her playing piano, then a sudden thud of the piano cover. *I couldn't decide what to play,* she'd lie, picking at a hangnail.

Now with Kreuzer still on the line, Billy backpedaled to piece together events. He should have called in sick and driven her last week. Instead he arranged day care because she wanted to drive herself. Suddenly he realized he hadn't checked the last refill date on the bottle. He couldn't admit *that* to Kreuzer. "Look, Mr. Mercedes Benz," he said, snapping, "maybe you should make house calls, maybe you should . . ." He made a fist and punched the air. "Asshole," he said to Stockton, "he hung up."

Stockton drummed his fingers on the counter. "You're being held hostage."

Billy returned to his microscope. He had tests to run on amber and cranberry fluids. *Hostage,* he thought, and pondered how to talk to Julia. *Kreuzer called me at work. Kreuzer? You saw him last week?* No answer. *Right? You saw him?* Did he see me, you mean. *Oh, so you went?* He doesn't understand, Billy, not like you. There it would be again, her half-answer, that hook. Love shifted. Dream and dread were on the same scale and Billy moved toward one, dragging the other. He wondered how long he could hang on.

Now with increasing agitation, Billy floored it toward Boxwood Court, fingering the steering wheel, wailing along with a new guy named Marsalis. Kreuzer called it a phase. More of a curse, Julia's refusal to be touched, toes, neck, calling hipbones. She seemed a magnet for despair, like it was her life's work. Other men cut off like this might force a woman, get vicarious pleasure out of chopping wood, or at least fuck the lab secretary. Not Billy. He was civilized and dependable, in search of clues to help her, but he was, as Stockton pointed out, a hostage.

Hostage he said as he rounded a curve. *Hostage* he repeated as he took a corner. His skin tightened in a straight jacket. *Hostage* he recited and barreled past a Don't Die of Ignorance billboard for that new disease. He drove, forever it seemed, to get to Julia and the kids and discover why, for chrissake, she hung up.

After Kreuzer's disturbing phone call, that very evening Billy tried to confront Julia while she loaded the dishwasher, the sink sky-high with plates and cups, soppy crusts, plastic tumblers with purple Kool-Aid. He nuzzled her from behind. She turned, looked at him as if she didn't know him. He asked what's for dinner.

"Me."

"Me too," he said, thinking Julia again playful.

She emptied a tumbler. Her eyes gloomed. "I think we've had a major misunderstanding," she said. Then Victoria let loose a full-boiling scream and Billy said Julia, Julia. He picked up Victoria and watched Julia hesitate whether to put the sticky tumbler in the dishwasher or cupboard. She set it on the counter, said give me my baby, and took Victoria to the window seat for feeding. Billy loaded the dishwasher, eye on Madonna and child. Kreuzer sure made him feel sketchy. If the brainy shrink saw this, would he say he had the right drug, or the wrong one?

The evening evaporated without anything major and next morning it occurred to Billy that Kreuzer's professional reputation was on the line. Why else would he call, adamant, somehow desperate too. It was up to Billy. All day he fortified himself how to address Julia. He got out on time and tore home to find Stoney snuggled next to Julia while she fed Victoria. The baby's touchy tummy filled without spit-ups. Julia wore lip-gloss and a ribbon in her hair. At the sight of Billy, Stoney squealed Daddy and raced through toys and trucks on the floor. Billy scooped him up. He smelled of peanut butter.

"Forget Kreuzer," Julia said, winding up.

"Really," Billy said, tossing Stoney in the air and catching him.

"Really," Julia said. "I ran out of pills . . . and, I'm *fine.*"

"When?" Billy said, a spasm launching along his spine. He held Stoney close. She didn't *know* when, a while ago, pills make me feel weird, what does it matter.

"You're almost there," Billy stammered.

"Moron," she said. Her volatility rose and she whipsawed between Daddy and Kreuzer. "Pills smooth out highs and lows. That's *mediocrity.* Now I know what Daddy meant." Billy hugged Stoney tighter. "I *like* highs and lows," she said. "Why spend money on Kreuzer? He creeps me out." She puckered her lips and said, "Gimme a kiss."

Billy bent forward, compliant, then put down Stoney and said, "Money's not the point, *Julia.*" He accented her name to emphasize her miscalculation, that highs were dangerous as lows.

"Look," she said, "the time I spend packing up the kids, driving there and back, worrying about that hillbilly aide at daycare just to tell shrink-head that I—you, we—had no idea how much work this was, well, who needs him to say, 'And how do you *feel?'*"

"How *do* you feel?"

She was *fine,* what else did he need to know? Then Victoria threw up, Julia started crying, and Stoney filled his diaper. And amidst the bawling and the refinance papers, the van needing brakes, the upcoming lab inspection, the landscaper and the carpet of Cheerios beneath his feet, Billy had no idea what more he needed to know. He *had* to find the cracks in her head and seal them. And so despite the chaos, he asked if she saw Kreuzer *last* week. She whimpered no. "Before that, the time before *that?*" She clutched her head. She can't remember, she's not discussing this anymore. Today was a high day. Now you've ruined it.

He ruined supper too, with chicken noodle soup and burned toast. Stoney finger-fed himself bits of chicken while in the den Julia's silence swelled, a note held so long its pitch changed while she clicked the remote control, click and clicked. Billy carried both kids upstairs, bathed Victoria first, then played with Stoney in his bathtub of toys. He got the kids to bed and came into the den, lit a candle and put on Coltrane. His head pounded but he toed the line and there on the new powder-blue love seat, he talked her into another Kreuzer visit. They went together. Kreuzer wrote a totally new prescription and Billy wrote the check at the pharmacy. And Julia promised to take the small, white capsules three times a day, just for her Billy.

That was a mere two days ago.

In the subdivision now, Billy heard a front-end loader carving a trail for more mortgages. There was a maddening overhead buzz of 747s and somewhere, an air hammer punishing cement. A police siren in the distance came and went, a necessary evil. And then he was home, a land-speed record, he'd brag to Stockton. He opened the back door, stumbled over wet towels and stepped on two little Lego guys with their Lego car. Stoney's race car drivers were smashed.

The house was quiet. The topsy-turvy house was *too* quiet. No radio, no Sesame Street, no… He stopped. *You should come home now,* she'd said, and he did. He thought he entered the wrong portico on Boxwood Court until he spied last evening's pizza with curled pepperoni. He crammed it in the trash. He paused inside his Greek Revival two-story to hear sounds of running water and rhythms of air conditioning, an odd arrangement in 4/4 syncopated time.

"Julia," he called. He walked into the den, his movements thick, sluggish. She sat on the love seat, Stoney's favorite trampoline, still barefoot. Her T-shirt clung to one breast, wet, as if Stoney's new water blaster had gotten her, and her cut-offs had dark splotches. She was paler than usual, exhausted, hair mussed like after jogging or swimming. Maybe she actually played Rubber Ducky with Stoney and it was too much. "Julia?" he repeated. A garbage truck went by, slowed, then the driver revved the engine pulling the noise away with him. Again Billy said, Julia, his mouth dry, mind flummoxed. Next door a dog named Arthur barked. Stoney wanted a dog like Arthur, but at this point a dog would be one more child.

"Julia!" Billy said, frenzied. He dropped before her. Those long thin fingers of hers feathered his cheeks. "It's so quiet here, why did you call me?" She gave him one last blank stare before her eyes rolled back and her legs torpedoed out. Her arms curled inward with hands balled up, shaking. Her swan-like neck twisted and quivered, tongue lolling until teeth clamped down and cherry red ran from the corners of her mouth.

He came apart. He shook her violently, screaming where's Stoney, where's Victoria, this cannot be, are you out of your mind, this place is haunted, call the cops. All the while an officer in military blue stood at the doorway, witnessing the damage, Billy's collapse. It was that officer who found the empty pill bottle among brightly colored toys on the floor after Billy tore through the streets at a vertiginous speed because what he heard in Julia's *come home* message spelled doom, and he was a musician who knew within ten notes what's going down. And he knew too, on some level, at some time, he never stood a ghost of a chance with a girl like that, a girl like that.

Surrender

Esther refused to surrender that morning. It all began after she'd been in the basement, loading three panties into the old Maytag. She had sprinkled in Tide and set the machine agitating. Then, slowly, she climbed those treacherous, steep stairs. When she arrived on the next to last stair, beet-red and out-of-breath, she paused.

Warren, her husband of forty-nine years, stood on the landing, eyeing her ascent. "It don't have to be," he said in a tone tiny-veined and blue.

"Out of my way," she replied. She pulled a hanky from her sleeve. She blotted her forehead. She exhaled heavily. He stood there, puzzled. Then he griped again, how it don't have to be. When she didn't answer, he leaned into the wall, lightheaded. Soon she was in the tight space on the landing with him. She planted one foot, then the other, and crept forward. She treaded the final step up into the kitchen and with her back to him, said, "You mind your own business." He braced a palm against the wall and toddled up into the kitchen. She looked over her shoulder to see if he had arrived safely. Their eyes locked and he said, "Every day, running the washing machine. It don't have to be." At that, he motioned toward the sink, above it, actually. His knobby finger joints looked like fiddleheads, swollen and shiny. "New curtains," he said, gesturing. "It don't have to be."

"You'll be the death of me yet," she said, cramming the hanky back up the sleeve. She grabbed Windex off the counter and bunched up a rag lying next to it. Then, on tippy-toes and leaning over the sink, she wiped splotchy windowpanes. He made his way to the small kitchen table and tugged a chair from its place. He squatted the best he could but dropped to the wooden seat, *plop.* He watched her from there, a curious mix of passion and critical distance. He had forgotten she fancied a life in interior design. He had forgotten she settled for wife and mother, niggling over embroidered pillowcases and footprints on just-waxed hardwood floors. Her pet peeve, though, was water stains on windowpanes. Now she worked vigorously, polishing the window into transparency for a daughter was coming to supper: pork roast, mashed potatoes, gravy, corn, cucumbers floating in cream, cloverleaf rolls and butter, homemade apple pie with a thin triangle of cheese atop. It was a meal fit for a threshing crew. God, she was glad to be off the farm—no more mudrooms and manure boots; no more sticky fly paper hanging from ceilings; no more cows tromping through the first few poppies. And no more Farm Bureau meetings with wives in sunflower dresses, gossip big as their backsides. She had finally made it to this little Cape Cod in Monroe. So today she will not surrender, what with these preparations, the excitement of company coming.

And he will not surrender either, mostly because the canals of his ears are overdue for wax removal. And when Esther does take him for cleaning and they wiggle in the hearing aid, he will turn it off, imagining secrets in silence. His dog, Fella, a handsome collie, heard secrets, too, and now Fella slept at Warren's feet. Every day, Fella waited until Warren opened the door to the attached garage. Esther would demand to know where he was going. He never answered. She knew it was time for a smoke in the garage. He needed those sagging lawn chairs on dank cement, Fella at his feet, odors of fertilizer and birdseed and recycling bins—no frilly curtains or fussy new upholstery. He lit up a Dutch Masters Perfecto and looked around the garage, seeing the 1931 Essex he got for $75 after trading in the Model T Ford Coupe. Then he told Fella about the time he shipped calves to the Milwaukee stockyards via rail. He received a bill from the railroad, saying the value of the calves wasn't enough to pay the freight. "Money I don't have," he said into the kitchen now, "all I can do is send you more calves." He laughed.

"He's telling that story again," Esther said to Kelly. Kelly's baseball-capped head and stocky body had tromped in, carrying stacks of *Martha Stewart Living* and *Architectural Digest*.

"There are no calves, Daddy," Kelly said. He looked at her with all the vacancy he felt in this strange new house. Kelly looked at her mother with intelligence weathered by her job as police dispatcher. Kelly looked, quite frankly, exasperated.

"Taste this," Esther said, in a tizzy about whether the gravy needed more salt or more Kitchen Bouquet. With one hand, she held up a spoon cloudy with gravy. With the other, she formed a drib chamber beneath. Kelly took a lick.

"Salt," Kelly said. She went back out to her Chevy Impala and slogged in carpet and tile samples. She deposited them on the coffee table. Esther came to look, ooing and ahhing, the spoon in her hand now clean as a whistle. Kelly thought they could start in the foyer and carry the theme (which will end up J.C. Penney) throughout the house. Esther nodded, giddy as a schoolgirl, and went back to the kitchen. She caught Warren at the counter, stabbing a pork slice off a platter. "You wait till it's served," Esther said.

"Oh *woman*."

Kelly stepped into the commotion. She cocked her head sideways at Esther. The tilt said, why-do-you-put-up-with-this?

"Mash the potatoes, Kell, would you?" Esther said. "And you," she said, pointing at Warren, "you sit down and wait your turn." She left the kitchen in a huff. She went to her bedroom. There she approached the chest of drawers. She opened the top, left drawer. She dug past panties and Cuddle Duds, full slips and half-slips, girdles and garter belts. She felt for the eight by ten manila envelope. Then, she fan-folded back her queen-sized, rosy bedspread, smoothed the matching sheets, and sat down. The envelope was secured with string around a disc and she unwound the string in a figure-eight movement. Then she coaxed out yellowed clip-pings from inside. They were newspaper advice columns on divorce. Often, she took forbidden pleasure in rereading the dog-eared pages, in just thinking about it. Now she pulled one at random and read the headline, DIVORCE NEVER EASY. *No matter how you seize it up, divorce is always nasty and never easy.* She was sure the writer meant *size it up,* but then again, *seize* sounded about right. She skimmed to the middle of the article. *Loneliness is very difficult for most souls. Some people prefer a dysfunctional relationship to living alone.* How would Kelly manage, still fresh from her and Ramon's Divorce Decree? *Are you planning a divorce? In the long run, you will be better off for it. YOU will find YOU.* Maybe she should share these with Kelly. A different clipping men-tioned "polar urges," present in everyone and how to build a path between them. She had tried, God knows she had tried. It was probably better to trash these keepsakes so Kelly, Rebecca, and George wouldn't find them when she's gone. (As if George, shacked up in Guadalajara, would care. Esther would disown him, but there probably was paper-work for that, too.) Certainly, her girls must never know she had considered breaking up the family. Tomorrow, she will destroy the evidence. For now, she scanned one more: *Marry the right person. This one decision will determine 90% of your happiness or misery.*

"Mom," Kelly said at the doorway. Esther jumped. Kelly moved in. "I thought you went to the bathroom."

"Yes," Esther said, "I should." She rose, fumbling with the clippings.

"What's all that?" Kelly asked.

"Oh," Esther said. "I thought I had some Good House-keeping hints on painting." She eased the crinkly papers back in the envelope. "I was wrong." Then she told Kelly to keep Daddy company while she stopped in the lavatory.

Kelly went back to the kitchen where Warren sat at the table, eating pickles and olives. He perked up when he saw Kelly. "Did I ever show you my arrowheads?" he asked.

"Maybe later, Daddy," Kelly said. "After supper." Kelly had seen the arrowheads fifty times. She had taken them to grade school every year for the history unit. In college, she had wanted to frame them on something artsy, maybe grass cloth, border them in brown velvet and hang them in Esther's living room. But Ramon thought it was a dumb idea.

"I found one today on the back forty," Warren said. "Was I surprised! Thought I'd picked that hillside clean." Kelly remembered Daddy's three-point plow, his suntanned hands sifting dirt in search of flint or stone. He had twenty-seven arrowheads, ranging in size from one inch to three. All contained sharp points, enough to kill. Now the arrowheads snuggled in bubble-wrap in a Thom McCann shoebox. "That makes twenty-seven total," Warren said, shoving back his chair. Kelly put her hand on his shoulder. She knew Daddy needed more and more watching. Last month he yelled for Esther to turn out the yard light, it's costing too much. So Kelly installed room-darkening shades to block city streetlights. Last week he wandered down the sidewalk at sundown, convinced Herefords had broken through the fence. Another time it was the horses, restless with a coming storm. Some day he will tumble down those basement stairs or slip in the tub or forget to turn off the burner. He will drive through an intersection and clip a bicyclist. At Cozy Care Village he could have his own flower garden, 24-hour care and someone other than Esther to zip his forgotten zipper. But diligent Esther was against Kelly on this idea: you take your father out of here, he'll die. This is his dream after forty hard years on the farm. No, Esther must hang on, but God there are days.

They made a triangle at table, the conversation flowing between Esther and Kelly, yakking through second helpings before preparing a doggy bag for Kelly, who told Fella,

"You have to share." Then the two women tidied up the kitchen and spread out Kelly's magazines like roommates decorating a first apartment. Warren disappeared to his room to read and soon his raggedy breathing rattled down the hall. Yakking continued over warm cocoa and Esther's All Good Cookie Cake. Esther revealed they'll try new medicine on Daddy. She dismissed Kelly's concerns that he might hurt himself or that he might hurt her. Nonsensical thinking, Rebecca called it. Besides, Esther wanted the scuttlebutt on Kelly's day in court, her triumphs. So Kelly told how she did it without a lawyer. She did not reveal Ramon's porn addiction or their escalating credit card debt. Finally, when it was way past Esther's bedtime, Kelly went after the Daddy dilemma once more.

"Really, Mom," she said, leaning forward. "How much longer can Daddy live here?"

"Long as he can."

"How long is that?"

"God only knows," Esther said. She passed some gas, silent but noisome.

Kelly, ignoring the odor, proposed a scheme: enroll Daddy in Cozy Care and take him there under the guise of visiting Alfred, a former neighbor. Take along his arrowheads, a *Farm Journal* or two, his begonias, and his favorite flannel shirts. Professional caregivers will handle his snarls. He means well, Mom, but his wires are fried. In a locked-down wing, he can do what he wants; his soul can wander free. Then

Esther could concentrate on a real life. "We can redo the bathroom," Kelly said. But for Esther it was too late (past eleven) to be having such talk. So they hugged goodnight. Kelly promised to come on the weekend to pick out perfect faucets. That's what Esther thought, anyway. Kelly, in fact, planned to fetch Daddy—there was no point delaying this.

Esther retired, her dreams rare and compressed. In the morning, she rose later than usual, pleased by the previous evening, how Kelly's divorce broke open both their hearts. There's a word for that but now she was behind schedule. She scrolled out a supply from the Kleenex box. She blew her morning nose. She heard Warren in the bathroom, the wall hollow between her fading wallpaper and the bathroom's blistering paint. Today she planned to review wallpaper books and paint samples. That, after taking Warren for wax removal and his weekly protime.

Warren coughed and spit. He sounded like the 1936 Plymouth with ice in the radiator and him trying to crank it. He hacked and hawked and hemmed. He made an awful racket. Molten chunks of phlegm and dead cells hit the toilet. Others landed on the floor. He coughed and spit some more. He sounded like he was choking. "Ahem," he said, finally, and cleared his throat, this time without spitting. She could see those fatty plugs on the floor. Later, she would clean them up for her cataracts were gone and for months she discovered fingerprints on walls, fur balls on carpets, and the besmirched picture window, too late in the season to wash. She blew her nose once more and dropped the tissue in the wastebasket. She worked a few rosary beads, an abacus counting his days while she waited for him to get out of the bathroom. He was ten years older than she. When he was gone, she planned to *have a ball* with Kelly—certainly not with Rebecca, that social climber and pretender in a Manhattan high rise. Becca, with a solitary thong peeking out of tattered, low-rise jeans, was her own flesh and blood. Imagine.

Now Esther's flimsy nightgown clung to her pancake chest. "Hurry up," she yelled. She shivered, clutching her gown to shroud what used to be buttercup breasts and his honey pot. She had once been a young farm wife with dress unbuttoned in a field of sweet clover. Oh Warren, you devil, the two of them carefree bees on the hillside, *yes baby*. A pull on the Lucky Strike, shared, everyone smoked then. His earth-tan hands clutched her in a scene for the wide screen—someone else's life, surely. She pounded on the wall. "Hurry up," she yelled.

The bathroom door opened. "Bitch, bitch," he said. "Man can't get any peace around here."

She hissed past him and closed the door. Urine trickled down her legs before she made it to the toilet. She sat down and finished emptying. Then the sink: first a cleansing of thighs and netherworld. Then the face: a splash of warm water, then cool, then cucumber toning mist from Rebecca. Next, Rebecca's face and neck cream from Switzerland. And glasses. Oh, that's right: no need since the cataract surgery. She dressed in pea green polyester pants and a rose blouse. She was at the stove in a *Kiss the Cook* apron when Warren clattered out of the den, assigned to him as bedroom last spring when she couldn't take it anymore. He stood there now, neither coming nor going, belt outside belt loops, cardigan buttoned wrong, cigar stench circling him.

She took one look at him. "Jesus, Mary, Joseph," she said, "give me patience." Fella limped to a sunspot, rare for November. Warren progressed to the kitchen table, ready to drink coffee, eat streusel coffee cake, and scoop warm liver sausage out of the frying pan he expected to be set before him. It was 7:30 a.m. The breakfast was late. It was thirty minutes late. Water for coffee hadn't even been drawn.

"What in the Sam Hill," he said. "No breakfast?"

"I'm working on it," she said as if to explain why the faucet was roaring and why she held a white pot beneath it. She was crying but without tears, used up long ago.

"Jesus Christ. Man can't even get a breakfast around here."

She set the pot on the back burner. She turned the burner on high. He opened the closet door and located his jacket and cap. "Where do you think you're going?" she asked.

"To rake."

"You did that yesterday."

"The sun is out. Rare, for November." She flew from refrigerator to table with butter, jam, cream, jelly, gherkins, honey, and cheese. He hesitated. "It's November, right?" She slammed the refrigerator door and reached for the sugar bowl in the cabinet, sniveling and pushing air with considerable effort.

Devoid of her answer, his mind flitted to milking and chores. And whether that Jersey cow had calved overnight. He hurried. He threaded the left sleeve up his arm and then, bent as a sunflower, wiggled to bring the right sleeve around. He winced as he rolled his right shoulder and arm, searching for that other sleeve. His rotator cuffs were shot. His hips felt petrified. That one rib, cracked by the Black Angus bull, healed crookedly and knifed him if he moved a certain way. So he bent slowly to avoid it, working with stiff shoulders and stiffer spine. "God damn it," he said. He made one more swing toward nailing the sleeve and missed. "Goddamnit to hell," he said.

And then, she crashed.

Someone in dispatch called Kelly right after notifying the ambulance crew. Now Kelly paced in the E.R. lounge, recalling the small step stool near the stove. It was always in the corner. Maybe he moved it and she tripped on it. The nurse said Esther had a small abrasion at the back of her head. *Did he hit her?* she asked, not once, but several sneaky ways. "Never," Kelly said. "Drop it." Later, Kelly would find the stool in its place, figure how Esther had clocked it, her angle of repose when found. Susie, the neighborhood nurse, drawn by the sirens, ran there. The table was set, Susie said, plates and cups and saucers, all clean, untouched. Now Susie cradled Kelly in her arms while behind closed doors, the E.R. staff measured the bruise on Esther's right hip. They tested her pupils. They considered her bones. *Nothing broken, imagine that. I hear she was a vitamin and herb freak.* They wheeled her to the cat scanner. There it was: three lobes, black as the ace of spades. Frontal, temporal and parietal had been cut off by a clot.

Soon Kelly stood at her mother's bed. "Mom," she said in a neutral and quiet tone. She knew how close she was to losing it. Esther's lids swelled like macaroon creams. One cheek sagged. The right side of her mouth hung low. Nothing moved except her chest.

Behind Esther's lids, colors of peach and soft rose flooded her wicker laundry basket. The sun was out, the wind out of the West. She picked up the basket, went down the stairs, threw her hip to the door, and waltzed to the wash lines. She set down the basket and grabbed the clothespins. Someone called to her. It was a little girl, pleading, *push me on the swing.* Esther put two wooden pins between her teeth as she pinched a sheet to the line. The clothespins tasted like hickory, nutty and sweet. She reached down for the pillowcases. That girl called again. Esther's arms flailed. Her legs dangled. The girl called *Mom, Mom, talk to me.* The girl was in a panic now and, try as she might, Esther couldn't reach her.

As for Warren, the kitchen still boiled with "Honey!" The sight of her slumped on the floor inflamed the kitchen. The collie, startled, lumbered in, and rutted his dry nose under Esther's neck and waist. Warren screamed, for authority or perhaps out of habit, a call for a sweetheart he had made cry right before she crashed. There was comfort in bickering. Anyone knew that. The stonewalling followed by kiss-kiss and make up—I'm sorry, sometimes I lose my head; me, too, I'd be lost without you.

That history was behind them now, Warren screaming, "Honey! Honey!" He screamed with a voice small and thin, a baritone who once yodeled to the woods to signal the kids picking trilliums that supper was on. "Goddamnit," he said, kneeling beside her. "Honey! Get up! Oh, honey, what's happened to you?" He bent one arm and crooked it under her armpit. He tugged. "Honey, honey," he cried, in a whisper now. He tugged again, adrenalin seeping, his strength wondrous. But she was dead weight. Nothing stirred except a flutter in her little bird chest. The collie whimpered and retreated under the kitchen table. Warren put down her arm and shuffled to the phone. His ticker beat like crazy. He tapped his forehead. What was that number? He looked at the refrigerator where she had written it in large red letters. And beneath the number were other instructions, should the time come: Where to find the will. Durable Power of Attorney. Who had copies of what. He was skeptical at the time. He had hoped for the big one on the dance floor. Or death by truck. Nothing like this ever crossed his mind. Now the large red numbers shouted at him. He turned over the newfangled phone. Push-buttons hid on the handset. He shook. He pushed number nine. Then he looked at the fridge. One. One. He did it and when someone answered, he knew his street address because that, too, was in bold on the fridge.

The record showed eight minutes from that phone call to sirens arriving at the little Cape Cod. Kelly photocopied the dispatch and ambulance reports. Now she sat in the spare bedroom, staring at milky white walls. She read and reread the two reports. Nothing unusual in the crisp efficiencies of Jack and Gregg, paramedics who had just started their shift. So, pained, she called Susie who lived four doors down. Together, they relived the scene in the kitchen, Esther on the stretcher, the collie whimpering, Daddy's frozen face, how Susie drove Daddy to the hospital where he sat in a swamp near Esther, crying, *Why? Why?* And the only salient answer had already rolled off the dispatcher's tongue: *Woman down. 1786 Sunnyvale Court.*

And Warren would go down, too, six days later. He would step into the garage for his cigar before the nice home care aide served supper. He would miss the small cement step he had navigated hundreds of times and collapse. His skull fracture was large. His brain whooped into what Susie called "contra-coup," the brain whipping and whopping from one side of the skull to the other, bleeding and swelling and drawing more blood. His coumadin-thin fluids poured out while he hollered, "Honey! Honey!" The aide came running. She knew her job. She did the drill.

That time, Kelly took the call. She dispatched the ambulance with Jack and Gregg at the end of their shift. Then she tore there herself. But those fluids on the garage floor, red luscious, were his last.

Meanwhile, Esther survived, paralyzed on one side and unable to speak. They banded and slotted her into a bed at Cozy Care. Two years later, she sat in a wheelchair in the dining room. An aide with three piercings and purple hair smoothed Esther's terry cloth bib. Then, she spooned up soft brown mush. "Come on, Honey," she said. "You've got to eat." Esther crooked a smile and opened her mouth, wide.

Tangled

Sunday, ten p.m. The doctor's weekend on-call is nearly done so he showers and has put on flannel pajamas just as the phone rings. "Hello."

A registered nurse at North Star Home blurts out, "Hi, Doctor, this man looks gray, pulse rapid and thready." She sounds wary. As if the patient were her own father. The doctor fights a yawn, imagining the ancient man, probably warehoused by distant kids. He's seen it before. He rubs his temple, scrunches eyes screaming for sleep as the RN's raspy voice says, "Rising fever, dropping pressures, confusion."

"Septic," the doctor says. "What does the family want?"

"Send him to ER."

"Okay, then," he says, peeved. He changes his clothes, then awaits the ER call that will come when he must drive to the hospital and admit the failing man. The doctor counts the time needed for each task: RN calls ambulance, now; RN prepares paperwork, ten minutes; ambulance arrives at nursing home, twenty minutes; ambulance arrives at ER, twenty minutes; man moved to ER stretcher, five minutes, depends on staffing; ER nurse and ER physician evaluate, thirty-five minutes, depends on case load. There, that's ninety minutes.

The clock ticks off the time, but no call comes. Was there a car wreck, a chain saw accident? Is the trauma team draining resources? He grows antsy and on edge. Finally, chewing a

Maalox, he phones the ER, announces, "I'm on my way." Once there, he approaches the ER stretcher and, greeting the ancient man for the first time, sees a nose spider-webbed with collapsing capillaries. The man has a name, Gibby. A widower with children, none of them here to see their father's doll's eyes, meaning his cranial nerves are shot. Gibby can neither track what he sees nor transfer sense or nonsense to and/or from the brainstem, mid-brain, or posterior fossa. In short, Gibby has—at age ninety-three—lived his life.

In California, a daughter, notified her father is in the ER, asks to speak with the admitting doctor. Her name is Margot and now she is speaking to, at, around, and for the tired doctor and his acidic stomach. Her words spill. "We all have plane tickets. All three of us. We're coming on Friday to see Daddy." Friday is five days away and the doctor believes Gibby will be gone by morning. He listens to Margot; his heartstrings thrum. He tells Margot about the doll's eyes. She was a nurse. She knows the imminence of doll's eyes. "He wanted hospice," she says. "If I returned to nursing, I would go into hospice."

"A good thing," the doctor says. "Too late now."

"I know," Margot says, voice gauzy and faint.

The doctor's eyes feel like sandpaper. His back is killing him. He is supposed to help, order labs, review vitals, do a physical exam and come up with an algorithm. If this, then that. If not that, then this. He is to run the drill of possibilities. Younger doctors do this with electronic gadgets; with thirty years' experience under his belt, he does it, faster—in his head. He admits Gibby and orders a routine IV, medications, and oxygen. He knows he could start a tsunami of X-rays, CAT scans, MRIs; the specialists would love it. He knows he should do something more, but what? He wants to be exact. He must be correct, nail the diagnosis, prescribe the treatment.

"Doll's eyes," Margot says. She is crying now, full tilt. Something inside the doctor wells up too, flushing sand from his eyes. Spaces between his vertebrae pinch, yet hold him in a position of service. He waits. He is present. He has learned there is healing in presence. Then, Margot composes herself, a little, and asks, "Would you do something for me?"

"I would."

"Would you give my father a hug? And tell him *Margot loves you very much.*"

The doctor goes to the room. The nurse stands there, awaiting a plan of action. The doctor goes to the stretcher. Diagnosis: dying. Treatment: hugging. He puts both arms around the Dad with doll's eyes, expecting to smell a body of rotting potatoes, unruly stool. Instead, he smells citrus and sandalwood, a middle note of cedar with jasmine. "This is from Margot," he says, directly into the man's ear. He hesitates. And then he speaks very slowly, the next five words wrapped with exactness. "Margot. Loves. You. Very. Much."

The man with doll's eyes squirms. The doctor gives one more hug, lingers a tad. By now the nurse in the room is misty-eyed, her lungs a sopping sponge. The doctor swallows. He releases Gibby, looks at no one, leaves the room, leaves the ER, and goes to his Subaru. It is the morning side of midnight. Trees toss their shadows against the sky. He steps through the wind, time ticking away. He starts the car and drives home, backbone bobbing down country roads. A blink of his eye catches a white-tailed deer in the ditch. He brakes, shaken, and makes it to his feather quilt. The rest of the night he rolls around in twilight sleep, chilled, tangled in the sheets.

Come morning, he rises with a crick in his neck. His head pounds. He is standing in the shower, water pelting to wake him up when the phone rings. He steps out, shivering. "Yes?" he says, holding the receiver away from his wet ear. At the mention of Gibby, he nods. "What time?" he asks. He nods. "I see," he says. "You may release the body."

Then he returns to the shower and soaps up, scrubbing briskly, thinking about the packed schedule at the office, how he's running late, how three Tylenol will be breakfast.

Hamburger

The news spread up and down the counter at Bill and Betty's Grill as the regulars revved up, saying it's Pete's fault for getting the kid a Harley in the first place, if only the kid had taken a safety course, if only his mother were alive, she'd a stopped such nonsense. There was blame on *Easy Rider*, too, if only it hadn't come out—Hollywood served teenagers a pipe dream. The naysayers were old gaffers drinking black coffee and smoking, plus a wispy little fellow in a seersucker suit who ate pudding in careful spoonfuls, wary of the simmering rage.

Even the sun took a hit and lost its oomph, wobbly rays scratching the window panes near a booth where two teenage girls in bomber jackets popped Bubblicious, passing a root beer float back and forth, glum and miserable, mascara streaking their cheeks.

"No one crashed in *Easy Rider*," a guy named Duke said. He motioned to the diner's walls, covered with fading posters of Elvis, Brando, and of Peter Fonda in *Easy Rider*. Fonda's eyes seemed to move, piercing. "Beats me how you can blame a movie for things people do. Like I said, no one crashed in *Easy Rider*. You see something I didn't?"

A chubby salesman loaded the last piece of apple pie on a fork before declaring, "Cycle crashes happen when a car turns in front of a bike. It's a fact." The salesman opened his jowls to the pie. An old gaffer asked what made him such an expert. "Insurance," the man replied. He rubbed his swollen mid-section. "Been with State Farm my whole life." He lowered the fork to the pie plate and pressed the tines into the remaining crust. "Cycles are hard to see," he said, licking the fork, first one side, then the other, before adding, "End of story."

"True, true," Duke said, shaking his head. "'Cept I heard that kid was out there alone on the road. No cars or trucks. Only the night wind and a kid on a Sportster XL."

"A Sportster XL?!" exploded a truck driver with a denim shirt ripped open to the navel. "That thing has great torque and pulling power. And, lower RPMs. She's nasty to kick-start."

"Why is it always a *she*?" asked Candy, a waitress with orange cheeks. She uncapped a green-tinted glass bottle of Coca-Cola as he winked at her and said, "She's hot, why else." Candy winked back before she said, "Well, then, maybe somebody started it *for* him, maybe someone else is involved." She served the driver a burger with the works while a grease cloud over the grill met pale-yellow light and paralyzed time. Then another guy reminisced about flatheads and panheads, cycles from the forties and fifties, and another, missing an eyebrow and an arm, told how if you ever get in an accident, the thing is, stay upright. You gotta remember, no matter what, keep that bike upright. Probably no one told the kid.

Duke sipped his coffee and decided to shut up. He had watched Pete work on the used Sportster for nearly two years, on and off, his project when work was slow. Pete had souped it up with mods to the engine for more zip and new pipes for more roar. Red, yellow, and blue flames shot up the front fender, painted by the kid himself, including lacquer on the flames. The bike positively glowed and Pete said he had told the kid at supper last week, *I made a few adjustments; she's really set now.* In several days, he and seventeen-year-old

Gabe were headed up north for the weekend. *We'll open her up and be in the next county before the sheriff knows what split his eardrums,* Pete had promised. They both had had a good laugh, knowing it would be about freedom and escape. It would be about the ride, the bike. A destination hardly mattered.

It was around six on Thursday when Rikki phoned and wanted to go for a spin. "Not yet. Dad wants to ride with me first."

"And?"

"I told you. This weekend we're going up north."

She whistled. "Did Captain America get Daddy's permission?"

"Captain America is a bike, Rikki, not a person."

There was a short silence. "Chicken," she said.

"Chicken? Aw, you can do better than that." He wrapped the phone cord around his index finger.

"Let's," she said. The request sounded light, airy. "We'll be back before Pete even knows." It was pure impulse—the language of a girl so damn sure of herself, she never stole the ball unless she could complete the play.

"I . . . I . . . I don't know."

"Come *on*," she said. "What can it hurt?"

"It's risky."

"Come *on*." Now it was a demand. "What's to risk? It's not like a Skeeter risk."

"What?" He fidgeted. Had she heard about Skeeter and the pig?

"You know. A dumb move. A *Skeeter* move."

They laughed hilariously. At the mention of Skeeter, a wave rose in him. "Well," he said.

"Alriiiiiiight."

He swallowed. "After this weekend," he said. "Just you and me. Promise." He pulled the spiral cord off his finger and began to wrap it again. She sighed, a silly, childish noise as if she were upset. As if she ever got upset. She had a motor in her hip, a perpetual motion machine, and now he could almost hear it hum. He thought of the afternoon they almost did it. Why had she stopped, then? What was it about the Sportster that made her push so hard now? He fell silent and inquisitive like the box turtle behind the house. Whenever he and his mother stumbled upon it, its claws gripped the little clay hill it claimed, and they had moved about the garden, respectfully, with an eye on it. The turtle's head retracted. Its beady eyes watched them, full of fear. Or fearlessness. He was fast becoming that turtle.

"Come *on,*" she said, again.

"No," he said. "No."

And a thing went into motion, a thing compressed and sensory, a thing layered with psychological details. It could not wait one more solitary night. A thing that included, he supposed, the leather biker vest she had given him for his eighteenth birthday, early. She had even sewn on the pocket (extra credit in home ec) an emblem of an American eagle. The plan was for him to turn eighteen up North, two days from now, he and Pete rolling in thunder from one county to the next. Had it been raining, perhaps he would have stayed put, believed his own *No.* Pete had drilled him about glassy roads, the slant of rain, and sudden oil slicks. However, it was not raining. It was April 16, 1974. The smells of awakening soil and peat moss were enough to defy gravity. It was not raining. He was thinking about this but probably not thinking at all (the way he didn't study when he was studying) when Rikki said, "Fine. Okay, *fine.*"

"You'll see," he said.

Then, with typical resilience, she started in about her game the night before. The basketball team had lost 34-30. "If we want to win," she said, "we have to cut down on mental mistakes and turnovers."

"It's all mental," he said. He could see her eyebrows bunch together, see the freckles spattered across her cheeks, how they burst into different colors when she became excited. He listened to her for the next few minutes, how Holly needed to stop being a ball hog, Jane needed to be more aggressive on post, and as for Suzy, don't get started on her. And then, abruptly, she said, "Shit. Dottie will *kill* when she sees the long-distance bill. I better go."

"Okay, then." He hung up and walked out to the shop. The snow had melted. An early robin huddled against the outhouse where last year his mother had planted clematis. High in the elm tree were fat blackbirds, their voices like crackling preachers.

He opened the shop door and saw that Pete was still at Looman's muscle car with the special four-barrel carburetor. The Sportster was parked near the front of the shop. The very sight of it made Gabe jump. He looked around the shop. He felt incredibly lucky. And, proud. His Dad was smart; he could fix anything. If anything ever happened to this bike, he could fix it. Pete rolled out from underneath the car, a wrench in one hand and beads of sweat dotting his receding hairline. "Heat shield," he said. "Thought I'd jerry-rig it up, get a few more miles out of it for Loomans." He lay on the dolly, knees bent, head straining at a forty-five degree angle, soot and dust deepening the lines in his forehead, around his neck and ears. "Cut me some wire yay long," he said, holding his hands eighteen inches apart. Gabe found the wire cutter on the shop table and snapped off the required yay length. Pete disappeared under the car, grunting with each turn of the wrench to knot the wire around the head shield. Gabe thought of saying *Anything I can do?* But he could hear the answer, *Naw, your homework done?* And then Gabe would say *Sure, besides I have study hall first period.* That would allow Pete to grunt through one more wire knotting before he'd say *Sounds good.*

Gabe ambled over to the Sportster and cozied up to it. He ran his hand over the shiny front fender. He smelled the cowhide seat. He ran his hand over the dyed flesh. He wrapped his hands around the handlebars. "Hey Dad," he yelled. "How about we take her out after supper?"

Pete rolled out from under the car. "I'm beat," he said. "This weekend. You just wait. We'll hightail it." Then he disappeared again under the car.

Gabe went back to the house and took the Sportster's key off a hook in the back hall.

He tapped it against his chin and then tasted it. It tasted grainy, bold. He slipped it in his pocket.

Pete came in shortly thereafter, hung up his frayed flannel shirt and work jeans stiff with axle grease and dirt. He showered and they sat down to hot dogs and beans. "Forest County," Pete said. "That's where we'll open her up." And then out of the blue he grabbed Gabe's hand and patted it. "You're a good kid."

Gabe liked having a Dad who was a kid himself, not a cave man like Skeeter had, a grump who talked more to cows than to family. Still, Gabe felt agitated. He knew it would do no good to bug Pete tonight. The man was exhausted, ready for his La-Z-Boy and Johnny Carson. And Gabe knew if he pushed the issue, Pete would turn mother hen, despairing and fluttering. So he did the dishes while Pete went to the bathroom. The toilet flushed and soon Pete was on his recliner, ready for the rest of the evening. Gabe waited until he heard him sawing logs. When his classic occasional nasal snort sung out, Gabe made his move.

In the back hall, he put on his steel-toed boots and leather vest with eagle on the pocket. He checked on Pete, then opened the kitchen door, went out, and closed it carefully, holding the doorknob and releasing it into the tumbler without a sound. By now, a slivered moon hung low in the sky. The sloping farm field behind the house smelled of earth recently turned over, of cow dung and cornstalks and molting grain. The land had been spring-toothed and was ready for planting, ready for new life. He went to the shop, lifted the wide overhead garage-like door, and slid it slowly on its tracks. It rattled over the crack in the frame and he held his breath, eyeing the house for any light suddenly switched on. The overhead door crackled in place; it held. Gabe raced back to the house and snuck a peek through the picture window.

Johnny Carson was into his routine and every now and then, Pete opened one eye. For several minutes, his heavy lids rose and fell like fog in the lowland. He watched Pete float in and out until his whole body twitched deeper into dreamdom.

Gabe tore back to the repair shop, kicked the kickstand, and rolled the bike down to the edge of the cement apron where it met a small blacktopped road. He felt happy and tough, smug and ecstatic. He felt unbearably strong, shoving the bike all the way to the corner where Droll's stood on one corner and St. Mary's Church on the other. Farther down, lights were on in several ranch homes built without a ranch. He looked around. Not a soul in sight, not even screwy Skeeter coming down the road to eat ice cream. People were either glued to the tube or already at Droll's, drinking tap beer. He swung one leg over the gleaming black bike and paused. His legs felt like sawhorses, braced and ready to balance the bike, to keep it upright at all costs. Pete had emphasized *Whatever you do, you keep that thing upright.*

Gabe turned the key and jumped full-nelly on the starter with his right leg. Nothing. What the hell, he thought. He and Pete had already taken it out twice, without any problems. The first time, Pete had driven, Gabe's arms ringed around him. They had found a new thrill in the Kettle Moraine high hills, taking rolling curves and tight turns with a full range of speed. When the wind was behind them, it was easy. With the wind in their face, it was skill. The second time out, Gabe drove. His bare hands gripped the handlebars while he gave it full throttle and they shot forward. Pete had yelled into his ear, *Let up, okay, easy now, crank her.* They had flown, motorcycle junkies craving more and more. Pete was cool and Gabe was his kid. Rikki was cooler and Gabe was her guy; he couldn't wait to surprise her. When she saw him, she'd explode like a wet spark. She'd squeal *Alriiiiiight.*

He pounced on the starter again, his leg rebounding from the impact. And from beneath him, the bike took air, alive and growling. He revved it up again but it didn't move. *Dumb shit* he said to himself—it wasn't even in gear. He shifted it into first gear, revved it again and sprung down the blacktop, muscular and full of purpose, headed toward Horseshoe Bend, the back way to Rikki, to catch her totally off guard. He rode, alone and understanding why Pete had said that anyone who gets on a bike is getting on life. Now he rode life, connected to spring, euphoria, ice melting, gushing, creeks overflowing. The Sportster's small headlight beamed straight ahead. Adrenaline flushed the road. He picked up speed, the sky an infinite space he could ride. He darted past shadowy outlines of barns, corncribs, and a tractor stuck in a field too wet for spring-toothing. He approached the anhydrous ammonia tank outside the trailer of a city slicker who spent weekends in the country. Some quirky art dealer named Reed Bartholomew Bartley. He sailed past Bartley's idea of escape. By now, he was lost in risk and the unknown, no longer impelled by a mission to make Rikki squeal. He wanted only to burn rubber. And so he chased the purest, most high-flying exhilaration he had ever known.

A rusted windmill appeared in the distance. Visible in the moonlight, it was a signal to Gabe to slow down. An intersection was coming up around the bend in the road, near where the windmill stood. Back then, such intersections didn't have stop signs. Common sense and a concern for fellow drivers were reasons to slow down, look.

Gabe didn't see anyone's headlights about to cross his path. But, infused with rural good manners, he slowed anyway, a little, not much, enough though. In driver's ed they said to cover the brake and now he didn't cover the brake but he did slow up enough, he'd have to say, enough. He would always say, *Enough.* Suddenly the bike started to wobble like the rear axle was loose or something. Pretty soon, the entire bike—and he—shivered and shook. It was living thunder. Had the rear wheel picked up a sleazy possum? A stray cat? *Fuuuuuck,* he said. *Fuuuuuuuck you.* Still, he was no sissy. And he remembered: *Stay upright, stay upright.*

However, in his inexperience, he forgot to let up on the gas and instead, he gunned it, a reflex reaction to beat the yellow before it turned red. And it was reflex too—that, and defiance— to stay upright. He fought, using all his power to maintain control, keep that bike upright. He pulled and hauled, biceps quivering under the strain. He worked it, worked it hard, but the thousand-pound Sportster began to tip. Within the rush, time stood still, the spotlight of memory before it was made. And then as he and the bike skidded across the grizzly blacktop, his last thought was: *This is going to hurt.* He hung on, a cowboy on a bucking bronco, challenged but still confident, a rush into his shoulders and arms, liquid steel, something supernatural like a man lifting an entire car to save a life, a man upright on a bike against all odds, feeling arrogant and proud. And unaware in his self-righteousness that he roared into oblivion. And that, within seconds, his leg would be hamburger.

Reed Bartley stuttered. "L-l-late," he said, meaning he had a late start coming out of Chicago. "C-c-coinki-d-d-dink," he added. It was pure coincidence he found Gabe in the dark ditch, the steam of the body rising. Here's the story as the sheriff's deputy wrote it down. *Mr. Bartley thought moonlight on the old windmill was a form of "outsider art." He stopped to admire it. Then he saw something move. It was the wheel of the motorcycle, spinning around and around. He admired the pulsing gleam, the shiny flank. He jumped out of his Pontiac station wagon and slid down into the ditch. The subject was unconscious.*

"When did you find him?" the deputy asked.

"L-l-lllate," Bartley said.

"What time, sir?"

"T-t-ten, I'd say ten. Awwwful," he said. "A puddle of blood. And that l-l-leg. The kid held it l-like it was a dying p-p-p-puppy." Bartley reported recognizing the razzled-up colors on the bike. He said he'd seen it in a local shop, rummaging for lug nuts and cast-iron engine housing.

"If you don't mind my asking, Sir," the deputy said. "Whadya do with that shit?"

"Paint them. Compose a collage," Bartley said without a stutter.

"Huh?"

"It's called art."

"Sign here," the deputy said. And Bartley signed.

Yes, No, I Don't Know

Rumors about Gabe and Sally began even before their rush job at the courthouse and reception at Hika Bay Tavern where Gabe did the toasting and Sal—nickname for Sally—did the eating, the menu being a quarter-barrel, broasted chicken, fries, and anemic beans. Afterward, they drove to their Southland Runabout, a rusting trailer slightly bigger than a dog kennel, parked at the old campground.

A month later, night had not made it to dawn when Gabe rolled out of the stiff mattress, shuffled to the kitchen, and opened a frayed curtain. He heard the Schnell Implement sign across the road, metal clanking against a pole in the wind. He peered out. A half-moon lit up tall grasses in the ditch. The sky was a burnt lilac. One ferocious cloud resembled a lion. In a few hours, he'd be hobbling among Schnell's rows of new and used John Deere tractors, tillers, and field mowers bigger than Kansas. When he wasn't selling, he would weld, hammer, or order mowers for next season, including parts to repair them.

He closed the curtain and poured a glass of milk. *He was going to be a father. How would he do? What if it were twins? What if it had Down syndrome?* He wrinkled his brow and took a gulp, then sat down at the table bolted to the floor. Sal had covered the table with contact paper, a checkerboard pattern in black and white. Every time he looked at it, his eyes jiggled. He lifted the curtain again and considered the implement yard. A pile of used tractor tires loomed in the dim enclosure. For a buck or two, a side-lying tire could become a flowerbed or sandbox. *A sandbox. Little Matchbox cars. A train set.* He emptied the glass. From the trailer's other end, he heard Sal. She was nearly three months, already signed up for prenatal class, eager to flex her muscles, push the kid out. Kids having kids, some would say, to which Gabe would reply, Heck yah and Sal, who played basketball, softball, and volleyball, would say with confidence, no pain, no gain, unaware as any nineteen-year-old would be that there are neither laps nor drills for giving birth.

He heard her pad toward the bathroom, open the plywood door, and flick on the light.

She screamed, a high-pitched shriek.

He turned, thinking *mouse, spider, plunger.* She wailed again, louder, and he was there in five hops, arms against the doorjamb, eyes squinting against a naked desolate bulb. He saw her curled lips, her cheekbones mottled and splotched. *What the hell*, he thought. She was tilted on her axis, holding up the walls of the small cubicle. *Soda crackers*, he thought. And then he saw her thighs, a river of red running down them. "Jesus," he said.

She yowled like a puppy with its tail in a door. She found the toilet seat and sat down in a spread-eagled fashion. Blood trickled steadily, the bright red kind when a wound was new, not the monthly burgundy smear. Her chin quivered and panic packed the corners of her mouth.

"Does it hurt?" he asked.

"No. Yes. I don't know!" She writhed back and forth.

Gabe momentarily retreated to his interior, flummoxed. The only time he had seen this much blood was when Skeeter's Dad tied a rope around hooves sticking out of a laboring cow and pulled and pulled until a newborn calf and blood and more blood gushed into the box stall. Sal began to hyperventilate. In the gloom, the distance between them expanded and contracted. The air in the small space stifled, recycled. "This isn't good," he said, moving toward her. She was panting and he touched her arm, his contact nervous yet empathic.

"Don't," she said.

It was a flash point and with great restraint, he said, "Like this is my fault."

She daubed at the blood and caught a gelatinous glob, the shape of a clenched fist yielding, slipping away. Across the road, the implement sign sounded like a gong calling Buddhists to worship. "No-o," she said, quieting now, the careful diffusion of emotion, piecemeal and slow. She ran every game strategy in her mind—lead a spade to his jack, time to bunt, go to a zone—and came up short, defeated. He, meanwhile, had a glimpse of the night he journeyed with his own plans, the detour he took, and how some simple thread kept him alive after he crashed the Harley, severing a leg, but still, alive.

And now this, their tiny babe, had neither strategy nor a thread to call on. Before their eyes, this little one dripped into the toilet like sewage. He watched his bride. Her lips tremored and her eyes had gone gray, flat washers with holes in the middle. Sorrow as the deepest thing had come to him when his mother collapsed and died before him. It had come again as he lay in the ditch, holding his detached leg. This sorrow was her first.

He watched her open her hand and spread her fingers wide. Slowly, she rubbed them to her soupy thigh. And then, her palm coated with blood, she pressed the fire-red-wet to her tummy. She marked the little belly with a handprint, then elevated both hands like a pagan in a ritual for the dead. "He didn't want to be here," she said, barely audible.

"Weren't we right for him?" Gabe asked, gazing at the blood print on her belly. He kissed the tips of his fingers, then released them, his breath and outspread fingers sending the kiss into the trailer redolent of dried hair spray and snuffed cigarettes. He moved closer. Their eyes met, two people in search of connection. Then he looked down. So did she, watching, as he lined up his thumb and fingers with her handprint on the smeary belly. She held very still, her cheeks laced with tears, snot blocking one nostril. He began to make a figure eight on the belly until there were no handprints, just a coating of crimson. "Maybe he didn't want us," he said, choking up, "but we wanted him." She collapsed into Gabe and he braced her.

In the half-light, there seemed no future, only the present, the sound of that implement sign clanging in the October wind.

Acknowledgments

At age fifty, I left a career in nursing to embrace my true calling: writing. Except I did not know how to write. What happened next was this: good fortune led me to talented teachers, including Dianne Benedict, Bruce Bond, Frank Conroy, Pam Painter, Gordon Mennenga, Sharon Oard Warner, Marshall Cooke, Christine de Smet, Mark Judge Poitier, Robert Hass, Kelly Dwyer, Carolyn Forche, Katie Ford, Laurie Kuchens, Melissa Pritchard, Caroline Leavitt, and Jonis Agee. Each one helped develop my multi-genre voice. For this, I am enormously grateful.

Indebtedness, too, to the Wisconsin Fellowship of Poets, Mead Poetry Circle, and the countless writers who journeyed with me, including Karl Elder, Dawn Hogue, Jean Biegun, Blair Deets, and Sylvia Cavanaugh. Heartfelt thanks to my cheerleaders Amy Mazzarillo and Jordan Leon.

And what luck to be discovered by Cornerstone Press at my alma mater. Much gratitude to director and publisher Dr. Ross Tangedal, managing editor Lillian Kulbeck, cover designer Abby Paulsen, and media/sales directors Sam Bjork and Sophie McPherson. A polished team of professionals.

* * *

Grateful appreciation to the editors of the following publications where these stories first appeared:

The Examined Life Journal: "Tangled"
8142 Review, The Hal Prize: "Yes, No, I Don't Know"
Eclipse: A Literary Journal: "Surrender"
Glimmer Train, finalist: "The Dresser"
Glimmer Train, finalist: "France"
Lullwater Review: "France"
Notre Dame Review: "Dancer"
Peninsula Pulse: "The Trouble With Ellen"
Permafrost: "Wife"
Pindeldyboz: "Almond Joy"
Porcupine Literary Arts Magazine: "Sugarplum"
Salamander: "Geraniums"
Sonora Review: "A Phone Call Away"
Talking Writing, Prize for Flash Fiction: "Sure"
The Mill Prize, Second Place: "They Said A Woman"
Wisconsin People & Ideas: "Miles", "Stones", "The Odds Against Something"

The following stories were cited by publications for awards:

"The Trouble with Ellen" (second place), The Hal Prize
"Miles" (third place), *Wisconsin People & Ideas*
"Stones" (third place), *Wisconsin People & Ideas*
"The Odds Against Something" (semi-finalist), *Wisconsin People & Ideas*

Kathryn Gahl is the author of *The Yellow Toothbrush* (2022) and *The Velocity of Love* (2020), both receipients of Outstanding Achievement Awards from the Wisconsin Library Association. Her fiction has been published in *Notre Dame Review*, *Glimmer Train*, *Wisconsin People & Ideas*, and elsewhere. For her poetry she was awarded the Lorine Niedecker Poetry Award from the Council of Wisconsin Writers in 2019.

www.ingramcontent.com/pod-product-compliance
Lightning Source LLC
Chambersburg PA
CBHW020024310726
48970CB00007B/2195